BONE
THIEF

BONE
THIEF

THOMAS
O'CALLAGHAN

PINNACLE BOOKS
Kensington Publishing Corp.

PINNACLE BOOKS are published by

Kensington Publishing Corp.
850 Third Avenue
New York, NY 10022

ISBN 0-7394-6329-2

For my loving wife, Eileen

Parents are the bones on which children sharpen their teeth.

Peter Ustinov

ACKNOWLEDGMENTS

I owe a very special round of gratitude to:

Matt Bialer, a magician of an agent, Dick Marek, who saw the novel within the manuscript, my very talented and insightful editor, Michaela Hamilton, Stephen Ohayon, Ph.D., a gem of a man, who inspired me tirelessly, Audra Koenig, Holly Cassino, Barry Richman, M.D., William Malloy, Frank Curtis and Noreen Nolan, a wonderful, wonderful woman. And, of course, the Group.

Lieutenant William F. Nevins, CDS, Commanding Officer of the Queens Homicide Squad (Retired) for his expert technical advice and skillful guidance. He represents NYPD at its finest.

My dear friend Priscilla Winkler, whose support through the years was greatly appreciated.

And to my loving daughter, Kelliann, and her bundle of joy, Kristin.

Chapter 1

It was an autumn day, brisk with the threat of a harsh winter. The air was filled with moisture. The weatherman had predicted rain.

A flock of laughing girls had braved the elements and had come to the park to see me play. Like a chorus of cheerleaders, they lined the sides of the playing field.

"Go get 'em, Colm!" their voices echoed as I took my position on the offensive line.

The play was called. The ball was snapped. I began to run, watching as the pigskin spiraled toward me. Just as I was about to catch it, I was tackled by an off-leash golden retriever intent on being part of the game. The collision with the dog leveled me.

"My God! Briosca knocked him out!"

"Give him room to breathe!"

"Someone call an ambulance!"

* * *

"Wake up! Wake up!"

My eyes opened to the dreariness of my tiny room. The dream evaporated, replaced by the nightmare of wakefulness.

Mother's eyes, grim and remorseless, stared at me, and I felt a tinge of nostalgia for the dog that had assaulted me, wishing to return to the dream, where the perils were predictable.

"Get up," she said. "Your father wants you."

Mother prided herself on being the obedient wife, and in that capacity, was exercising her duty to execute Father's wishes, no matter their eccentricities. She had been ordered to awaken my sister and me and to bring us down to the subcellar, where Father skinned his birds.

A chill came over me when I sat up. I knew it wasn't the temperature of the room. My body was girding itself for the approaching horror.

My sister, Rebecca, came racing into my room, the remnants of sleep still fresh in her eyes.

"Colm, Colm, again?" she whimpered.

Mother returned and led Rebecca and me downstairs. We were prodded through the cellar, passing a gurney where a gutted heron, an egret, and a peregrine falcon waited to be skinned, stuffed, and mounted.

Down in the subcellar we were brought before Father. He sat at the blood-soaked worktable, crouched on his rickety stool, where he could coil and strike like a venomous snake. His pockmarked face, weathered by time and ravaged by overindulgence, surrounded deep-set eyes. Eyes that seemed lifeless, like those of a hooked fish. The glow at the end of his cigarette struggled to stay lit, gasping for oxygen, breathing the emanations of his alcohol-drenched sweat.

Mother, who always looked as though she were about to be thrown from a plane, rummaged through the pocket of her soiled apron and produced a vial. She unscrewed the cap and shook out two yellow tablets.

"Time for your chemo," she said.

"To hell with the chemo! I wanna be buried with hair on my balls!" Father bellowed, swatting the pills out of Mother's hand.

"Oh, Bugler," Mother sighed.

"I don't have much time, Evelyn. The children must learn this trade. Gather 'round the table, kids. Watch my every move."

I looked at my sister, who had positioned herself across the table from me. Mother and Father acted as if we had been summoned to this dreadful place for the first time. We were not. We were part of the hellish ordeal nightly.

It was as though Father had read my thoughts, for he sneered at me as he reached for a large bird from a wooden shelf. "This here is a pheasant from Lancaster County, Pennsylvania," he grumbled. "A twelve-gauge Mossberg brought the sucker down. Now watch, I'm placing the bird on the worktable, spread eagle, breast up. I'm stuffing the beak with cotton to catch the blood."

I closed my eyes and fought back the urge to vomit.

"Pay attention!" Mother barked, swatting me on the back of my head.

Father's angry eyes found mine and rested there for what seemed like an eternity. Finally, withdrawing his glare, he picked up a lance and continued the lesson. "This here's a lance, and I'm gonna use it to cut below the pheasant's neck to its asshole. You wanna open the skin only. Stay away from the flesh. See how I peel away just the skin with my fingers?" Father stopped. He looked to Mother. "Evelyn, where's the damn flour?"

"Rebecca, get the package of Pillsbury from the kitchen and bring it here," Mother ordered.

Becky scurried up the stairs, her ponytail flopping behind her. When she returned, she was holding a sixteen-ounce bag of enriched confectionery flour.

"Look, kids, I'm sprinkling the flour on the bird's skin. It sops up the scum."

A second wave of nausea hit me. I looked at Becky. Her face was ashen, her eyes half closed.

"Now, I'm using a surgeon's curved scissor to snip the critter's legs. There. No more legs. That'll make it easier to skin the rest of him. See. Wha'd I tell ya? Just look how nicely this skin slides off. OK, who can tell me what comes next?"

"Off with its head," I muttered.

"That's right. I'm using a boning knife to lop off its head. We'll put the head aside and work on it in a minute. First, I've got to ream a hole at the base of the neck with these here wire cutters. Like that. OK, now, it's time for the head. Damn it, Evelyn, where's the borax?"

"Rebecca, look under the sink."

Becky rushed up the stairs again, returned with the carton of borax, and handed it to Father.

"On second thought, hold the borax. These are coming out nicely. Why ruin tomorrow's breakfast?"

He had palmed the pheasant's head and was using a spoon to scoop out the bird's brains, which he plopped into a Tupperware bowl.

"These are for my scrambled eggs," he said, handing the bowl to Mother.

"Colm, these go in the fridge upstairs," said Mother.

I flew up the stairs and placed the bowl in the fridge. A third wave of nausea seized me. I headed for the toilet near the back of the house.

"What's taking you so long?" Father bellowed, stopping me in midstride.

"*Right away, Dad,*" *I stammered as I rushed down the stairs and sidled up to the table. Risking another swat from Mother, Becky and I closed our eyes, for we knew what came next.*

Thankfully, Mother stood mute as Father reached for the melon scoop and, staring into the pheasant's dark pupils, plucked out both eyes.

"Colm, line up two number twelves. Make sure they're brown."

"Yes, sir," I replied.

My assignment was to retrieve the cardboard box that held the glass eyes, select the ordered pair, and bring them to Father. I marched toward the metal shelving that lined the rear wall of the subcellar, pulled down the corrugated box, and lifted its lid. A multitude of artificial eyes glared up at me. As always, I shuddered.

"What's keeping those eyes, Colm?"

A shriek came from atop the basement's shelving, shooting splinters of fear up my spine. A skittering sound followed.

"Bugler, what was that?" cried Mother.

"Daddy, we got rats!" Becky whimpered, her brown eyes pooling with tears.

"That ain't no rat," Father grinned.

A second shriek, more bone piercing than the first, discombobulated me. The box leaped out of my hands, launching the agate eyes into their own frenzied trajectories. My father's face went through a transformation. The muscles of his jaw knotted. A furrow cut deep into his forehead.

"Now look what you've done!"

He stood up. My heart burst.

His face became warlike. He let loose a cry, unfathomable and archaic, like the howl of a Celtic warrior.

My sister and I watched in horror. I knew my life hung on

his very breath. He could choke me with his brute hands or spare my life.

He ground the strewn eyes under the heel of his hiking boot, leaned his distorted face into mine, and said, "I could snuff you out, son. And it wouldn't matter much to the sun or the moon or the stars."

The sound of a blaring siren jarred Colm's consciousness to the present. A homeless woman pushing a Key Food shopping cart had collided with a Volvo, activating its alarm.

In a flash, he refocused on the task at hand. That afternoon he had followed the housewife as she drove that Volvo from the Kings Plaza Shopping Mall to this dimly lit parking lot outside Ralph Avenue's retail strip.

Her sole purpose for going to the mall was to meet with him for the first time. Colm took pleasure in knowing he had stood her up. But what thrilled him more was that she had now become his quarry.

Seated behind the wheel of his van, he watched as she dashed out of the video store toward the Volvo. She got to her car and depressed the panic button, killing the siren.

Colm stared at the stiletto heels she had donned for their first encounter, at her meaty fingers clutching the rented tape. Inside his parka, he touched the rag soaked in Halothane. The homeless woman drifted from sight. His target was now alone in the deserted parking lot.

He struck.

As he dragged the housewife's body to the sliding door of his van, his gaze fell upon the videotape she had dropped on the parking lot's asphalt. He picked it up.

It's a Wonderful Life with Jimmy Stewart and Donna Reed.

That was a flick she'd never see again.

He'd watch it for her.

Chapter 2

Colm spilled a tube of Max Factor Burnt Umber lipstick, a Lancome compact, and a Tampax tampon from her pocketbook onto the meat-cutting block in his basement's kitchen, in what Colm liked to call the operatory. The room was fitted with all the gadgetry needed for his murderous spree, and was dingy in comparison to the grandeur of the rest of the mansion.

He sniffed the tube of lipstick and the compact, and lingered on the virgin tampon. Her scent enveloped them all.

She was sitting before him, duct tape sealing her mouth and binding her arms and legs to the chair. She reeked of fear, but Colm saw only the terror in her eyes.

"I can't tell you how thrilled I am to finally meet you," he said, pulling up a chair. "The personal touch is lost when corresponding over the Internet. It did permit me to gather volumes of information about you, but in exchange you learned nothing about me. That's not fair. Wouldn't you agree? I can't tell you why, but it's important to me that you go to your grave knowing who it was that sent you there."

The woman's eyes widened. Tears streamed down her cheeks. Colm continued.

"My name is Colm Pierce. Although my birth name was O'Dwyer. My adoptive parents, the Pierces, thought my name should be changed. Wonderful parents, the Pierces.

"Please forgive me if I'm boring you. I just thought you should know my name. Oh, and by the way, although I've been toying with the idea for the past few years, you're my first."

He stood up. Behind his head five meat hooks dangled from a stone ceiling.

Gastric juices tumbled in the pit of her stomach. He imagined the taste of bile that surely coated her throat. Her breasts were swollen from the terror. Were her nipples sore?

He reached inside her purse and withdrew a leather wallet. In it were four plastic sleeves, suitable for photographs. Three of those sleeves contained snapshots of a little girl.

"I don't rob cradles," he muttered.

He slouched toward her.

She braced herself, expecting an assault.

There was none. Instead, he caressed her face and whispered her name.

"Deirdre."

He walked to the stove and opened the oven door. Rubbing his fingers on its blackened walls, he returned to his captive, streaked her cheeks from ear to ear and encircled her eyes with soot.

"Don ghrian agus don ghealach agus do na realtoga," he

chanted in Old Irish. To the sun and the moon and the stars.

He left the room. When he returned, he was pushing a gurney. It held a tray of surgical instruments. Selecting the Bard-Parker scalpel, he turned to face his Deirdre.

She trembled as the skin of her neck welcomed the glimmering blade.

Chapter 3

The ambient air that hung above the cemetery was as cold as the bodies the graveyard encased. The sparrows that usually trumpeted their presence were elsewhere, seeking shelter from the rain that was about to fall. Only the lonesome cry of a cricket pierced the stillness.

Police Lieutenant John W. Driscoll, his face etched in grief, reached out his hand and let it fall on the grainy texture of his daughter's granite tombstone. Tears moistened his eyelids.

"Good morning, my little one," he breathed, eyeing the stone's epitaph: "A Ray of Sunshine," words that spoke the language of his heart.

He envisioned his daughter's smile, and his lips responded in kind. "Daddy's here," he whispered.

In life, she had always known how to lighten his heart when all else failed him. And in return, he made sure that she was never darkened by memories like those of his own childhood at the hands of an alcoholic father and a despondently depressed mother. No, Nicole had never felt what he'd felt: like an orphan, shipwrecked.

It was six years since the accident that took the life of his daughter and nearly killed his wife. And in those six years, he had visited his daughter's grave site religiously.

"I brought you a present," he murmured, reaching inside his jacket pocket, from which he produced an Egyptian alabaster music box. He placed it on the cold stone and lifted its lid. The first few notes of Vivaldi's Concerto in D Major rang in the stillness of the grave-yard.

"This is for your collection," he said.

His cellular purred. "Driscoll here. When? Where? I'll be there in twenty minutes."

He genuflected on the lawn and leaned the music box against the tombstone.

"They need me," he sighed, and kissed the stone.

Chapter 4

Driscoll guided his rain-swept Chevy along the meandering roadway that sliced through Prospect Park, then parked his cruiser alongside the yellow-and-black police tape that cordoned off the crime scene. He hated rain. He had promised his wife, Colette, that someday they would settle on an island with no clouds, discard his shield, collect his retirement pay, and never drift far from shore. His dream remained on hold.

He swept back his sandy hair and approached the abandoned boathouse where the remains of a woman had been discovered. He winced at the expression of dread on the face of the rookie cop who greeted him. The bottom of the officer's trousers was stained, and the stench of vomit hung in the air.

"You first on the scene?" Driscoll asked.

"Yes, sir."

"First homicide?"

The officer nodded. "I feel like I'm caught in a nightmare staged at a slaughterhouse."

Inside the boathouse, the scent of fresh blood was dizzying. Its acidity assaulted Driscoll's sinuses. He approached Larry Pearsol, the city's Chief Medical Examiner, who was hunched over what was left of the victim. Jasper Eliot, Pearsol's assistant, was busy photographing the remains.

"What do we have, Larry?" asked Driscoll

"Our guy is vicious. She's gutted like a fish. I can't find a bone in her, and the head, hands, and feet are missing."

The eviscerated remains lay sprawled on the rotting wooden floor. The boneless flesh vaguely resembled something human. Its breasts said female.

The sight of the corpse disgusted Driscoll. This crime was particularly heinous, its perpetrator barbaric. What would drive someone to commit such an atrocity? And why take the head, hands, and feet? What was that all about?

As he stared down at the mutilated remains, he was reminded of his mother's mangled corpse after the New York City Fire Department cut her dismembered body out of the entangling steel of a Long Island Railroad passenger train. His mother had ended her life in the summer of 1969 by hurling herself in front of the oncoming train. Driscoll had been eight years old. He had accompanied his mother to the station that day. She had made him wait at the bottom of the stairs, telling him she had to meet the 10:39 from Penn Station. As the train had screeched into the station above, a river of what he believed to be fruit punch cascaded down, splattering the asphalt and the windshields of passing motorists. A woman had jumped out from behind the wheel of her car, screaming, "My God, that's blood!"

The memory of his mother's suicide haunted him every day of his life.

"Lieutenant? Are you all right?"

It was the voice of Sergeant Margaret Aligante, a member of Driscoll's elite team. She had just arrived on the scene.

"I'm fine."

"For a minute there, I thought you had seen a ghost."

"Whad'ya make of it, Larry?" Driscoll asked, ignoring her remark.

"Brutal. Capital B. And I'd say this is the drop site, not the murder site. No blood splatter. Forensic's been all over the body and all over the site, but they've yet to come up with a single strand of trace evidence."

"This rain doesn't help," said Margaret.

"Looks like the boys may have missed something," said Driscoll as he leaned in over the butchered corpse. His eyes had detected a tiny fragment of material protruding from the mutilated labia. His gloved hand provided protection and discretion as he pulled the object from the fleshy wound.

MCCABE, DEIRDRE

ID NUMBER: 31623916

EXPIRATION DATE: 2/04/08

CLASS D CORRECTIVE LENSES

ORGAN DONOR

The New York State driver's license showed the face of a youthful redhead smiling for the camera.

"Here lies Deirdre McCabe," said Driscoll. "And some sick bastard went to a lot of trouble to introduce us."

Chapter 5

There is a sanctuary in this hustling city, a peninsula in the New York archipelago spanning the Atlantic Ocean and the greater Jamaica Bay. It is a community of freckle-faced children and burly blue-collar workers. They call it Toliver's Point. This strip of land, a home to gulls awaiting its summertime awakening, lies trapped between sea and sky, situated just beyond the footing of the Marine Parkway Bridge on the outskirts of New York City.

A wooden dock juts one hundred yards out into the bay. On its tip stood Driscoll. The Lieutenant was drawn to this particular spot. Drawn to its silence, to its natural coastal beauty. Behind him sat the tranquillity and calm of Toliver's Point. But before him, on the other side of the two-mile-wide body of water, prowled a killer.

Putting that reality aside, his thoughts drifted to earlier times. It was Colette who had discovered Toliver's Point when, as a landscape painter at New York's Art

Students League, she had fulfilled her assignment to locate the most scenic spot in the city. She had found the
location irresistible, and vowed to establish a home there
as soon as she had raised $25,000 for the down pay-
ment. After five years as a pattern artist at Bertillon Tex-
tiles in Manhattan, she had saved enough money to put
a deposit on her first piece of oceanfront real estate, a
summer bungalow in Toliver's Point.

The first night Sergeant John Driscoll was invited to
the peninsula, he thought he had been transported to
some distant island where she was Calypso to a young
and inexperienced Ulysses. After he and Colette married, the bungalow was renovated and winterized and
became for them a year-round home.

One afternoon in May, as Colette was driving Nicole
to her weekly flute lesson, a Hess gasoline tanker side-
swiped their Plymouth Voyager. The bleak images still
haunted Driscoll's consciousness. Colette's twisted
minivan, its shattered windshield, his daughter's lifeless
form, the overturned eighteen-wheeler, his wife's mangled hand boasting the wedding band, the wail of the
ambulance, the hellish dash to the hospital . . . his
grieving.

After the accident that robbed him of fourteen-year-
old Nicole and threw his wife into a permanent state
of unconsciousness, his world changed. Driscoll the
happily married man and loving father became Driscoll
the caretaker and grieving dad. The bungalow that was
their paradise became an intensive care unit. In the
middle of what was once her artist's loft, Colette lay in a
positioning bed surrounded by a Nellcor N395 pulse
oximeter, an Invicare suction machine, a Pulmonetic LTV
950 home-care ventilator, a Kangaroo model 324 en-
teral feeding pump, and an EDR super-high-resolution

electrocardiograph. Her inert body was wired to amber screens. Her circulation, respiration, and cardiac tremors were being vigilantly monitored by a multitude of sensors. Constantly attended by a registered nurse, Colette waited, listless, comatose.

It had been no small feat to care for his wife at home. He had been forced to flex his authority and call in favors from friends in high places to convince the hospital's administrative staff to condone such an unorthodox arrangement. But that's where he wanted his Colette. The in-house treatment had been costly beyond his wildest imagination. He had to delve deeply into his pension to offset what was not covered by Blue Cross. But, to him, the expense was worth it.

The Lieutenant left the dock and turned toward home. Sullivan's Tavern, which lay at the beach end of the pier, beckoned. It had become a regular haunt for Driscoll, where bartenders Jim and Christopher helped him wrestle with his demons of despair.

But not tonight.

In the pocket of his Burberry topcoat he carried a jar of natural emollient, skin cream brought from Trinidad by his friend, Detective Cedric Thomlinson. Made from natural fruit oils, it was widely used by Caribbean women to moisturize and nourish the skin, and Driscoll wanted the nurse to apply it to his wife's inert body.

The jar was deforming the pocket of his topcoat. Before he had known Colette, Driscoll wore polyester suits purchased at NBO on Washington's Birthday, the great holiday of sales. He saluted patriotism with frugality. But Colette had introduced him to fine English tailoring. She believed it was more advantageous to own one exquisite suit, well made and designed, sewn to withstand the wear and tear of a harried life, than to boast five mediocre ones that were dull, uninspiring, and shoddily made. Her logic was irrefutable. Overnight, she had donated his wardrobe to the Salvation Army and bought him three luxurious suits at Barney's annual sale, five Dior shirts at clearance, two Ferragamo ties with a gift certificate at Bloomingdale's, two pairs of Kenneth Cole shoes at a One-Day-Only Two-For-One extravaganza, and her favorite men's cologne, Halston 14.

Driscoll had become hooked on fine English cloth—expensive wools and beautiful silks. His wardrobe became his only indulgence. After a purchase of a jacket by Bill Blass or a pair of slacks by Ralph Lauren, he could sense Colette's approval. He still dressed for her, not for the unanimous distinction of being New York City's best-dressed detective, nor for the moniker "Dapper John" his well-cut suits had earned him.

Driscoll carried his height with a forceful stride that made his 6'2" stature seem intimidating. There was a swagger to his walk, not unlike that of Gary Cooper's in *High Noon*. Precinct women found him irresistible, but Driscoll was impervious to feminine adulation.

Another remarkable feature of Driscoll's face was his expressive lips—lips that were kind and generous, that did not belong to his Celtic jawline but were more Mediterranean, almost Latin. They responded to his emotional states, dilating when contented, contracting under stress, vibrating when anxious. There was a nonverbal language his lips communicated. Colette had learned to read his heart and transcribe his thoughts by observing his lips' tremors. Because of those lips, Driscoll couldn't boast a poker face that, in his profession, would have been an asset.

And now, his lips thin, he walked the deserted shoreline, heading for the bungalow and Colette. Arriving on the porch, he turned the key in the lock of their front door. Oil paintings that once seemed to have lived and breathed welcomed him. They too had become lifeless, a silent salute to their creator, who lay motionless in the center of the loft. The scent of fresh-cut peonies and artist's turpentine had been replaced by the sharpness of Betadine antiseptic and the sterile smell of bleached hospital linen.

Colette lay with her eyelids closed and her lips parted, inhaling pure air brought to her lungs through plastic tubes that invaded her nasal cavity. Her skin was ashen, lusterless. Her once radiant hair was matted, flattened on her scalp.

"*Bon soir, ma cherie,*" he murmured, kissing her forehead.

"We had a lovely day," sang Colette's Jamaican nurse, Lucinda, who was busy massaging his wife's feet.

Driscoll unpocketed the jar of emollient, and Lucinda's eyes widened.

"I haven't seen that since I was a little girl in Kingston," she said, unscrewing the jar's lid and inhaling the fragrance. "Ain't nothin' better for the skin." She began to apply the cream to Colette's ankles.

"You can take a break when you're done, Lucinda. I'll fill in for you," said Driscoll.

The nurse replaced the cap on the jar of emollient and placed the jar on Colette's nightstand. She excused herself and headed for her room.

Driscoll was alone with his wife. He reclined in the armchair next to her bed, where electronic instruments monitored life signs, supervising the maintenance of her existence.

"Let me tell you about my day," he said. "I visited the

dock at Sullivan's. Remember, honey, the time we launched the catamaran from there? Your face went ashen when we hit the water, and whiter still when the first wave nearly toppled us over."

Colette's breathing faltered. The respirator displayed a quavering line. After ten seconds, an alarm would ring. Driscoll leaped from his chair and watched the digital chronometer showing the passing of seconds. Three . . . four . . . five. Panic seized him. Was she going to die right here and now with him watching, powerless to keep her alive? Seven . . . eight. My God, he was losing her.

No. Her breathing returned to normal. The line showed her lungs were working again, ventilating her body.

What had just happened? Had she been dreaming? Was he in her dream? What had taken her breath away?

Driscoll loosened his tie and collapsed back into the chair. He flicked on the room's Sony receiver and loaded a new CD into its feed. The sound of Jean-Pierre Rampal's flute filled the loft. He rambled to the kitchen, retrieved a bag of frozen scallops from the Frigidaire, and placed them into the microwave to defrost. It was Colette who had introduced him to French cooking, and he had relinquished his diet of Quarter Pounders and fries for the nuances of *coq au vin, agneau à l'estragon, escalopes à la colonnade,* and *tranche de boeuf au madere.*

Tonight's dinner would be *coquilles chambrette,* a combination of sea scallops, lemon juice, Worcestershire sauce, cognac, and wine. It took him fifteen minutes to prepare the dish. He brought his meal to the easy chair beside Colette's bed.

Suddenly the heart monitor beeped. The pattern of

electronic zigzagging had changed. The rhythm seemed more agitated.

"Lucinda!" he shouted.

The nurse came running in, dressed in a robe.

"There's a change in her heartbeat! It's up to 98!"

"I see that," Lucinda said, eyeing the monitor. "But, she's not in any danger, sir. It would have to climb above 110 for there to be a problem."

"Why did it change?"

"I don't know, sir."

She turned a knob on the monitor that darkened the screen, then turned the knob back to its original position. The agitated pattern returned.

"Machine's working fine," she reported.

The music stopped. It was the last selection on the Rampal CD. The zigzagging of the heart monitor returned to its original pattern.

"She's back to 62," Lucinda announced. "It dropped when the music stopped."

Driscoll hurried over to the wall unit that held his stereo system and hit play on the CD player. He then depressed the right arrow button eleven times until he had recalled the last selection that had played. The sound of Rampal's melodious flute filled the loft again.

"That's La Ronde des Lutins, from Bazzini," said Driscoll, his eyes riveted to his wife's chalky face.

"Her heart rate is climbing again. It's up to 99!" gasped the nurse. "She's reacting to the music. But that would be impossible."

"That was Nicole's favorite flute piece," said Driscoll, absently. "She used to practice it over and over again."

"Lord Almighty," breathed Lucinda.

Sadness and despair filled Driscoll as the musician's crystalline notes played on. He knew there was no chance Colette would awaken from her coma. He placed no hope in that. There was only one unresolved question rolling around in his head. He knew it would go unanswered, but he wondered nonetheless. Was it his daughter or his wife that was now speaking to him from the grave?

Chapter 6

To Driscoll, Sergeant Margaret Aligante was a looker. Five-feet-seven, and a figure that would rival any of Veronese's models. She carried her High Renaissance body with confidence, using her physical charisma to her advantage. Driscoll knew that suspects she interrogated were often distracted by her curvaceousness and sensuality. She was a Brooklyn girl, born and raised in Red Hook, an Italian neighborhood where the men worked as firemen, cops, and truck drivers. It surprised Driscoll that, as a teen, she had run with the Pagano Persuaders, a street gang that intimidated ten city blocks. But that had soon ended. She had decided to become a police officer. She had registered at John Jay College, completing the four-year curriculum with a 3.96 grade-point average; complemented her education with a smattering of courses in criminal behavioral science, forensic psychology, and profiling methodology; and studied the martial arts of aikido and tae kwon do.

Margaret graduated from the Police Academy in 1991. Her first assignment as a patrolman had her monitoring the arteries of the 72nd Precinct, between Third and Fifteenth Streets in Brooklyn. In six years, she had earned her gold shield, passed the Sergeant's test, and was working undercover with Vice. After that, it was Homicide with Lieutenant Driscoll for the past four years.

Driscoll had asked Margaret to sit in as he conferred with Gerard McCabe, the murder victim's husband. A somber silence filled Driscoll's office. The two police officers waited compassionately for McCabe to pull himself together. Then Driscoll said, "You should know we don't have a DNA profile yet, but it is your wife's license."

"What kind of a person would do this to a woman?" McCabe's hands were trembling, and his face was as pale as chalk.

"Your wife's Volvo was found parked in a retail strip on Ralph Avenue and Avenue L. Would that have been a normal stop for her?" Margaret asked, not answering his question.

"She must have stopped at Video-Rama, on her way back from the mall. The tapes were two days late. She said she'd drop them off for me. I'm a pharmacist who never has a chance to get out from behind the counter. My God, does that make me responsible?"

Driscoll understood his guilt. "Mr. McCabe, it was a simple shopping trip with a stop at the video store, the kind of errand thousands of housewives make every day, in every town in the country. What happened to your wife was not part of the picture. Something ugly and unexpected intervened." He looked at the distraught man with sympathy, trying to keep his own emotions at bay. "There are some personal questions I'll need to ask."

"I understand."

"Were you and your wife having trouble, sir? I mean, was your marriage OK?"

"The marriage was fine."

McCabe had flinched, and Driscoll had caught it. The man was hiding something. Something wrong with the marriage? Had his wife taken a lover? Had that gone bad? Bad enough to end in her slaughter?

"Do you know of anyone that may have had a grievance against your wife?" asked Margaret, picking up on Driscoll's lead.

"Who wouldn't like Didi? She was a wonderful woman."

"Define fine," said Driscoll.

"Excuse me?"

"Fine. Before you said your marriage was fine."

McCabe's eyes narrowed. Driscoll had struck a nerve.

"I see where you're going with this. You're thinking this had something to do with infidelity. Well, you're wrong. Dead wrong. I'll admit our marriage has baggage. What marriage doesn't? You live with someone long enough, the passion dwindles. But if you're thinking Didi was having an affair, you'd be way off-target. That I'm certain of. Believe me, I'd know."

McCabe's eyes held fast to Driscoll's.

The Lieutenant let it go. He reached out his hand and placed it on the grieving man's shoulder. "I'm sorry I can't change what happened to your wife," he said. "But I will make you this promise. I'll do my best to catch this man, although in this case I'm not sure it's a man I'm after."

"What do you mean, not a man?"

Driscoll's eyes drifted toward Margaret's.

"This time, I think we're after a ghoul."

Chapter 7

The heinous murder put the political machinery of the city in motion. The Police Commissioner and the Mayor himself were leaning on Captain Eddie Barrows, who made it clear to Driscoll that he was to have some leads in the case, now thirty-six hours old, before the next newspaper headline thrashed the police department for its ineptness. Both the *Post* and the *Daily News* had aptly labeled the killer "The Butcher" and had forecast a long and arduous investigation because, as the *New York Post*'s Stephen Murray put it, "The NYPD is clueless." The front-page coverage by both newspapers sprouted seeds of paranoia in New York City's populace.

Driscoll paced the floor of the Command Center. It was a large room on the fourteenth floor of One Police Plaza. Though it featured a panoramic view of the Brooklyn Bridge and the lower New York harbor, the homicide detectives referred to it as the dugout. It was where strategy was planned, orders rendered, and where all particularly vicious crimes and high-profile cases were investigated. The pea-green walls of the dugout were lined with photos and the minute details of this latest abominable crime. Margaret and Driscoll were briefing their associate, Detective Cedric Thomlinson.

"I hear the driver's license was shoved into her vagina like it was an ATM slot," Thomlinson remarked, pouring himself a cup of coffee. "Maybe the guy's got credit problems." Detective Thomlinson's Trinidadian roots gave him a sunny and uninhibited perspective on reality.

"I've got more snapshots," Driscoll offered.

"I'll pass," said Thomlinson.

Driscoll stopped pacing, coming to a halt beside a large map of New York City that was thumbtacked to the east wall of the Command Center.

"This is where her Volvo was abandoned," he said, the tip of his finger on a small blue pennant that punctured the Canarsie section of Brooklyn. "And here is where her body was found." He sprinted his finger to a red pennant inside Prospect Park. "A ten-mile stretch between the Volvo and the dump site."

Hearing himself speak of the dead woman, Driscoll considered the parallel to his own life. Hadn't villainous fate interceded and robbed him of his wife as well? Sure, Colette's body was intact. She hadn't been boned. But she might as well have been, for her soul had been stolen.

"Back home in Trinidad, when bones are missing, we're usually looking for a ritual sacrifice." Thomlinson said. "Whad'ya got on the victim?"

Whad'ya got on the victim? Driscoll's mind raced.

His wife loved art. It was her life. She built her world around it. She loved her family. Nicole was her sunshine on a rainy day. She was my wife, goddamn it! She was my wife. Do you know what it's like to lose the love of your life? And to lose that love at the merciless hands of some bastard who has no regard for the law, and little regard for the grieving spouse?

"Lieutenant, whad'ya got on the victim?" Thomlinson's voice echoed, dispelling Driscoll's anger and instantly bringing him back to the matter at hand.

"The victim was a housewife and mother whose only mistake, it seems, was in dropping off videos after dark in a dimly lit parking lot," he said.

"What kind of movies we talkin' about?"

"She returned *South Pacific* and *The King and I*, and rented *It's a Wonderful Life*. That one's still missing."

"Broadway musicals and a seasonal love story. Downright innocuous. Simple romantic movies," said Margaret.

"Now what provoked our guy?" Driscoll pondered. "This bone scavenger? Cedric, do you know how many bones there are in the human body?"

"Aahh . . . two hundred?"

"Two hundred and six. And judging from what he did to the torso, I'd say the son of a bitch removed each one of them. That's dedication. That's tolerance under stress."

"And our boy's meticulous," said Margaret.

"This ain't no sexual crime. No run-of-the-mill butchering. We're looking at the artwork of an educated vandal. A white-collar psycho," said Driscoll. "But how much of this was planned in advance? Did he know his victim? Had he stalked her? Will he strike again?

One thing's for certain, our subject is arrogant. He flaunts his crime. Hell, he identified his victim for us."

"Was there any semen?" Thomlinson asked.

"The lab says no," said Margaret.

"How 'bout how he savaged the body? Now that says overkill."

"I don't think his primary intent is killing," said Driscoll.

"Are you for real?" said Thomlinson.

"We're looking for a thief. A bone thief."

"Then why are we handling the case? It should'a been Robbery that caught it." The black detective grinned and lit a cigar. With one eyebrow arched like a drawbridge, he blew out a cloud of smoke that filled the Command Center.

"What you said before about a ritual sacrifice may have some merit," said Driscoll. "Could we be dealing with voodoo in the Big Apple?"

"It might be worth a looksee."

"What's going through your head?" Driscoll asked, sensing that Thomlinson wasn't satisfied with the voodoo theory.

"Still got the look of a sex crime to me." Thomlinson leaned back on the rear legs of his chair and expelled a series of smoke rings, poking at each one with his finger.

"And what makes you so sure?" said Margaret.

"Look where he left the ID. Only a disgruntled lover is gonna use her slit as a mailbox."

"Go on," Driscoll urged.

"I think she wanted out, but her Romeo wasn't willing to call it quits."

"So he mutilates her?" said Driscoll. "He took her bones, goddamn it! That doesn't fit the profile of a jilted lover."

"You guys ever hear the story of the thief of hearts?" Thomlinson asked.

Driscoll and Margaret shook their heads.

"In the summer of 1976, in Trinidad, several women were murdered. Their hearts had been plucked out. A big investigation followed. Bodies kept piling up. Beautiful girls. No hearts. Suddenly the murders stopped. Three years later, the mayor of this little tourist town shoots himself. He had written a letter before pulling the trigger. In it, he admitted that he was the one who had killed the eight women he had once loved. They had all betrayed him with other men. If he couldn't have their hearts, no one would."

"But our ghoul takes bones," said Driscoll, his finger pressing hard on the hanging 8-x-10 glossy of the mutilated corpse. "And this ghoul has no regard for human life. The McCabe woman weighed 116 pounds and stood five-feet-two. My Nicole had ten pounds on this woman, and three inches. We're talking a frail target. It must have been easy to overtake her. For all we know, the poor woman might have died from fright before being slaughtered. And that would have been a blessing."

Driscoll picked up a wooden pointer and tapped its tip on the red pennant inside Prospect Park.

"I've got a bad feeling about this murder," he said. "I have a hunch we're looking at victim number one. What we must do, and do now, is get inside the mind of this crazed killer. What sets him off? What drives him to commit such a vicious crime? The key, as I see it, is in understanding what the bones mean to him. He's got a real good reason for taking them, and our job is to find out what it is."

Chapter 8

The rain that pelted the city for the past three days had finally stopped. Driscoll pulled the Chevy into an open parking space just outside the video store where Deirdre McCabe had last been seen alive. The "after view," as he liked to call it, seemed surreal. The present passivity of the crime scene disturbed him. It seemed like any other slice of America, not the place where demons danced. He thought of the Bensonhurst section of Brooklyn and the stretch of roadway that serves as a service road for the westbound Belt Parkway. On that particular roadway David Berkowitz, better known as the Son of Sam, staged his last bloody assault on an unsuspecting couple who were parked in, what was for them, a lover's lane. Are there any signs to indicate that an abominable act had taken place there? No. That "after view" has taken on the embodiment of a quiet and cozy lover's lane once again, and the tranquillity of life goes on around it.

Driscoll got out of the cruiser to better scan the area, the same area that the crime-scene crew had scoured, producing no tangible evidence, and he counted eight parked cars and one utility vehicle, a Ford Bronco. None were occupied. The space where McCabe's Volvo had been parked was now empty. It was a good thirty feet from the video store. Had the killer been waiting in the dark? Watching her? If so, from where? Did the victim know her assailant? Had this been a tryst gone bad? There were no apparent signs here that a murder or an abduction had taken place. But, given the fact that the Volvo was left behind, the abduction, more than likely, had taken place in the parking lot.

What bait had he used to lure her to his vehicle? Serial killer Ted Bundy liked to wear a false plaster cast on his arm and wrist and pretend he couldn't lift a parcel into his Volkswagen. Time and again, his soon-to-be victims would come to his aid, helping him load the bulky item. Or had the McCabe woman met the killer in the shop and gone willingly to his vehicle? Or had he simply overpowered her, an unsuspecting and frail woman returning from a quick visit to a local retailer? In any case, the killer probably had his own auto.

With more questions than answers, Driscoll headed for the store.

"Hi! Welcome to Video-Rama," a cheerful voice sounded. "May I help you with your selection?" The clerk, a young girl of high-school age with tawny blond hair in a ponytail, had gentle blue eyes that crinkled when she spoke.

"I'm Detective Driscoll," the Lieutenant announced. "I was hoping to speak to the manager, Ms. Clairborne."

"I'm sorry, but Ms. Clairborne works the evening shift. She won't be here for another fifteen minutes."

Driscoll checked his watch. It was a quarter to six. He'd kill the time browsing the racks of videos.

Below the advertisements for Coca-Cola and micro-wavable popcorn, Driscoll saw that the shop's walls were lined with rack upon rack of current releases. The center of the store, he noted, was devoted to celluloid treasures of years gone by. Driscoll meandered to a kiosk displaying a collection entitled Film Classics. *Gone With the Wind, My Fair Lady, On the Town,* and an entire collection of Hitchcock favorites stared back at him. The beautiful face of Grace Kelly in the arms of a young and debonair Jimmy Stewart caught Driscoll's attention. He picked up *Rear Window,* returned the gaze of leading lady Kelly, and remembered Colette.

On a bright, sunny April day early in their courtship he and his date were picnicking on the rolling hills of the Sheep Meadow inside Prospect Park. Prospect Park, he thought. How ironic to have such a remembrance while investigating the death of a woman whose body had been discovered in that park. Perhaps his unconscious was at work trying to obliterate the horrendous find. *Good transcending evil,* he thought. His eyes were drawn back to the smiling face of Grace Kelly, but his mind was now littered with thoughts of the terrible homicide. The spell had been broken. He took one last look into the gleaming eyes of Grace Kelly and smiled sadly.

"May I help you?" a voice sounded.

"Quite a film," he said, returning the video to its appropriate slot in the display.

"Yes, it is," replied Ms. Clairborne with a smile. "I understand you have some questions regarding Mrs. McCabe, the poor soul. Supposing we go inside my office, shall we?"

The woman stood about six feet tall. Her blue and gray business suit hugged her lean frame. Driscoll was reminded of Mrs. Haggerty, a grade-school teacher not well liked by her students, but admired by him since she seemed strict but fair.

Once inside the office, Ms. Clairborne motioned for Driscoll to have a seat, and then sat down behind a desk cluttered with trade magazines and big-screen paraphernalia.

"How can I help you, Lieutenant Driscoll?" she asked.

"I understand you were working last Friday evening. The night Mrs. McCabe came into the store."

"Yes, I was. I always work Friday evenings. It's our busiest night."

"Do you remember seeing Mrs. McCabe?"

"Yes. In fact, I waited on her myself. She returned two videos, and rented one. *It's a Wonderful Life.* I remember because Jimmy Stewart is a favorite of mine."

"Was she with anyone?"

"No. She was alone. She always came in by herself."

"Did she seem nervous or edgy, or act as if she were meeting someone?"

"No. She was her usual pleasant self."

"Did you notice if she spoke to anyone in the store? Anyone at all?"

"Not that I noticed. But I couldn't swear to it."

"What kind of person was Mrs. McCabe?"

"Why, she was a lovely person. Very polite."

"Was anyone else in the store at the same time as Mrs. McCabe?"

"Mr. Thornwood was here with his two teenage granddaughters. They were in the New Release section, which is on the opposite side of the store from where

Mrs. McCabe was. She was in the section where we feature the Classics."

"So they didn't interact?"

"No, I don't think they even saw each other."

"Anyone else?"

"Yes, two OTs who browsed the racks and then left without renting anything."

"OTs"?

"Out of Towners. People who don't have an account with us. These OTs were two women."

"Ms. Clairborne, have you had cause to let anyone go recently?"

"No. I've never had the occasion to fire anyone."

"Ms. Clairborne, are your records computerized?"

"Why, of course."

"I'll need a list of all your account holders, and especially a listing of everyone who rented or returned a video on the Friday in question."

"I'm not sure if I can do that."

"Ms. Clairborne, I wouldn't ask you for anything that I absolutely didn't require. It's vital to the investigation."

The woman pondered his request for a moment and then said, "Wait here, I'll be right back. It'll take a minute or two for the computer to print out the records."

"Thank you, Ms. Clairborne."

Driscoll pulled out his notepad and wrote: *Have Thornwood interviewed at his home. The granddaughters, too. Check all the stores on the strip for the two OTs. See if they were picked up for shoplifting. Have Cedric run the account holders list for criminal records. Check with the local precinct to see if there were any radio runs to the area that night.*

Ms. Clairborne appeared with the printouts. "Here you are, Lieutenant."

Driscoll accepted them and thanked her again. "One more thing before I leave. Have you noticed any trouble on the strip lately? Any retailer complaining about strangers who don't belong around here?"

"Oh, no. This has always been a safe neighborhood."

I wonder if Mrs. McCabe felt that way, thought Driscoll.

He handed Ms. Clairborne his business card and told her to call him if she thought of anything else. Driscoll returned the woman's smile and left the store. He glanced at the sheets of paper in his hand and wondered if the answer lay there.

Chapter 9

The rushing sound of the subway car was melodic. Colm waited on the platform for the A train to come to a stop, savoring its panting from fatigue and rust. His medical bag sat at his side. He was eager to meet his new date.

A girl was pacing the platform, forlorn, disheartened. Had she just broken it off with some lover? he wondered. He could comfort her were it not for his date. Maybe some other time.

The girl entered the subway car just before he did. The doors scraped closed. Colm positioned himself in front of the girl, watching as her fluted fingers entwined around the subway car's stainless-steel pole. Under a fluorescent bulb he stared at her, this wingless cherub. Her face would have inspired Raphael. Her body was pure ether, tinged with sensuality. In the gash between two buttons of a linen vest he could detect the incline of a breast. The garment concealed her secret, the

aroma of untouched flesh. Was she aware of her car-
nality?

The girl looked sixteen, perhaps a year or two older.
The weight of a knapsack strapped to her shoulders
caused her torso to arch and her breasts to jut forward.
Her hair was brassy blond. Cut short. She wore no
makeup, no jewelry. Her eyes were stratospheric blue.

He imagined her skeletal frame under her external
beauty. She would rival any one of his treasures.

She got off the train at the Beach Seventy-fifth Street
station. His urge was to follow, but his legs refused his
mind's order. There was another girl waiting for him.
He stayed on board. He'd let this one go. In a matter of
seconds the train arrived at his stop.

"Beach Sixty-seventh Street," the loudspeaker crackled, and the doors opened.

He descended the stairs, palming the rickety railing.
A gang of high-school teens stampeded up the staircase,
nearly knocking him down. His fingers longed for a ser-
rated blade.

The sun greeted him at street level. He smiled at the
sight of so many abandoned bungalows and headed for
the boardwalk, thrilled that his date had picked such a
remote section of the city for their rendezvous.

He climbed sun-soaked wooden steps. The boardwalk
was empty. He was sure she had said Beach Sixty-seventh Street. Had he been stood up? He scanned the
beach. A handful of sun worshippers dotted the narrow
strand. By the ocean's edge, a young woman was dabbling her toes in the waning tide. Sunshine streamed
through her gossamer dress. Could that be his date? It
was hard to tell from a distance.

He removed his shoes and socks and strolled toward
her. A thought lingered on the rim of his conscious-

ness. All the ingredients were present for a truly romantic encounter. He thought of the girl on the train.
Wouldn't it have been satisfying if he could teach his
heart to crave the tenderness of a woman? The notion
disoriented him, but in a few seconds his resolve returned.

He caught up with the girl at the shoreline.

"Hello, Monique," he said.

"Hello."

"Or should I call you Ariel?"

"Ariel? Why would you call me Ariel?"

"Because you look just like the Little Mermaid," he
grinned.

Chapter 10

The sun had climbed above the horizon and was hidden behind lead-colored clouds. The turbulent tide, its waves brown with sludge and darkened seashells, crashed onto the shore, delivering polluted brine. Though morning had broken, there were no gulls on the beach.

In the company of her Labrador, a jogger ran the boardwalk, oblivious to the brooding ocean and its contaminated waves. Yet the absence of gulls unnerved her. They had also been her running companions, welcoming her morning endeavor. But not today.

Without warning, the Labrador broke from its leash and dashed toward the boardwalk's staircase, then bolted down onto the beach and under the boards. The jogger brought two fingers to her mouth and let loose a high-pitched whistle. The dog did not respond. The jogger raced down the steps in pursuit of her dog. Just under the boards she found the gulls. They were screeching boldly, flying in her face, and splattering what appeared to be blood in every direction. The sound of the gull's fluttering wings and frantic squawking was as deafening as it was terrifying. The jogger was paralyzed with fear. Again, she brought two fingers to her mouth but couldn't manage a whistle.

"Brandy!" she hollered. "Brandy, please!" she cried.

The dog reappeared in the midst of the blood-soaked birds. The jogger fell to her knees and wrapped her arms around the Labrador. That's when she spotted it. Clenched firmly in the dog's white canines was a trove her pet had looted from the gulls.

"Drop it, girl. Drop it," she commanded.

The obedient dog let go of the trophy. The jogger suddenly recognized what it was the dog was carrying. It was a freshly torn human breast, its nipple adorned with a tiny ring of glittering gold. The jogger screamed. Grabbing hold of the dog's collar, she pulled her pet out from under the boards and let loose another scream. But both screams were lost to the clamor of the hysterical gulls.

Chapter 11

As he glanced at himself in the Impala's rearview mirror, Driscoll realized he needed a shave. He unlatched the glove compartment, picked up the Braun cordless razor, and prayed the batteries weren't dead. They were.

He tossed the razor back in the glove box and proceeded to the boardwalk at Beach Sixty-seventh Street in Rockaway where, he feared, victim number two had been found. As he crossed the Marine Parkway Bridge, thoughts tumbled inside his head. It was the same MO as the McCabe woman, and the victim's head, hands, and feet were missing. That particular aspect of the first crime had been held back from the news media, so it ruled out a copycat killing. These two atrocities were the work of one man. New York had a serial killer on the loose. Driscoll was certain of it. And he knew it was his job to find him before he struck again.

Arriving at the boardwalk, he got out of the Chevy

and walked briskly toward the wooden staircase that led to the beach. He made his way toward the area cordoned off by yellow-and-black crime-scene tape. A small crowd of onlookers had clustered around the site.

"What have we got?" Driscoll asked Medical Examiner Larry Pearsol.

"Your boy thinks he's an artist. He filleted this one and nailed her remains to the underside of the boardwalk." Pearsol pointed to the hollow where two uniformed officers from the 100th Precinct stood sentry. "It took a small battalion of policemen in riot gear to roust the goddamn gulls out from under there. They were feeding on the rotting corpse."

"Time of death?"

"I'll know more when I get her up on the slab. I'm guessing she's been under there for at least seventy-two hours."

Driscoll glared at the flock of gulls that had perched themselves on the sand some twenty feet away.

"Oh! And Lieutenant, there's a slight twist to this one. Crime Scene says she was killed here."

"They finished processing the site?"

"That they are. Here comes Hobbs now."

Driscoll took a ninety-degree turn and was greeted by Walter Hobbs, the Commanding Officer of the Crime Scene Investigating Unit.

"Good morning, Lieutenant."

"Talk to me, Walt. Tell me you found something."

"Well, we know he killed her here. That much is for sure. The blood tells us that. The sand is saturated with it, there's blood spatter everywhere, and there's no trail of it in or out. He boned her. Just like the woman in the park. Even left the driver's license. Monique Beauford. She was nineteen. Your boy's got a knack for carving,

John, and just like the first victim, he took the head, hands, and feet. What he does with them is anybody's guess. He left us with what remains of the torso and the upper and lower extremities. A good portion of the body was pecked away by the gulls.

"He used three-inch flooring nails to fasten her to the boards. Nothing particularly uncommon about the nails. You can get them at any Home Depot. Judging from the indentures surrounding each nail, we figure he used a ball-peen hammer or something close to it. Blowfly maggots feeding off the flesh mean she's been in there for at least three days. Any tracks your guy left, he was quick to cover. Sand is terrible for footprint casting anyway. We found what may be trace evidence. Some fibers. Cotton, I'd guess. Probably clothing. Let's hope we catch a break and they lead us somewhere. The lab boys will tell us if he left any of his DNA on her. We found no trace of semen.

"Now blood. That's a whole other ball game. With all that slicin' and dicin' he may have nicked himself in the process. We'll be looking for any blood that wasn't the victim's. We'll also run her blood through toxicology. She was probably drugged like the McCabe woman. It's not likely she walked under the boardwalk willingly. It's hard to tell if she put up a fight, considering the condition of the body. Larry'll search for any defensive wounds during the autopsy. I sure would like to know what he's doing with the head, hands, and feet."

"You and me both."

"Like I said, we'll know more after the autopsy. I'll contact you with the toxicology results and with anything else the evidence points us toward. We're gonna keep the wooden planking intact until we get her back to the lab. Who knows? Maybe he slipped up, and we'll find a print on one of the boards or on one of the nails." Hobbs turned his back on Driscoll and began to walk away. Stopping in midstride, he turned and faced the Lieutenant. "Oh, yeah. There's one other thing. Your vic was fond of jewelry."

"How so?"

"You'll see."

Plainclothes detective Ramon Ramirez approached Driscoll. He had a haggard look about him, and walked with a limp. He was the 100th Precinct's homicide detective who caught the squeal when it was called in earlier in the day.

"Good morning, Lieutenant," said Ramirez, who had met Driscoll only once. "I guess I'll be handing this one over to you."

"You catch the call?"

"Six-thirty-five in the A.M. A woman called 911 from a cell phone. The emergency operator got a no-hit on the number she was calling from. The caller remained anonymous, as well. She reported finding part of a dead body under the boardwalk at Beach Sixty-seventh Street and hung up. That was it. Part of a dead body. Nothing more. The precinct dispatched a patrol car and me. When I got here, a cluster of crazed gulls were ripping apart what looked like a woman's tit. I swear to God. A woman's tit! When I approached them, one of the suckers flew off with it. Well, what was left of it. By that time, it was the size of a tennis ball. A tennis ball with a nipple. The strangest thing you've ever seen. The rest of the gulls, dozens of them, were shrieking and flying wildly in and out from under the boardwalk. I called Emergency Services. They dispatched a team of officers to clear out the birds." He gazed over Driscoll's shoulder at the gulls. "Tough motherfuckers, those birds.

Anyway, I went under the boardwalk. You can stand a little hunched over for eight feet or so, but after that you need to crouch down. I'm tellin' ya, you've got one hell of a dead body under there. I called in Forensics right away. Larry Pearsol and company were here in fifteen minutes. And now you're here."

"And now I'm here," said Driscoll as he eyed the desolate surroundings.

"I'll tell ya Lieutenant, I don't envy your job. I know this is victim number two. That means the heat's gonna be on real quick."

"You've got that right. You know, I think it's time for me to take that walk under the boards. It looks like everyone's been there but me."

Driscoll headed for the cavernous hollow directly below the boardwalk, where he was greeted by two uniformed officers. "Sir, you may want to use these," one of them said, offering Driscoll a jar of Vick's VapoRub and a flashlight.

Driscoll applied a dab of the ointment under each nostril and slipped on a pair of surgical gloves, then crept his way under the wooden expanse. Despite the Vick's, the stench of rancid flesh made him gag. He decided to inhale through his mouth.

Ten feet in, he found what the birds were feasting on. The mutilated remains of a human body had been nailed to the boardwalk's planking. Muscles oozed greenish brine, hosting feeding maggots. Flesh glistened, effervescent under the flashlight's beam. Something metallic caught Driscoll's eye. A gold ring. It pierced the center of a piece of hanging flesh. That must have been her hand, he thought. But that can't be. The killer absconded with the hands.

"Son of a bitch," Driscoll groaned. It was her clitoris, pierced by a gold ring. Why did the killer leave it there, exposing it the way he did? Was it by accident? An act of negligence committed by a distracted murderer? Or, was there a message in his not removing the ring? A message between the unknown suspect and the investigator? With a gloved hand, Driscoll discreetly fingered the ring. Was the killer a body artist, a flesh piercer that had once punctured the tender membranes of this girl's privates and inserted this metal loop? Chemical analysis would reveal the alloys that composed it. The killer had to know the police would find the ornament's manufacturer. And so the flesh artist, possibly the killer, would be found as well. Was he taunting the police? Was this a game?

Driscoll picked up the New York State driver's license that was lying in the sand just below the remains. Monique Beauford. Age nineteen. *This killer may be an exhibitionist,* he thought. He leaves his handiwork behind as though it were a work of art, and uses the driver's license to identify his kill. The McCabe woman was found in a public park, and now this victim is discovered at a public beach. Was there a message in that?

Driscoll looked into the face of the picture displayed on the driver's license. A young, brassy blonde returned his stare. "He may have slipped, you know. Unwittingly, he may have slipped," he said. There was now a thread of commonality to these murders, not only in how the two women were butchered, but in where the killer chose to leave them: in public recreational sites, knowing they would be found.

Driscoll removed a plastic evidence pouch from his breast pocket and placed Monique's driver's license in it. He then examined the nails the killer used, and prayed the wounds were postmortem.

"I'll catch this son of a bitch. That I promise," he vowed as he turned his back on the victim and headed back to the beach.

Chapter 12

Cedric Thomlinson checked his watch and turned off the engine of his Dodge Intrepid. He was five minutes late for his meeting. He walked solemnly toward the heavy oak door that led to Saint Rose of Lima's community room, and slipped inside. There was a large crowd, a mix of men and women, all of them police personnel, and all with the same purpose: to garner the strength to keep from drinking.

Thomlinson was greeted by Father Liam O'Connor, a Jesuit priest, a bulk of a man, sixty-five years of age, with a shock of white hair streaking otherwise gray. He was a Certified Alcohol and Substance Abuse Counselor and had run the Police Department's Confidential Alcohol and Drug Abuse Program for thirty years. His successes recovered, regained their lives, and went on to become productive police officers. His failures didn't. Some of them ended their careers by ending their lives. It wasn't uncommon for a despondent police officer to put the barrel of his service revolver in his mouth and pull the trigger.

"Hello, Cedric. How are you tonight?" asked Father O'Connor.

"Doing fine, Father. And you?"

"Aside from a touch of arthritis, I'm doing fine myself. Thanks for asking."

Thomlinson smiled and meandered over to his assigned seat within a circle of chairs. He glanced around him. The faces remained the same, some revealing hope; some, despair. Every once in a while a new inductee. The Department averaged two a month.

"How ya doin?" Thomlinson muttered to the rookie police officer to his right.

There were far too many young officers in the room caught up in the four-to-four lifestyle. These were officers who started out doing steady four-to-twelve shifts, then continued on to the bars until they closed at four A.M. Hence the classification: four to four. Most of the rest of the crowd were whiskey faced veterans holding on until retirement. At forty-two, Thomlinson felt caught somewhere between the two. "Caught" being the operative word.

The muted chatter that filled the small room ceased as Father O'Connor took his seat and began his invocation: "Almighty Father . . ."

That was all Thomlinson heard, for at that point his mind drifted back to the events that led him here in the first place.

He and his partner, Harold Young, were undercover working Narcotics. They had set up Jamal Hinsdale, an insidious drug dealer, for a medium-sized buy, and had entered a dimly lit hallway with marked money. There were to be no arrests that afternoon, just a controlled buy. Jamal stepped out of the shadows and approached them.

"Everythin' cool, my man?" said Jamal.

"Yeah, mon. Everything's cool," said Thomlinson, despite the fact that he was very hungover from a night of binge drinking, and his view of the world was a blur.

That's why Thomlinson never saw where Jamal's gun came from. Shots exploded in slow motion, the first one catching Thomlinson just above the right shoulder blade and knocking him down. There were several more shots in rapid fire, followed by an eerie silence. When the smoke cleared, both Harold Young and Jamal Hinsdale were dead, and the stench of gunpowder and spilled blood filled the air. Thomlinson called for the Ghost, his backup team. They were already on their way. He heard the sound of sirens approaching, and the sound of tenants in the building opening their windows to look out. When the backup team finally reached him, all hell broke loose. Police radios crackled, a host of uniformed and plainclothes officers came running, and the sergeant in charge barked orders. As they put Thomlinson in the ambulance he heard very clearly what that sergeant said. And that was that Thomlinson still had his gun in his holster.

The official report stated that Thomlinson was situated behind Detective Young and therefore could not fire without hitting his partner. The Mayor and the Police Commissioner settled for what they got: a dead hero cop, a wounded hero cop, and a dead drug dealer. Young's funeral made front-page news. Another hero lost in the war on crime. But, in two years' time, only the people who knew him well would remember his name. Thomlinson would never forget him, and would never forget the gun battle and the true circumstances surrounding it. For it was Thomlinson's binge drinking that helped bring down a fellow police officer. His partner, no less.

For his part in it, Thomlinson was awarded the Department's second-highest medal, the Combat Cross. He was then transferred to the elite Homicide Squad, headed up by Lieutenant John Driscoll. It was every detective's dream assignment.

But the street cops believed a story closer to the truth. Every time he walked in their midst, conversations stopped. Looks of disapproval surrounded him. He knew what was said about him as soon as he left the room. His partner was killed, and he had never even pulled his gun. That was tantamount to being incompetent or a coward, two things a cop could never be. Everywhere he went within the department, he was known as the cop who never pulled his gun.

His drinking became heavier after that, but since he could no longer hang out in cop bars, he turned to drinking alone. Many a morning, he woke up at the kitchen table with an empty bottle and a loaded 9 mm staring him in the face.

He began to duck work, often missing his first or last tour of duty, too drunk to make it in. When on duty, he would make excuses to go to his car, where he kept his stash: a sealed bottle of Jamaican rum. Other times, he simply disappeared for hours, returning with a mouthful of breath mints or some gum.

Driscoll was no fool, and after a few weeks he took the hardest step a police commander ever had to take. He called the representative from the Detectives' Union and had Thomlinson "farmed." Driscoll knew he was ruining Thomlinson's career, but he hoped he was saving his life.

"The Farm," as it was called, was an old retreat house

located so deep in Delaware County that the nearest town was twenty-five miles away.

Thomlinson was stripped of his gun and shield and whisked away. He was given a choice. He could complete the program, or be fired. Those were his only options. The program, administered by a group of Certified Alcohol and Substance Abuse Counselors, consisted of six weeks of alcohol counseling that included regularly conducted one-on-one therapy sessions, and group therapy with past and present alcoholic police officers. It was interspersed with religious encounters as well. Lights-out and lockdown was at eight P.M. each night, and there were guards at every door.

Once you completed the program, you were sent back to Command without your gun or your shield, and were required to attend the self-help program run by Father O'Connor. At the end of one year, if the Department psychiatrist deemed you fit, you were returned to active duty. Your gun and your shield were returned, and supposedly your personnel record never reflected any of it. Of course, everyone knew better. There were few secrets in this man's department.

It had been twenty-nine months since Thomlinson graduated from the Farm. He was now 868 days sober. His gun and shield had been returned to him, and he was eternally grateful to his commander and true friend, Lieutenant John W. Driscoll.

"Cedric, do you have anything to share with us this evening?" Father O'Connor's question rocketed Thomlinson back to the present.

Thomlinson stood up and repeated his usual routine about how he had taken up drinking because his partner had been killed in front of him. He knew it was a lie, the priest knew it was a lie, and everyone else in the room knew it was a lie. But no one challenged him, so he sat back down.

As the meeting was drawing to a close, Thomlinson's cell phone rang. He stepped outside to take the call.

It was Driscoll. He had sobering news. They had found victim number two.

Chapter 13

Margaret poked her head inside Driscoll's office. "Lieutenant, there's a call for you on line two. You're not gonna like who's calling. It's from the office of the Chief of Detectives," she said.

Here it starts, thought Driscoll. From this day forward, every higher-echelon moron with a star on his shoulder would be looking to get into the act. He picked up the phone and hit line two.

"Stand by for Chief Walters," came the voice on the other end.

"Hello, John. How are you holding up?" asked Walters. Walters was the second in command at the office of the Chief of Detectives. He was an old-time Bureau veteran, and he understood just how the game was played. Thank God it was Walters, thought Driscoll.

"I've been better, Chief. How are things there?"

"Heating up, John. Santangelo wants to see you at

nine o'clock tomorrow morning in the conference room. He says to bring the pretty sergeant with you."

"Will do," said Driscoll begrudgingly.

"Take care, John. See you in the morning."

As soon as Driscoll hung up the phone, his head began to pound. Goddamn it, he thought. "Things are heating up" was an understatement. They'll want a head to chop off if this case doesn't turn around soon. Well, this head is staying right where it is.

At eight-thirty the next morning, Margaret and Driscoll were ushered into the oak-paneled conference room on the twenty-first floor of One Police Plaza. Bill Walters was already there, as were several Captains and Inspectors from the Detective Bureau all seated around a large table.

Walters took Driscoll aside and whispered, "Santangelo's in rare form today, so be careful." Driscoll nodded, grateful for the tip, and took a seat next to Walters. Margaret sidled up next to Driscoll. At precisely nine, the door opened, and Chief of Detectives Joseph Santangelo walked in. He was a man who was universally despised throughout the Bureau. Behind his back, his squad commanders sarcastically called him "the World's Greatest Detective" due to his constant meddling and ridiculous suggestions. Basic investigative work escaped him. Over the years, the nickname had been shortened to simply the "World's Greatest." He had risen directly from the rank of Inspector to Chief of Detectives, skipping over several more qualified candidates. It was widely rumored that he had some politician in his pocket. Nothing else could explain how he had gotten so far. After seating himself at the head of the table, he nodded to the midlevel ranks and turned his attention to Margaret.

"How nice to see you again, Sergeant." He fancied himself a ladies' man.

"Thank you, Chief." The man made her skin crawl.

"Now, John, what have you got for me?" he asked, turning his attention to Driscoll.

"Chief, we've been proceeding in the usual manner, but nothing concrete has turned up yet."

"Goddamn it. That's not what I want to hear. I've got the Police Commissioner calling me every hour. The Mayor's office has been all over me, and the goddamn press is up my ass. And all you can tell me is that you have nothing concrete? What the hell are we paying you for?"

Walters broke the tirade.

"Chief, John is our best squad commander. Everything that can be done is being done. Maybe it's time to start a Task Force. Let him pull in some people from other squads."

"Give him whatever he wants," barked Santangelo. "But if I don't see some progress, he's gone. Can I make it any clearer? This guy is butchering women on my watch, and I won't stand for it. I won't." Santangelo looked at his watch. "I've got a briefing with the Police Commissioner in five minutes. I'll leave Chief Walters to work out the details with you. Whatever the hell you need. Just get it done, or I'll find someone that will. Can I make it any clearer?" The Chief stood up, and made a quick exit. Driscoll wanted to haul off and punch the bastard.

Walters leaned over and put his hand on Driscoll's shoulder. "Don't take it personal. It's just his way."

Driscoll scanned the room. Everyone avoided his

gaze but Margaret. He placed his hand over hers and gave it a squeeze, letting her know that he was all right.

"OK, John, whadya need?" asked Walters.

"Three and thirty," Driscoll replied, letting the Chief know he wanted three sergeants and thirty detectives. "And Chief, I don't want any deadbeats."

It was well known in the Bureau that when a Task Force was formed, a sharp squad commander would unload his worst detectives. That, Driscoll was hoping, would not be the case here.

"Your call. You put the names together and give them to me. How are you fixed for cars?"

"I figure I'll need ten additional cars, and a surveillance van."

Walters turned his attention to a slim, suited man seated across the table from him.

"Inspector Malloy, you will arrange that with Fleet Services. And call Gallagher over at the Technical Aide Response Unit (or TARU, as some call it) and give him a heads-up. Anything else, John?"

"Not that I can think of now, Chief."

"You gonna run this out of your office?"

"Yes, sir. I have everything I'll need there."

"OK, any questions? No? Dismissed." All the nameless suits got up and walked out.

"John, you and Margaret stay here for a minute," said Walters. When the room was empty, the Chief spoke. "I know you two are doing everything you can. Don't let Santangelo wear you down. If any squad commander can get to the bottom of this one, you can. If you need anything on the QT, you come directly to me. You got that?"

Driscoll nodded his head.

"I'll want daily updates. And be careful of press leaks.

You speak only to me. No one else. And John, one other thing."

"Sir?"

"Stay clear of the FBI."

"Yes, sir."

On the elevator ride to the Command Center on the fourteenth floor, Driscoll's thoughts were of Walters. He was a clearheaded professional, not a loudmouthed buffoon like Santangelo. For that, Driscoll was grateful. And while Driscoll's thoughts were of Walters, although she didn't know why, Margaret's thoughts were of Driscoll. A brave and unwavering Driscoll. *Hell, he's a married man, for God's sake.* Margaret bit down hard on her lower lip.

Chapter 14

Margaret had interviewed Mr. Thornwood and his two granddaughters, the customers in the video store where the McCabe woman was last seen alive. The interviews had added nothing to the investigation. Ms. Clairborne was right: Thornwood and his girls hadn't even seen Deirdre McCabe. There were no records of any shoplifting on the part of the OTs, and the local precinct, the 68, had had only two radio runs in the area of the video store that night. One drunk-and-disorderly, and one single-car automobile accident involving an elderly woman who took a turn too sharply and clipped a parked car. Thomlinson had run the store's account holders' list for criminal records. Nothing active. Thomas Whiting, seventy-two, had been arrested in 1984 for stock fraud, and Alice Hathaway, now forty-five, had been busted for prostitution when she was twenty-three.

Driscoll mulled over these "revelations" as he put up with bumper-to-bumper traffic on East Broadway. He and Thomlinson were headed for the Medical Examiner's office on First Avenue. Because of a water main break on Allen Street, all traffic had been diverted onto Canal. Driscoll placed the emergency flasher atop the cruiser, turned on the siren, and veered the Chevy north on Centre Street, leaving behind a string of cars and taxi-cabs.

The NYPD was now galvanized. The total resources of the department were at Driscoll's disposal. Cedric Thomlinson was to be Driscoll's house mouse, the lead detective who would speak with Driscoll's authority and coordinate the efforts of the additional police person-nel. In spite of what each member of the Task Force thought of Thomlinson, they knew he was acting on di-rect orders from the Lieutenant, and therefore, so were they. In his new capacity, Thomlinson had already been in contact with Telephone Control, the NYPD's own in-ternal telephone equipment server, and asked that ten additional phone lines be installed inside the Com-mand Center. He would soon be calling TARU to se-cure the electronic equipment that might be needed. That electronic equipment would include such items as listening devices, telephone taps, trap-and-trace units, and videotape equipment. Thomlinson would also oversee the force's telephone tip line. The tip line was a separate phone line the public was encouraged to call with information that may be relevant to the case. The number was furnished to the news media and to the publishers of the daily newspapers, and was included at the close of every broadcast or newspaper article about the case. It usually prompted a number of crank calls and dead ends, but each call was assigned to a detective, and it became his or her responsibility to track down the lead.

As the Lieutenant continued north on Centre Street, he glanced over at Thomlinson and could tell his friend's anxieties were getting the best of him. He knew that Thomlinson was craving a drink. Driscoll watched as his newly ordained house mouse reached in his vest pocket and produced a Macanudo. That was always a sign. When he wanted to drink, Thomlinson would settle for the taste of tobacco over the taste of booze. Driscoll noted how anxiously he peeled away the cigar's cellophane wrapper, pressed the Chevy's cigarette lighter, and waited patiently for it to pop back out. It didn't.

"Check the coil," said Driscoll.

Thomlinson did. It was cold to the touch. "Got any matches?" Thomlinson asked.

"There should be some in the glove box."

Thomlinson rummaged through the clutter in the glove compartment and produced a book of matches with the name of SULLIVAN'S TAVERN embossed on its cover. He struck a match and fired his Macanudo.

"I gotta tell ya, Cedric, there was something very haunting about that cadaver under the boardwalk. The killer's obviously staging his victims. It's up to us to decipher his message."

"The guy's a psychotic exhibitionist," said Thomlinson, exhaling a thin stream of smoke from his cigar.

Driscoll wouldn't argue that. He asked Thomlinson, "Tell me something, why do you suppose he's so hell bent on IDing his victims?"

"We'll need to get inside his head to answer that one."

Inside his head, thought Driscoll. *Now there's a one-way ticket to the Twilight Zone.*

The Lieutenant turned right off of Centre Street at East Houston and then made a left onto First Avenue.

335 First Avenue, the City Morgue, loomed in the distance.

"Our guy's a collector," Driscoll remarked, as he pulled the Chevy into a parking space and turned down his visor, revealing the NYPD's "OFFICIAL BUSINESS" placard. "He must be taking the bones as souvenirs from his kill."

"Maybe the guy's a movie buff. Remember that *Predator* flick, where the alien comes to earth on a hunting spree? After each kill, it collected the victim's skeleton and hung it on a tree. What's the chances this guy's got his own relic garden?"

"He's gotta be putting his trophies somewhere."

Once inside the building, the pair rode the elevator to the sixth floor and marched down the long corridor toward the double-glass doors marked "CITY MORGUE."

The main room of the morgue was spacious, with white-tiled walls and a high ceiling. High-wattage halogen bulbs illuminated eight naked cadavers lying atop stainless-steel gurneys. Two corpses, their chests and abdominal sections gaping, were attended by a team of morgue assistants busily dissecting and weighing the individual organs.

On a separate gurney, unidentifiable rotting flesh was being meticulously examined by Larry Pearsol, the Medical Examiner, and Jasper Eliot, a coroner's assistant.

"Welcome, Lieutenant. Good to see you again, Cedric," said Pearsol. "This one's yours," he gestured with open arms. "We've got the internal organs out of the way, and I was just about to record my findings."

Driscoll winced at the remains. He saw shreds of boneless flesh, and slivers of odorous skin and muscle.

"You get Crime Scene's report?" Pearsol asked.

"Yes. They came up with zilch. All the blood was from the victim. The cotton fibers could have come from any one of a thousand sources, and they found no trace of any other forensic evidence on the body or at the site. It's almost as if a ghost is performing these murders."

The ME depressed the button activating the Uher recorder and spoke:

"Item C296B21. Arrival date, October 19, 2005. Monique Beauford, tentatively identified by New York State driver's license. Remains consist of a female torso with partial extremities attached. Examination reveals multiple beak lacerations, and absence of a skeleton and a right breast. Internal organs are torn. Further micro-analysis is required, with DNA and pathology examination to follow. Victim's bones have been surgically removed after evisceration. First cut measures 26.5 centimeters, beginning at the base of the abdomen and ending at the labia majora." Pearsol turned off the recorder and gestured to Driscoll. "He gutted her like a fish."

"Your guy likes to slash and carry," said Jasper Eliot.

Pearsol hit the on button and continued: "The second and third cuts are lateral incisions to both thighs, allowing extrication of the bones from the upper legs. The incisions measure 29 and 30 centimeters, respectively. The victim's patella, fibula, and tibia are missing, as well as externus and internus malleolus."

"The gulls got some of the choice parts," Jasper Eliot whispered to Driscoll. "What's he want with the bones?"

"That's what we'd like to know. Larry, kill the recorder for a minute and talk to me."

"You got it." The ME hit the switch and turned to face Driscoll. "What we have are the remains of an undernourished Caucasian female, possibly anorexic. She dyed her pubic hair blonde. Nestled within it is an old tattoo of a faded heart. Kinky. About five-eight, five-ten, weighing between 105 and 110 pounds. My initial examination of her genitalia shows no indication of a recent assault or violation. In the flesh of her shoulders I found circular wounds, half a centimeter in diameter, eight in all, probably postmortem, left by three-inch nails."

"That's how he hung her on the boards, by the shoulders. Tell me about the piercing."

"An abundance of scar tissue surrounds the perforation."

"Does that tell you when she got it done?"

Pearsol unscrewed the top to an aluminum canister and emptied its contents. The ring made a clinking sound as it hit the base of a glass dish.

"Judging from the scar tissue, I'd say she's been wearing it for a couple of months, give or take a few days," he surmised.

Driscoll stared at the ornament, a gold band with jade studs. "I'd like to know the composition of the ring as soon as possible."

"One step ahead of you, Lieutenant." Jasper Eliot handed Driscoll a computerized printout detailing the chemical analysis of the ring: "11.1 milligrams gold, 26.2 milligrams copper, 2.6 lead, 2.3 tin, 8.7 steel and 3.7 resins. Studs: imitation jade. Estimated worth: $16.32."

"Larry, what about the body piercer?" Driscoll asked, scanning Eliot's report.

"Well, he's a perfectionist. The guy knows his flesh. No nail gun used here. These suture marks are perfectly symmetrical. Impeccable work. You're thinking, maybe the body piercer and your perp are the same guy?"

"Can't overlook it." Driscoll punched in a number on his cell phone.

Margaret answered on the third ring.

"I want a list of body piercers," Driscoll said. "Start with the tristate area."

"Aren't earrings against Department regulation?"

"Very funny. It may be a lead."

"Sorry, sir."

"I gotta run. Get on that list right away."

"You got it." Margaret grumbled. *He's gotta be kidding. Does he know how many body piercers there'd be in the goddamn tristate area?*

Thomlinson picked up the ring. "If this could only speak . . ."

"Can you make it speak, Larry?" Driscoll asked.

"I'd say the ring was handmade. Probably by the guy that did the piercing. They like to make their own jewelry. And your victim, she was into pain. I can tell you that much."

"How's that?"

"The ring was inserted without an anesthetic. Body piercers use a local, a mix of paracin trichloride and Novocain. It always leaves a trace in the surrounding membrane. A signature. There's none here."

"Let's hope that'll help us ID the piercer," said Driscoll.

As Pearsol returned to his recorder, Driscoll's thoughts drifted. What does a homemaker have in common with a nineteen-year-old aside from being female?

And what lure did this madman use to attract these two unfortunate women? Staring down at the butchered remains of Monique Beauford, Driscoll was instinctively certain of one thing. These killings would continue, and they would keep him and the city of New York on one hell of a roller-coaster ride.

Chapter 15

Margaret was pleased with herself. She had managed to squeeze into one of her old Vice outfits, and damn if she still didn't look hot. The leather pants were skin tight, and the midriff top showed off her flat stomach to full advantage. A push-up bra and some red fuck-me pumps completed the package.

She opened the door to the strategically positioned TARU van and stepped inside. All the guys in the van stopped what they were doing to stare. Wolf whistles filled the air.

"Knock it off, assholes," Margaret said. "This is a professional police operation."

Danny O'Brien, the TARU technician, handed Margaret a small, round metal object.

"That's the transmitter, Sarge. Figure out where you're gonna hide it."

Margaret walked to the back of the van and turned

her back on the men. She reached inside her bra and hooked it on.

"Need any help with that?" hollered O'Brien.

"In your dreams," Margaret said as she did a one-eighty and faced the technician.

"Seriously, Sarge, the skel is all set up. Speak in normal fashion. If you get into any trouble just say the word pinhead, and we'll be in there in two seconds. Remember, pinhead."

"O'Brien, how many years did I do this in Vice? I'm quite familiar with how a skel works. You clowns just be ready to move if and when I give the signal."

As she went to exit the van, Driscoll took her by the arm. "You be careful in there. Don't take any chances. If it doesn't feel right, you holler. You understand me, Sergeant?"

"Why, John, you do care," she smirked, and with a flip of her hair, out she went.

Francis, a self-proclaimed body piercer extraordinaire, scoped the patron in close-fitting leather as she browsed the shop's window.

"Come on, honey, step right in," he chanted, projecting his words telepathically to the lingering customer.

"I'll be damned," Francis marveled as the shapely brunette turned the handle on the door.

Undercover Sergeant Margaret Aligante tiptoed in, her eyes taking in the panoply of gold, silver, platinum, and steel studs embedded in the vinyl epidermis of a naked mannequin. *A freestanding work in progress*, thought Margaret.

Her working undercover, she hoped, would help loosen Francis's tongue. That was also the opinion of her confidential informant, her street snitch, who steered her toward this particular body piercer. The snitch made Francis out to be the type of guy that was leery of the police but would turn in his brother if it meant saving his own ass. And that was exactly what Margaret was looking for: a turncoat.

Margaret quickly scanned the interior of the tawdry shop. Two movie posters, one for *Crash* and the other for *Hellraiser III,* adorned one wall. They stared down at three crushed velvet love seats arranged in a U shape. Freestanding lighted candles provided stark illumination while sandalwood sticks burned, perfuming the room. Margaret thought the grouping resembled a small altar. Photographs of pierced eyebrows, ears, noses, lips, and other body parts wallpapered the opposing wall, assaulting Margaret's senses. The far wall boasted antique engravings of ancient Picts, Melanesians, Maori natives, and Australian aborigines pierced to the hilt. A life-sized statue of an African Ibo warrior, his body heavily illustrated and pierced, looked down at her.

"Can I help you?" The voice startled Margaret. A tall man wearing a black-leather vest, with tattooed arms and an exposed chest, smiled at her. Several silver hoops punctured his bushy eyebrows, while fishermen's hooks pierced both ears.

"Tell me, where I should wear this?" she asked, producing Monique's ring.

Francis examined it carefully.

"That's a wedding band. Jade studs. Cool. You'll want to wear it someplace special, no?"

"Is that one of your specialties? Implanting jewelry in special places?" she asked.

"Three times a week I'm asked to hook a ring like that onto one of several places on the body."

"How 'bout a woman's clitoris?"

"There too."

"So that's a common request?"

"Very."

"Some people would call that surgery."

"You bet it is."

"You got a license to operate?"

"I need one?"

"Some would say you do."

Francis shrugged.

"You could really hook a ring this size to a clit?" she asked.

"Piece of cake."

"How do you do it?"

Francis leaned his pockmarked face into Margaret's. "You leave that to me. A drop of medical magic, and you won't feel a thing."

"What if I wanna feel a thing?"

"No Novocaine for you, then."

"You pull teeth, too?"

"If I find any down there," he smirked.

She held back on the impulse to slap the man's face.

"There's a catch," Margaret said, biting the tip of her tongue, containing her anger.

"Don't tell me? You're a hemophiliac."

"No. I want two. One for my finger, and one for down there. And I want the rings to match."

"No problem. But you gotta bring me the other ring."

"Can't you supply it?"

"That's a specialty item. Handmade!"

"I thought you were a specialist."

Francis stopped speaking and stared fixedly at Margaret, this woman who was asking so many questions. The markings of fear slowly carved themselves on his face. He sensed danger. "You're in the wrong bodega, Miss. Hasta la vista."

His stare drifted to the sheen of a police shield brandished by Margaret, its glint reflecting off of the room's overhead lighting. "C'mon, where's your sense of humor?" he said with a sheepish grin.

"Is this your handiwork?" she said, producing the forensic team's photograph of Monique's genitalia, which displayed the inserted ring.

"That's not one of mine."

"Then whose is it?"

Anger and defiance replaced his fear. He grabbed a tattered Yellow Pages directory. "Here! Body Piercing! There's four pages. Take your pick."

Margaret's hands grabbed his forearms like a vise, pressing them hard against the Formica counter.

"Don't try fucking with me," Margaret growled. "You need a medical degree to draw blood, and I can close you down faster than you can say health violation." She flipped open her cellular phone. "You're just seven digits away from an inspection by the Board of Health."

"That's police harassment."

Margaret punched in a series of numbers.

"Oh shit," he groaned as Margaret placed the handheld receiver close to Francis's ear.

"You have reached the New York City Department of Health. If you are calling from a touch-tone phone, please press 1."

Margaret's finger complied.

"If this is an emergency, please press 2 . . . If you are reporting a violation of health code, please press 3 . . .

If you are calling to speak to someone in our AIDS Awareness Center, please—"

"I think 3 is the one we want, don't you?"

"Turn that thing off."

"You gonna tell me what I want to know?"

Francis nodded.

Margaret hit the disconnect button and folded the cellular phone.

"You know what they do to whistle-blowers in my line of work?" Francis whined.

"I don't give a fuck. I want to know who made the ring, and who did this piercing."

"He'll string me up by my balls!"

"Don't make me hit redial."

"OK, OK, OK. But you gotta forget what I look like."

"I got a short memory. Now give me his name."

"But—"

"Name! Now!"

"Jack the Ripster. He's known for his jade studs."

"Where would I find this pillar of society?"

Francis sighed. "Last I heard, the Ripster was operating out of a trailer on Houston Street."

"What's his real name?"

"Lester Gallows."

Margaret exited the shop and felt the immediate need for a shower. It wasn't the smell of sandalwood incense that she was looking to expunge, it was the entire sordid experience. The lingering vision of Francis's pockmarked face filled her head. Was it the fact that this man pierced the genitalia of so many women that filled her with contempt, or was she simply amazed by the number of women who found it fashionable to submit to such a piercing? She had always considered herself to be a modern-day thinker, but the vision of an ornamented clitoris was, to her, a complete turnoff. But she was not paid to pass judgment on what she considered vulgar. As she headed back to the TARU van, she was reminded of why she had come to Francis's body piercing shop in the first place. She was tracking a vicious killer and she hoped the information she had extracted from Francis would lead her to the man that brutally slaughtered Monique Beauford and Deirdre McCabe.

Chapter 16

It was a sunny autumnal Saturday in New York, but city parks were filled with few revelers. The populace of the city was in panic mode after learning about the latest slaying. It was the lead story on all the local network newscasts, and the city's newspapers were heralding the shocking details as well. The headline in the *Daily News* read "Second Victim Butchered in Rockaway," while the *New York Post* led with "NYPD Fears Serial Murderer on the Loose."

But the newspapers and the networks were also lending a hand in the investigation. They were running Monique Beauford's photograph, the one depicted on her New York State driver's license. The public was also given the force's tip line number and was asked to call the Task Force if anyone had any information regarding the crime.

Detective Steve Samuels, a member of Driscoll's newly formed team, had been given the assignment to check out the address on the victim's driver's license and show the dead woman's photograph around. It was the only address the Department of Motor Vehicles had on record, but it was now a boarded-up tenement in North Brooklyn. Most of the adjoining buildings were boarded up as well. There were only four families living on the block. One of those families, an older woman and her two adult sons, remembered Monique. She was a loner, they had reported. Never seen in the company of anyone else. She had moved from the now-condemned building years ago. They didn't know to where. Samuels canvassed the neighboring streets, where a bodega, a soda distributor, and a dry-cleaning shop were still open for business. No one there recognized Monique's photo. And no calls regarding Monique were ever received by the Task Force.

Chapter 17

The static chatter emanating from Driscoll's police radio filled the Chevy's interior as Driscoll and Margaret made their way down the East River Drive, heading for Lester Gallows's trailer on Houston Street. They had just left the Command Center, where Driscoll had been called upstairs and lambasted by his superior, Captain Eddie Barrows. The Lieutenant was being put to the test. He knew he'd be directing traffic in Brooklyn if he didn't soon turn up a lead.

"Don't ever aspire to head up a Task Force, Margaret. When things turn sour, the heat is on like a pizza oven," said Driscoll, his eyes riveted on the road ahead.

"Barrows must be in the crosshairs, too. No?"

"I'd say so. The flack is flying from the Mayor's office on down. I'll bet you at least three people will be reassigned before this is all over. I'm just praying I'm not one of them."

"Say a little prayer for me, will ya?"

"You're insulated. I'll be their number-one target."

"The Mayor losing ground in the polls sure as hell doesn't help matters, does it?"

"The pressure's always relentless when politics is involved. But it's not politics that's gonna catch this guy. We are. This psycho is bound to slip up. They all do. And when he does, we'll be there to nab him."

"The son of a bitch."

"So much for business. What's going on in Margaret's world?"

"I started a new yoga class."

"Oh, yeah?"

"Yeah. You ought to try it. It's great for stress relief."

"Does it come in pill form?"

"Not yet."

"Let me know when it does. Extended-release capsules would be even better."

"Really. It wouldn't hurt to consider it."

"Between the job and Colette, I don't have much time for anything extracurricular."

Margaret felt as though she had detonated a land mine. "Has there been any change in Colette's condition?"

"None."

Driscoll hated that word. *None.* It was so final. So hopeless. Yet he knew it was the one word that succinctly summed up the chance of his wife ever regaining consciousness. Goddamn it! What he hated even more was his inability to do anything about it. He missed his wife terribly; the sound of her voice, her crooked little smile, the tilt of her head when she was in a seductive mood. Hell, speaking of *none,* he hadn't had sex since the week before his wife's accident. He remembered the mood of that night as though it were yesterday. He had worked a twelve to eight, and on his way home had stopped off at Hudson's wine shop for a bottle of Mondavi Merlot, her favorite wine. It made her frisky, she told him. They dined on steak au poive, listened to Francis Albert Sinatra, and moved from the dining room into the bedroom, where they made ravenous love while Old Blue Eyes's voice tiptoed in from the adjacent room, adding to the magic of their lovemaking. After the subtlety of murmurs and whispers, the pair fell asleep in each other's arms. On awakening, Driscoll found himself alone in his bed. The smell of strong coffee filled the bungalow. He lumbered into the kitchen, where he found his wife preparing a breakfast of toast and eggs. What he would do to recapture that moment, to turn back time, to set things right, if only to say goodbye.

The sound of a horn honking brought Driscoll back to the present. The Chevy inched forward in bumper-to-bumper traffic. The silence that had settled between Margaret and him was broken by Driscoll, attempting to close the door on his shattered dreams and slip back into the minutiae of life, hoping it would dispel his despair.

"I don't mean to downplay the yoga classes," he said. "I'm sure they do wonders for you. But, if I had the time, working out in a gym would be more my style."

"I tried that. Too many Arnold Schwarzenegger wannabes in sweat-stained polyester. A total turnoff for me."

"Tattoos on a woman."

"Tattoos on a woman?"

"Yeah, tattoos on a woman. My total turnoff."

"C'mon. An intimately placed miniature tattoo wouldn't do it for you?"

"OK. I stand corrected. In just the right spot, a tiny rose or a miniature heart might."

"Thank God! The man's alive."

A smile creased Driscoll's face.

"So, which is it?" she asked.

"Which is what?"

"A rose or a heart?"

Driscoll's smile broadened. "It would depend on how discreet the placement."

"I have a tattoo," said Margaret, with the grin of a Cheshire cat.

"Lemme guess. The rose. And judging from the blush that colors your cheeks, you've picked one helluva place to hide it."

"Damn it. You really know how to take the fun out of flirting."

Silence returned to the pair. This time it was Margaret who broke it. Margaret, whose attempts at a love life always ended in disaster. So why was it she was suddenly attracted to her boss, of all people? Margaret was one tough cop, but when it came to relationships she felt totally inept. She thought of herself as a pre-adolescent neophyte. Relationships were to be avoided. But still, the attraction was there. That was unmistakable. She decided she'd have a go at it and hope for the best.

"Tell me. Would you ever consider seeing a woman again? I mean as a friend, that is."

"I thought that's what we were. Friends."

"We're good friends." Did she want more? The thought frightened her, yet filled her with exhilaration at the same time. Goddamn it! What the hell was going on in that psyche of hers? She couldn't deny it. She was becoming attracted to all the little things he did and how he did them. *He's married, for God's sake! As in taken.* Still, the curious attraction continued. "I just thought we could go out. We don't have to call it a date. Just two friends going out. That's all."

"Whether you're calling it a date or not, I thought it was the man who was supposed to ask the girl out."

"That went out with Y2K. Besides, if I waited for you to ask we'd be nearing Y3K."

"Oh, I get it. This is Relationships in the Twenty-first Century 101, and that makes it lady's choice. Is that it?"

"That's right. Whadya think?" There. She'd said it.

"You know my circumstances."

Land mine time again. "Say no more. I know the drill." *Time to lighten up a bit. Fluff it off.* "Hey, you can't fault a girl for trying. But, one of these days, John Driscoll—"

"Just not today. Or anytime soon."

"That's fine. A girl can wait." My God! Did she just say that?

Chapter 18

The colorful mural that adorned the side of the trailer on Houston Street featured Saint Sebastian bound to a Corinthian column. Arrows pierced his flesh.

The sign above the trailer's door read:

BODY PIERCING. IT'S NOT FOR EVERYONE
PROPRIETOR: JACK THE RIPSTER

Driscoll followed Margaret up the two rickety steps that led into the trailer and opened its aluminum door. Pushing aside a beaded curtain, the pair emerged inside a narrow reception area. A teenage girl, her hair styled in a Mohawk, waited there anxiously, dragging on a joint. Driscoll put aside the impulse to handcuff her.

"Want a hit?" the girl asked, offering the joint to Driscoll.

"No thank you," he replied.

The Lieutenant stared at the tapestries of torture

that blanketed the trailer's walls. One featured a ton-
sured monk, stripped of his habit, stretched across the
rack. Tears welled, frozen in the cleric's eyes, as the
hooded executioner wielded the iron rod. A second depicted a medieval beheading in progress. A third displayed the body of a nubile young girl impaled on the
lance of an armored knight.

A seam down the center of that particular tapestry
opened, and a huge man entered the reception area. A
leather apron draped him like a breastplate.

"Lester Gallows?" Margaret asked.

"I am. And you must be cops. Another license violation? I assure you—"

The teenager scooted toward the exit and disappeared.

"This isn't about a license," Driscoll answered.

"What, then?"

"Suppose we ask the questions," Margaret said. "It's
about this." She showed him the ring.

"Where'd you find that?"

"You just answer the questions," Driscoll said. "Does
the ring look familiar?"

Gallows took the ring from Margaret's hand. "It's
mine all right."

"Do you remember who bought it?"

Recollection flashed in his pupils. "Yeah, I remember . . . blond bombshell . . . a little skanky . . . Wanted
to try out the ring right after I put it in her. I told her
she's gotta let it heal first, but she wanted to get it on
right then and there. So I balled her. What the hell.
Then she wanted me to put in another one. I told her
I'd make one to match. The bitch never came back."

The audacity of this man offended Driscoll. Driscoll
thought of his daughter, Nicole. How could this man

speak so cavalierly about a young woman? He'd seen a lot on the job, but this type of irreverence he found disdainful.

"What did you do with the other ring?" Margaret asked.

"Still have it."

"We'd like to see it."

"It's in the back."

"Let's go get it."

Driscoll and Margaret followed Gallows into the back room. A bloodstained dentist's chair sat in its center.

"Some operatory," Margaret grimaced.

Gallows opened drawers, then unsealed cardboard boxes, porcelain jars, and metal canisters. "Where is the damn thing?" he grumbled.

"Better be here," said Driscoll.

The man's hand reached for a Russian doll. Snapping back its head, he emptied the contents of its hollow chest into his massive palm. Out popped a gold crucifix, a penis-shaped pen, a miniature knife, and the ring. A smile formed on Gallows's face.

"Did you get her name?" Margaret asked.

"Monique."

"Monique what?"

"Beats me. She paid cash."

"Wha'd you know about her?"

"Not much. Only in here once."

"When was that?"

"About two months ago. She told me what she wanted, and I fitted her with the ring. No anesthetic for this one. She seemed to get off on the pain. I told her to come back in a week so I could take out the sutures, but she didn't want to wait. Like I said, she insisted I do her then, right there in the chair." Gallows studied Driscoll's stare. Realization registered. "Someone killed her. That's what this is about. Right?"

"Been to the beach lately?" Driscoll asked.

"I hate the beach."

"What's not to like?" asked Margaret.

"I'm a hemophiliac. The sand is littered with jagged shells and broken glass."

Driscoll's mind raced. Had something ugly ensued between Gallows and the girl to turn him into a killer? Or was he merely an opportunist gaining profit on a new wave of exhibitionism, and nothing more?

"I know what you're thinking," Gallows said. "But I don't get off on murder. I get off on scarification."

"When do you know when to stop?"

"Hemophiliacs don't do homicide. That's for real, man. You can look up the statistics."

Driscoll continued to stare at the man. He had done the piercing and had gotten off on the intimacy with the girl. That was for certain. But did he kill her? His instincts said no.

Chapter 19

Colm saw red: the blazing red nail polish that painted the brunette's fingernails, the crimson adorning her toes, and a spot of red marring the waxy white of her eyes. In her fevered attempts to free herself from her bindings, a vein had exploded, flooding her retina with blood. Both eyes now teared, screaming of the atrocity committed on her flesh, while the sheen of those eyes reflected the frenzy of her executioner. But Colm was immune to the mute cry for clemency that her gaze transmitted.

Her resistance to the paracin trichloride and parasolutrine mixture was unnerving. His Casio flashed 2:48 A.M. He had waited the required fifteen minutes for the 20 cc's to perform their wonder, but to no avail. He reloaded the syringe and injected her vein with another dose of the elixir. It was now 2:51 A.M. The second dose did the trick.

Colm's heart stirred. He picked up her pocketbook and scrounged inside.

"Amelia Stockard," he read from a credit card. "Such a classy name. Let me tell you, Miss Stockard, your e-mails were more amusing than most. And to think you once dated the late Charles F. Brunner, a former Sanitation Commissioner of Hoboken. Well, that entitles you to one hell of a resting place, young lady."

He grinned at his unconscious captive, then hoisted her over his shoulder and headed for the meat hook that hung suspended from the crossbeam in the center of the operatory. Once there, he turned her body to face him, and lining up the hook with the third and fourth rib, he pressed her body against its point. The steel pierced the right lung on its way to the heart, which it entered at the left ventricle. A spasm rocked his hostage. Her lungs flooded with fluid, and she began to gurgle. Blood dribbled from her nose and trickled onto her fuchsia blouse.

The sight of the blood staining her blouse disturbed him. He unbuttoned the garment, removed it, and tossed it into the kitchen sink, which he had filled with warm water and a squirt of Woolite.

Her Playtex bra was now blood soaked as well. He used a small scissors to slice it free, and tossed it in with the blouse. Her skirt, stockings, and panties followed. He positioned a bucket under her feet to catch the remaining blood. How ashen white she had become, in contrast to her scarlet flow.

Once she was bloodless, Colm unhooked her and loaded her onto the meat-cutting block, where the surrounding sawdust gave off a brassy smell.

The boning knife was pitiless to the muscles surrounding the humerus, hacking away the resilient tendons without scoring the bone. He turned his attention next to the brunette's hindquarters, then on to her lower extremities.

After decapitation by cleaver, he dunked her head into the vat of sulfur trioxide and watched its jubilant effervescence. It was less toilsome to dislodge the flesh from the skull with the acid solution. It avoided nicking the gentle veneer of the bones. Past mistakes had taught him that facial bone was more subtle and could be easily damaged by a sharp tool. The hands and feet would be next.

Ray Orbison's "Pretty Woman" blared from the surround-sound speakers. It was the perfect accompaniment for the meeting of blade to flesh. He had chosen well. His musical taste was impeccable.

Chapter 20

The fibulas and tibias of the brunette's legs just fit the kiln. It was designed to fire clay pottery, but was quite adequate for drying human bones. It was important that all of Colm's relics be dehydrated and preserved. Without moisture they'd survive the insult of time, like those Inca kings who emerged intact after centuries buried in the dry sands of Peru. Colm stood by, motionless, embraced by the searing heat that permeated the small room, while the kiln performed its magic.

The ring of the oven's timer shattered his reverie. He opened the kiln door and stared at his trophies, appreciating their purity. The bones were whiter than white, chalky. He longed to hold them, but he'd have to wait until they sufficiently cooled. Only then could the fondling commence.

A buzzer sounded, profaning the solemnity of the ritual. Colm shivered like a night creature in his burrow, narrowing his eyes to tiny cracks, straining to detect the slightest stirring from the outside world.

The buzzer sounded again. The resonance was unmistakable. He had a visitor at the gate. He turned on the security monitor. The image of a young girl filled the screen. She was no more than four feet tall. Her blue blazer and plaid, pleated skirt draped a thin frame. She had a curious smile, and she was alone.

"Shouldn't you be in school?" he asked, his voice crackling through the outdoor speaker of his palatial estate.

"Would you like to buy some shortbread cookies?"

"Cookies. Now there's a thought."

Colm buzzed her in. The gate unlocked. He had plenty of time before she reached the door. Swiftly, he turned off the heat and headed for the vestibule. The doorbell sounded. He opened the door and invited her in.

"And you are from Saint Agnes Elementary," he said, eyeing the insignia on her blazer.

"Sister Mary Sean is collecting for our missions in San Salvador."

"Our missions?"

"Yessir, because of the war there are many orphans."

The girl, perhaps twelve, looked more fragile in person than she did through the security monitor. Her glassy eyes revealed signs of malnutrition. Poverty was etched all over her skin.

"I do have a sweet tooth," he said.

"The cookies have been blessed by Monsignor Carlucci."

"Delighted."

"Smells like something's burning," she whispered, sniffing the air.

"You've got me there. I'm an awful cook."

Colm disappeared, leaving her in the vast, well-appointed living room. When he returned, she was nowhere in sight.

It was going to be a room-to-room search, was it? All twenty-two of them, throughout the mansion? The thought intrigued him. He had never hunted a Catholic schoolgirl before.

"What took you so long?" she grinned, emerging from behind an Oriental screen, her snooping interrupted.

"I thought, for a minute, you wanted to play hide-and-seek," he replied.

"No time for that. I'm here on a mission," she said. "And that is to help the missions. Gee, I made a joke." She giggled. "Anyways, it's really, really important to help our missions, so can I count on you to buy some cookies? Please?"

The vision of her skeleton, her bones, like twigs of malnourished brush, exhilarated him. But her ashen skin told of unnamed deficiencies and genetic defects. She'd make a pale trophy in a room full of glorious relics.

"Would you like to taste one of the cookies?" she asked, opening the near-empty box with spindly fingers.

Colm envisioned the bones below those fingers, like white pebbles chiseled and polished by the tide. The urge to suck them was compelling. His craving became intense.

"I'd like that," he murmured.

She approached, offering a chocolate-covered shortbread like a priest dispensing the Eucharist. The proximity of her fingers was maddening. "Come on, take a little bite."

He quickly took hold of her hand, his lips avoiding the shortbread and nibbling her pinkie instead. His head lolled in bliss. To mask his perversion, he gulped the cookie whole.

"Those are three dollars and fifty cents," she stammered, tears welling in the corners of her eyes. She withdrew her hand and gawked fearfully at the tip of her pinkie finger. "Maybe I should go now."

"Feed me another."

"I'd hafta open a new box."

"Please do. I'll pay for it."

With trembling hands, she unwrapped the box's cellophane and exposed row after row of glazed cookies. Reluctantly, she brought a second one to his lips.

This time, desire emboldened him. He slid his tongue into the hollow of her hand. She didn't budge, frozen now in fear.

"You could win a statue of the Blessed Virgin," she whimpered. "If you buy two boxes, your name goes into the raffle. Please let me go home."

As the clock struck, sounding the hour, the buzzer at the front gate interrupted his rapture. Colm had another visitor. He gave the girl a puzzled look.

"Goody, goody," said the girl. "That must be Mommy."

Chapter 21

All things considered, it wasn't a bad day. Goulee had gleaned enough copper and brass pipes for two quarts of Thunderbird. It pissed him off, though, that he had to split the loot with the sanitation foreman. After all, he was the one crawling around in all the filth.

"C'mon down, Goulee, today's my lucky day, and you gotta leave," hollered the foreman from the bottom of the trash heap.

"What're ya talking about, Henshaw, it can't be three-thirty yet," Goulee yelled back, tugging on what looked like the narrow end of a fishing pole.

"Never mind watchin' the clock, ya prick. Get down here. Now!"

Goulee gave one last yank on the fiberglass rod and threw up both hands in frustration. "Give me a minute." He took out a spray paint canister and marked a circle where the fishing pole was embedded so he could resume his search on his next visit. That is, if the trucks didn't offload more trash on top of his find. The dump was huge. The odds were in his favor.

"C'mon, numnuts. Put a move on!" Henshaw's lucky day meant his waitressing girlfriend was getting off early, and he could steal away to her house for some horizontal mambo before her husband came home.

"I'm comin'. I'm comin'. Keep your fucking pants on!" Goulee hollered as he stepped grumpily over the mounds of refuge.

That he was endowed with only five toes, all of them attached to his left foot, made his stepping precarious. What he sought was solid footing. He balanced himself on a thin fragment of discarded plasterboard. It didn't hold his weight, and his body cartwheeled. An avalanche of garbage cascaded down, smothering Henshaw. Goulee was lucky, though. He had landed on something soft and gelatinous that had spilled out of a plastic trash bag.

Chapter 22

The stench from Goulee's find gagged both the Medical Examiner and Driscoll.

"Jesus H. Christ!" Driscoll exclaimed.

The abomination stared at them under the flash of the camera manned by Jasper Eliot, the coroner's assistant. Illuminated was boneless membrane and tissue, along with blood-drenched cartilage that was full of maggots.

"This one looks like it's been in a blender. It's hard to tell if it's human," said Pearsol.

"What's that mound?" Driscoll asked, gesturing toward a protrusion in the middle of the bloody mush.

"An air bubble. Fermentation does that."

Driscoll took a pair of surgical tongs and reached for the blood-soaked bulge. Steel teeth clenched a spongy mass.

"Mother of God! It's a fetus!" Driscoll cried out. "And what's that thing in its middle?"

With surgical pliers, the medical examiner freed a plastic card.

Driscoll wiped it clean and read its inscription:

COURTESY OF SAKS FIFTH AVENUE
TO OUR PREFERRED CUSTOMER, AMELIA STOCKARD,
ACCOUNT NUMBER 2476-3876-1204

A flurry of flashes radiated as Jasper Eliot followed the find with his high-speed camera.

"Amelia Stockard? That name sounds familiar," said Larry Pearsol.

"It should," said Driscoll. "She's the Magnolia tea heiress. Worth more than fifty million dollars."

"She was pregnant. There's a man involved. Could be your elusive assailant."

"Maybe. Maybe not. We'll need to track him down to find out. But one thing's for certain."

"What's that?"

"Move over, *New York Post* and *Daily News*. This particular murder will make international headlines."

"That's sure to put the heat on."

"In a hell of a hurry."

Driscoll pulled out his cellular and punched in a number. Cedric Thomlinson answered the call and spoke quickly. "Lieutenant, the scene down here is like a madhouse. Newspaper reporters and TV crews are camped outside the building. Santangelo's been on the horn four times. He wants to know what progress we've made in the case."

"Well, he's not gonna like the latest development. Amelia Stockard is our latest victim."

"Holy shit! That was the Magnolia tea heiress they found at the dump?"

"That's right. Now listen carefully. I want you to get hold of Butler and Vittaggio. Fill them in on the latest development, then send them to Saks Fifth Avenue. Have them get the rundown on Miss Stockard's charge card, number 2476-3876-1204. They're to see the security manager and keep it on the QT. I want a list of purchases for the last year, and I want to know if anyone else was authorized to use the card. They're to get me her current address as well."

"I'll get on it right away."

Detective First Grade Liz Butler was part of the Task Force. She was a top-notch police officer, with a keen investigative mind and tenaciousness. Her partner, Luigi Vittaggio, stood on equal ground. Driscoll knew they would both do a thorough job. Now if only he could keep the press and the newscasters at bay. But this was New York City, the capital of the world, and as far as news was concerned, the death of the tea heiress would rival the sojourns of Patty Hearst.

Driscoll turned his attention back to Larry Pearsol. "Can you take a DNA sample from the fetus and run it against the known sex offenders list?" It was a long shot, but Driscoll wanted to cover all possibilities.

"Sure, but it may take a couple of days."

"Larry, I may not have a couple of days."

Chapter 23

Colm had been at it since 6:00 A.M. when his shift had begun, and it had proved to be another grueling day. The workday's end seemed out of reach, and he was in the grip of despondency, finding no immediate escape or relief. His vocation offered some insulation from his demons, but everyone else he was forced to work with annoyed him, and his mood was growing increasingly bleaker. He glanced at his watch. It would be another forty-five minutes before he could put the day behind him and meet his date. Time seemed endless.

He leaned back in his swivel chair and closed his eyes. For some reason, the memory of his first visit to a hospital floated to consciousness.

It was to the Williston Medical Center in South Burlington, Vermont. He remembered the shushing sound his gurney made as it zigzagged through the hospital's bleach-scented corridors on its way to a cloistered ward on the third floor. His wrists and ankles were restrained, held fast to the metal transport by leather straps. In a dreamlike state, brought on by a potent dose of diazepam, he had difficulty remembering the events that had led up to his arrival at the hospital. And where were his parents? Why weren't they at his side? He sensed something ominous had happened to them. And what was that smell? It wasn't coming from the winding corridors of the hospital. No. It was coming from his own tattered clothing. In his drug-induced stupor he had difficulty affixing a name to the scent, until it suddenly dawned on him: it was the smell of smoke. Had he been in a fire? He looked up at the orderly that was guiding his gurney. He tried to speak but had difficulty forming words. It was as though someone had put a stranglehold on his vocal cords. Drool was all that escaped his mouth. He tried to communicate through tear-soaked eyes, but all the orderly saw was Colm's glassy-eyed doelike gaze.

Into the elevator they went, where the orderly exchanged pleasantries with a talkative nurse. Colm felt ignored. Peeved at the dismissive orderly, he fought the urge to swipe at the man, despite his restraints. Then, with a jolt, the elevator came to a stop. His gurney was on the move again. More winding corridors. He heard the definitive sound of a woman's voice crackling over a loudspeaker. She was directing doctors and nurses to different departments within the hospital.

"Ride's over," said the orderly as he slid the gurney to a stop in front of an eight-foot high steel door. The door had a plastic sign affixed to it: PEDIATRIC PSYCHIATRIC WARD. After pressing an admittance bell, the orderly stared through a wire-meshed pane of glass in the door's center. His call was answered by a willowy-looking man dressed completely in white. Colm figured the man to be a doctor.

Wordlessly, the orderly relinquished his responsibility, and Colm was placed in the care of this pristine-looking man. Again, the gurney was in motion, this time inside the confines of the dreary ward. The bossy directives that had filtered through the hospital's loudspeaker were replaced with the guttural sounds of people in emotional distress. This cacophonic chorus of human wreckage came from every direction. Terror-stricken, Colm looked to this newly assigned caretaker with pleading eyes.

"You're going to be all right," his new watchman said as he lowered the height of the gurney and unfastened Colm's restraints. He then led Colm into a small room with a bed and a simple wooden chair beside it. Colm sat in the chair and began to cry.

The shuffling of feet in the corridor outside of Colm's office brought him back to the present. It was precisely 3:00 P.M. Quitting time. Driven, he got up from his chair and walked to his closet. In the darkness of that intimate space, several items of clothing were impeccably displayed on wooden hangers. It was a casual look he would need today. He selected a Polo shirt and Levi's slim-fit jeans, then slipped into a pair of Sperry Topsiders. Thus armored, he was ready for his next encounter.

He left the building, ambling lightheartedly toward the parking lot where he had parked the van. In just under an hour he would arrive at the Kings Plaza Shopping Mall. The anticipation exhilarated him.

Colm strolled the bilevel plaza, stalking his own reflection in the store windows, until he reached the Croissant Shoppe. That's when he saw her, demure yet provocative. Time to act like any other shopper in need of a coffee break. After she stopped watching him, reasonably certain he was not her date, he circled the girl and sat nearby, in a corner of the restaurant where he could study her. Her garish attempt at makeup disturbed him. Despite the cones of nipples that indented her cotton halter, she looked boyish, with masculine legs. From his vantage point, he could see the reflection of her nubile form multiplied in the mirrored walls of the eatery. The expansion made him dizzy.

Her impatience was growing thinner by the minute. He knew she believed her date was a no-show.

She walked briskly to the counter and ordered a cappuccino that she sipped angrily, scalding her tongue. She squatted on a bench, slid a Virginia Slims between her lips, and was about to light it when she spotted the NO SMOKING sign. She bit her nails and stared at her watch. She confirmed its reading with the large industrial clock dangling above the cashier and, exasperated, stormed out of the shop, coffee cup in hand. Her hasty dash caused her to spill some of the cappuccino on her denim skirt. Aggravated, she threw the cup in the trash and made her way down the windowed corridor.

Colm was in heaven. He had watched her every move and felt her every emotion. He decided to follow her.

She turned into Aubrey's Bookstore. Her attention span was infinitesimal. She moved from hardcover to paperback, opening and closing jackets, leafing through pages, then replacing each book on its shelf, only to start all over again.

A girl called out her name. "Clarissa!"

A smile formed on the face of his intended.

Who was this other girl? A friend? A classmate? A lover, perhaps? She certainly was not part of the plan.

Together, Clarissa and the newcomer walked out of the bookstore, their laughter ringing under the glass cupola of the mall. They continued down the corridor, turning hurriedly into Sweet Delights, a confectionery store. Colm followed.

The variety of candies, their shapes and colors, the fragrance of licorice, vanilla, fruits, and sugars inebriated him. *Sweets for the sweet*, he thought. He filled two gilded gift boxes with sugar-glazed fruit drops and approached the cashier. "Please present these gifts to my two friends over there . . . after I've left the store. And make no mention of me."

"No sweat. How 'bout I tie a ribbon on top? Just two bucks more?"

"You read my mind. How much do I owe you?"

"That'll be . . . fifteen-forty-nine. But no credit cards under thirty dollars."

He handed the teenager a twenty and vanished from the shop, hiding behind a polymer ficus that stood beside the store's entrance. How he reveled at their astonishment, their nubile giggles, their pixilation. Like children presented with new gifts, they quickly ripped open the boxes and marveled at their candies. Clarissa, the more vivacious of the two, picked out a blood-red confection and popped it in her mouth. Her eyes beamed with delight. Her friend did the same and grinned. The pair strolled out of Sweet Delights, visibly giddy. Obviously, Clarissa had gotten over her no-show date.

When they reached the bank of elevators, they hugged and kissed and promised to call each other later that evening. Clarissa was now alone, and Colm could get back to his stalking.

Upon its arrival, he entered the elevator with her. They were finally together, inside the glass cage. Just the two of them. He took a good look at her. She was made of the finest stuff. Ebony eyes, alabaster skin, porcelain nose, silky hair. The thought of her bones made his skin tingle. "Isn't an elevator a wonderful thing?" he said.

Surprised, Clarissa smiled. "You don't get out much, do you?"

He began to whistle a familiar melody.

"That's from *The Wizard of Oz!*" she said, grinning.

"Correct. You just won a trip for two to Hawaii! You and your guest will be staying at the lush Waikiki Grand Hotel, overlooking beautiful Diamond Beach."

Clarissa gave him a look.

The elevator reached the exit-floor landing, and she stepped out.

"Wait," he pleaded. "The ride's not over."

"It is for me."

Colm caught up with her in the parking garage, daringly burrowing his fingers inside her halter, rubbing the ridges of her vertebrae.

She bolted from his touch, running headlong into and under the front wheels of a Ford station wagon packed with kids. "Someone call 911!" the driver's voice rang out.

As shoppers encircled Clarissa's inert body, Colm approached his intended. Pulverized calcium was all he saw.

Two police cruisers arrived, followed by an ambulance. Colm's head ached unbearably, as though shards of glass were lacerating his brain. He turned away from his misfortune and ambled for the shelter of his waiting van.

His hand reached for the glove compartment, scrounging for a bottle of Tylenol. He popped open the cap. The bottle was empty. Colm flung it against the van's windshield.

"Goddamn it," he cursed as he put the vehicle in gear and headed for the exit ramp.

Chapter 24

Clarissa's blood pooled on a fast-moving gurney, then trickled onto the mosaic tile, trailing a line of crimson through the winding corridors of the ER.

In a matter of minutes, the gurney was rushed into Trauma One, where the young girl's comatose body was injected, probed, and connected to a cluster of instruments that flashed vital data on amber screens.

"Suction!" ordered Doctor Stephen Astin, a stethoscope to the victim's chest. "We've got pulmonary blockage."

As a nurse intubated the patient, pink froth filled the plastic tube, draining pieces of lung into the metallic sink.

"Hypotension!" hollered Astin. "Give me two units of O-negative, and a mixture of Ringers and dextran. Now! And get her scanned for correct type."

A bluish hue receded from Clarissa's face as the suction cleared the pulmonary alveolus. Intravenous infu-

sion pumps were dragged in to inject fresh serum into
the girl's arteries.

"Anyone know who she is?" asked Astin.

"Clarissa Parsons," the lead nurse replied.

"Any relation to the DA?"

"She's his daughter."

"I'll be damned," said Doctor Colm Pierce as he entered the room holding a collection of X-rays.

Chapter 25

When Driscoll arrived at Police Headquarters, he was immediately surrounded by a swarm of newspaper reporters and television newscasters. Microphones were jammed within inches of his face, while TV cameras captured his every movement. The reporters asked question after question.

"Lieutenant, are you any closer to finding the killer that's murdering our city's female citizenry?"

"Is it true Miss Stockard was pregnant?"

"Do you have any news at all that you can share with the public that might make them feel less fearful?"

Driscoll's gaze fell upon Jessie Reynolds, one of New York's more considerate newscasters. She had been following the crime beat for years. When he spoke, his comments were directed at her. "Ladies and gentlemen, the Department has a team of thirty dedicated detectives assigned to the case. I assure you that every effort is being made to capture the madman that has declared war on New York City."

"What about Miss Stockard?" a voice cried out. "Is it true she was going to have a baby?"

"I can't answer that question. The Medical Examiner's office has not yet finalized its findings."

Driscoll's cell phone rang. He fought his way through the crowd of news-hungry reporters and stepped inside the lobby of One Police Plaza.

"Driscoll here."

"Lieutenant, it's Liz. We've got an address for you on the Stockard woman. She lived at 128 East Ninety-fourth Street. An apartment house turned condo on the Upper East Side. She was the only authorized shopper on her Saks charge card, and we have the list of purchases for the last year. Nothing really stands out except for a bottle of men's cologne she purchased two months ago. Everything else is routine."

"Liz, I want you and Luigi to go to her residence and give it a thorough search. See if it leads us anywhere. Question the super. I need to know who her acquaintances were and if she was romantically involved. Before you leave the building, slide a tip card under each of her neighbor's doors."

"You got it."

When Driscoll pocketed his cellular, he thought about the volley of questions that were just directed at him. What business was it of theirs whether Miss Stockard was pregnant or not? That particular question offended him. It served only to feed the frenzied newsmongers. *How despicable and crass humans could be*, he thought as he headed for the bay of elevators that would take him upstairs to the Command Center.

As Driscoll rode the elevator to the fourteenth floor,

his cellular rang again. This time it was Larry Pearsol, the Medical Examiner. He let Driscoll know that he had run the DNA from the Stockard fetus against the known sex offenders list, but he had gotten a no-hit.

Luck wasn't with him today, Driscoll thought. Maybe it would be tomorrow.

Chapter 26

Driscoll was behind the wheel of his Chevy heading for 128 East Ninety-fourth Street, Amelia Stockard's residence. Detectives Butler and Vittaggio had run into a snag. The building manager had refused to let the two detectives search the deceased woman's condo without a proper warrant.

Liz Butler had been in contact with Andrea Gerhard, an assistant district attorney. Since it was unknown where the Stockard woman was killed, Ms. Gerhard had agreed to write a crime scene warrant for the Stockard condominium, on the premise that dead people have no expectation of privacy. Thomlinson had already sent an officer downtown to pick up the warrant and have it signed by Judge Creedey. By the time Driscoll reached the East Ninety-fourth Street complex, the signed warrant, its truthfulness attested to by the affiant, was in the hands of Detective Butler. But when he pulled up in front of the six-story building, Butler and Vittaggio were standing outside.

"What are you two doing out here?" he asked. "You've got the warrant, right?"

"Yeah, we got the warrant. But we thought it best to wait for you," said Detective Vittaggio.

"How come?"

"This ain't no south Jamaica crack house, Lieutenant. It's a multimillion-dollar complex. The lobby looks like something out of *Architectural Digest*."

Driscoll nodded. He understood their apprehension. The last thing they needed was some Park Avenue lawyer accusing them of stealing a dead woman's Rembrandt.

"Well, I'm here," said Driscoll. "Let's go."

The sign on the door read BUILDING MANAGER. *A fancy name for a super*, thought Driscoll. After a knock, the door opened, and there stood Jonas McPartland.

"Back again?" he asked.

"I'm Lieutenant Driscoll. You've already met Detectives Butler and Vittaggio. We now have a warrant to search apartment 4E."

"Oh my! You guys are quick. I'll still have to check with the Board's attorneys."

McPartland was not what Driscoll expected. He was impeccably dressed in a Brooks Brothers three-piece suit. He was short, with close-cropped hair and horn-rimmed glasses. He seemed rather effeminate to Driscoll, a far cry from some Moe with a rag sticking out of his back pocket pushing a janitor's bucket.

"Mr. McPartland, we are here as a courtesy to you.

The warrant is signed by a judge, and we will enforce it with or without your Board's OK."

"Of course, Lieutenant, of course. We always try to cooperate with the authorities. I just wanted to check with my superiors. We don't usually have this type of disturbance in the building. It's very unsettling."

"I understand, Mr. McPartland. It would be helpful now if you would provide us with a key. It will save us from breaking down the door."

"Oh, please don't do that. What would the residents think? Just give me a minute." The little man scurried away and reappeared a few seconds later, holding a set of keys.

"Lead on, Mr. McPartland."

When they reached the apartment, McPartland opened the door and then turned to walk away. Driscoll said, "No, you stay. You're going to witness the search. This way there can be no accusations later that something is missing."

"As you wish. I'm here to help."

The apartment was bigger than Driscoll's house. It was immaculate. Everything was in its place, giving the appearance that no one lived there.

"Did Ms. Stockard live alone?" Driscoll asked McPartland.

"Why, yes, yes she did. She did have a woman who cooked and cleaned, but she went home after dinner every night."

"I'll need any information you have on that woman."

"Of course."

"Lieutenant, take a look in here." It was Liz, calling from the master bedroom.

"What have you got?" Driscoll asked, stepping inside the room.

"Men's cologne. It's about three-quarters full. I'll bet my pension it's the credit-card purchase from Saks. Strange, though, there's no other sign of a man anywhere. No clothes in the closet. No razor or toothbrush in the bathroom. Even the toilet seat is down."

And that's why you need a woman to search a woman's residence, thought Driscoll.

"Lieutenant." It was Detective Vittaggio.

Driscoll followed the voice to the den. Vittaggio was standing behind a regal-looking oak desk.

"I found a cell phone bill, but I can't find the phone. I called Cingular, and the number is still active. I dialed it from my own cell phone. It rang twice, and then a man's voice answered. I didn't answer back. I hung up. Somebody's using her phone."

Driscoll felt a sudden surge of adrenaline course through his body. "Mr. McPartland, you lock the door, and don't let anyone in unless I say it's OK. Liz, call the local precinct. Have them send a uniform up here to stand on the door. Luigi, call Cedric and have a couple of people sent over to interview Mr. McPartland here and to run down the cleaning lady. We've got to get to TARU to trace that cell phone. Come on, make your calls, and then let's move."

Chapter 27

Driscoll punched in Margaret's cell phone number as he drove, but got only her voice mail. Where the hell could she be? He dialed his office, and Cedric Thomlinson came on the line.

"Cedric, you got any idea where Margaret is?"

"Not a clue. I'll beep her and have her get back to you."

"Fine. You do that. And if anyone else needs me, I'm heading for the batcave."

"The batcave" was a police euphemism for the TARU Command Center. To get to it, you needed to find the nondescript driveway that led to the underground stronghold. That was where all the heavy-duty electronic toys were housed. Even in the NYPD, few people knew of its existence, and even fewer knew where it was.

Butler and Vittaggio were standing three-quarters of the way down the block when Driscoll made the turn onto Lefferts Boulevard. *Well,* he thought, *at least some-body knows where it is.* His money was on Butler. He parked the Chevy and walked over to the pair of detectives. Butler spoke first.

"I called Danny O'Brien and gave him Stockard's Cingular cell phone number. He's inside working it up for us now."

"That's good, let's go talk to him."

Security was tight. They had to pass through several locked doors to gain access. When they finally made it to the TARU Command Center's office, Danny O'Brien was waiting for them.

"Lieutenant, Luigi, Liz. How is everyone?"

"We're good, Danny, we're good. How far along are you?" asked Driscoll.

"I got a friend over at Cingular. She's given me a list of the outgoing calls, but she's gonna need paper from us somewhere along the line. We'll need a judge-ordered subpoena to triangulate."

Driscoll nodded in agreement.

"My friend is checking cell sites for us as we speak. We should know where he's been making the calls from in a few minutes. But remember, I promised her paper. She's risking her job for us right now."

"Liz, call that DA friend of yours and see what she can do."

"Will do." Liz Butler stepped away to make the call.

"So what's our best bet, Danny?" asked Driscoll.

"If he's using the phone, we can locate the general area through the cell sites. Once we're in his ballpark, we can use the triangulater to pinpoint exactly where he is. I've got one set up in the van. It's ready to go once we get the subpoena."

"Good. How long is this gonna take?"

"All depends. First we have to find out what cell sites he hit the last time he used the phone."

Liz walked back to where Driscoll was standing. "I spoke to Andrea Gerhard. Her boss wants her to come over here so she can write the subpoena and fax it to him."

"No way. We don't need some assistant DA snooping around. It'll only stall the investigation."

"Sorry, Lieutenant, but without a subpoena we're breaking the law," said O'Brien.

"OK. I guess we have no choice." Driscoll nodded to Liz Butler, who stepped aside to place a second call to the DA's office.

Driscoll's cell phone rang. It was Margaret. Driscoll got right to the point.

"How fast can you get to the batcave?"

"Ten minutes."

"OK. Ten minutes it is."

A smile creased O'Brien's face. "We've located him. He just called a cab company in Easthampton. Gerhard better get here fast."

Chapter 28

Assistant DA Andrea Gerhard held out her hand and smiled. "Nice to see you again, Lieutenant."

Driscoll was taken by surprise. He had no recollection of ever meeting the woman. She was thirtyish, with blond curly hair and sparkling blue eyes. She wore a smart black business suit, with a long jacket that pulled in at the waist and flared out at the hips. *Sharp dresser,* he thought.

"I can see by your expression that you don't remember me. We met at the District Attorney's Homicide Conference about a year ago."

"Why, Ms. Gerhard, of course I remember you," he lied. "There's no way I could forget a pretty face such as yours." He found himself flirting, but then was interrupted by Danny O'Brien.

"Lieutenant, the subpoena?"

"Andrea. May I call you Andrea?"

She nodded.

"I'm not sure how much of this Liz discussed with you by phone, but what we need is a judge-ordered subpoena to triangulate, to track cell sites and trace outgoing calls from a missing cell phone."

"Is it missing, or stolen?"

"At this point, we don't really know for sure. All we do know is that the phone belonged to a homicide victim, and that someone is still using it."

"That's good enough for me. I'll call Judge Fulton. He used to be a prosecutor in our office. I'm sure I can convince him to sign off on it. I'll need one of your detectives to act as the affiant and swear to the subpoena's veracity."

"Absolutely. Liz, you're to assist Ms. Gerhard."

"Now if you'll guide me to a desk and a telephone . . ."

"Danny, OK to use this as an outgoing line?" Driscoll was holding a receiver to what appeared to be a simple telephone, but since he was inside the batcave, he thought it best to ask.

"Of course," said O'Brien.

Driscoll handed the receiver to Gerhard.

"Thank you, Lieutenant." There was that smile again.

Driscoll turned his attention back to Danny O'Brien. "What's the last read you have on him?"

"Same as before. Easthampton."

"OK. I want to know the minute it changes."

Margaret walked through the last of the security doors and joined Driscoll.

"What do we have, John?"

Driscoll quickly explained the situation.

"What do you need me to do?

"Get on the horn to Cedric. Have him start putting together a roster and get a tactical plan going. I want everyone held until I say go. We'll need all the teams in the field on this one, and I want everybody packed and ready to move when I give the order."

"I'll get right on it."

"He's moving," O'Brien shouted. "He just hit cell sites in Westhampton, Speonk, and Mastic."

"He's headed back toward the city," said Driscoll.

"He must be in a car," Vittaggio added.

"Judge Fulton just approved the warrant. You're good to go," said Gerhard. "Now all I need to do is fax the details to my boss."

O'Brien pointed to the fax machine.

Margaret poked Liz. "Who's that?" she said.

"Assistant DA. She's writing the warrant for us."

Margaret eyed the pretty blonde. Why was she sensing competition?

"Lieutenant, we should be moving," said Liz Butler.

"My next order of business. Liz, you and Luigi take the Southern State Parkway. Margaret and I will take the Long Island Expressway. Danny, get somebody to drive that van, with you and the triangulater following me."

O'Brien had his ear to the phone. "He's passed Patchogue, Sayville, and Oakdale already."

"Traffic must be light."

"Islip and Bayshore," shouted O'Brien.

"He's not in a car," said Driscoll. "He's on the Long Island Railroad. Those are railroad stops."

Driscoll caught Margaret's eye. "Cedric has extra manpower set up if you need it," she said.

"That's good news. Now call the Long Island Railroad police. We have to stop that train before it hits Jamaica. If he makes it there, we'll never find him. What's the last stop before Jamaica?"

"Lynbrook," someone hollered.

"Margaret I don't care what you have to tell them, but have that train stopped at Lynbrook."

"Liz, Luigi, go. Meet me at the Lynbrook station. Danny, get to the van and get ready to move. You're to keep me informed by phone."

Driscoll turned to leave with Margaret.

"Wait," said Andrea Gerhard. "Here's my card. Call me and let me know what happens. I have to go and file the warrant now, but you can call me anytime. My home number's on the back."

Driscoll took the card and thanked her. His eyes followed her as she walked away. As he turned back, he caught Margaret's glare. *Men!* was her thought. *You shouldn't ever trust them.* Why did she feel so vulnerable? So violated?

"When your mind is back on the business of catching the bad guy, you'll be happy to know that I got through to the Long Island Railroad police. They'll hold the train at Lynbrook until we get there. I also gave Cedric the heads up. He's sending over a team."

"That's good news. Let's go. I'll drive."

They drove in stony silence for a good five minutes. Driscoll made the left from Darcy Street and headed onto the interchange that would take them to the Grand Central Parkway. He hit the flashing lights and eased into the left lane.

"Margaret, call the Chief of D's and put us out of the city," he said, breaking their silence.

"Yes sir, Lieutenant, anything you say."

"All right, Margaret, what's the attitude for?" He knew full well what was wrong, but decided to let her air it out.

"There's nothing wrong. I'll make the call right now."

"C'mon, let's not let personalities get in the way of this."

"Personalities!" she exploded. " 'You can call me anytime. My home number's on the back,' " she said, mimicking Andrea Gerhard's voice. "The bitch! She doesn't even belong in a police facility, and she has you kissing her ass."

"I was not kissing her ass. We needed her to write the warrant. Without it, we had nothing. Sometimes you have to play ball."

"She wanted you to play ball, all right." Margaret folded her arms and stared out the passenger-side window.

"Margaret, if that upset you, I'm sorry." He reached over and touched her shoulder. She gave him a sidelong glance and brushed his hand away. Silence returned as Driscoll gave her a moment or two to cool down.

Margaret finally spoke. "I don't think you should let the Chief of D's know we're out of the city. If you do, Santangelo will want to know why. Are you ready to let him in on this?"

"You're right. He'll just screw things up. We'd be better off running silent until we know exactly what we have."

They were moving onto the Southern State Parkway from the Cross Island when the car phone rang.

"Lieutenant, it's Liz. The railroad cops have the train stopped at Lynbrook. I had the conductor make an announcement that there was trouble on the track ahead, and that it should be cleared in a few minutes. What do you want us to do?"

"Stand by, Liz, we're only a few minutes out. Hold everybody till I get there."

"There's a railroad police captain here. He wants to know what's going on."

"Tell him you don't know, and that your boss is on his way and will explain things when he gets there."

"OK, Lieutenant. I'll hold him off as long as I can. Cedric's reinforcements are here, and Danny just pulled up in the van."

"That's good. I'm just passing Exit 14 on the Southern State. We're five minutes out." Driscoll hung up and pulled off the parkway onto Franklin Avenue, heading south. He made his way to the Long Island Railroad parking lot on Sunrise Highway, where he killed the lights and pulled up beside the TARU van. Margaret and he then got out of the cruiser and climbed the stairs to the platform.

Liz and Luigi were talking to a team of Long Island Railroad uniforms when Driscoll approached.

"Captain, this is Lieutenant Driscoll, my boss," said Liz. "Lieutenant, this is Captain Warner of the LIRR police."

"What's this all about?" asked Warner.

Driscoll motioned for the captain to walk away so that they could talk privately.

"Cap, we think we may have a homicide suspect on the train. We're not sure what he looks like, and I think the uniforms might scare him away. He's got our victim's cell phone, so what I planned on doing was put my people in every car, dial the number, and see whose phone rings. He has no idea that we know about the phone, so he has no reason not to answer it."

Warner was silent a minute, twisting his walrus-like mustache with his right hand. "OK, that sounds like it'll

work. I'll keep my men on the perimeter in case anything goes wrong. Try not to kill anybody on my train,
will ya?" Warner did an about-face and headed toward
his men. Driscoll looked skyward and thanked God
there were still some reasonable men left in other police departments.

The Lieutenant then gathered his people around
him and assigned each team one of the four cars. He
was about to tell Margaret to dial the number when
Danny O'Brien appeared with what looked to be a satellite antenna with two prongs sticking out of its middle.
On his head, he wore a pair of headphones.

"Lieutenant, I'm triangulating him now. He's on the
phone." O'Brien passed the first two cars and stopped
at the third.

"He's in here. In here!" O'Brien said, desperately
trying to keep his voice down.

Liz Butler and Luigi Vittaggio took the front door,
and Driscoll and Margaret, the back. On Driscoll's signal the conductor opened the doors, and all four detectives entered the car. There in the middle of the car
sat an unkempt-looking white male with his feet on the
seat in front of him, talking on a cell phone. O'Brien
pointed excitedly.

Butler and Vittaggio approached from the front, and
Driscoll and Margaret closed in from behind. Liz Butler
stood before him and said, "Hi." As he looked up,
Vittagio stuck his gun in the man's ear, and Driscoll
grabbed both of his arms.

"Police," they all screamed at once.

Driscoll and Butler got the man's hands behind his
back and cuffed him. Margaret took the phone and
pressed the button that displayed the phone's cell number.

"Bingo!" she said. "We got him."

"Wait! Wait!" The man protested. "It's OK. It's my girlfriend's phone."

"Get him out of here," said Driscoll, staring down an assembly of alarmed passengers. "Liz put him in my car and sit with him. Margaret, grab his stuff and meet me at the car."

Margaret picked up the bag next to the once-occupied seat and walked out of the car.

"We're gonna search your belongings," said Driscoll.

"OK, OK. Whatever."

Driscoll found Warner at the end of the platform and walked over to him. "Thanks, Cap. I appreciate all your help."

"Like hell you do. You appreciate me staying out of your way. I wasn't born a Captain, Lieutenant. I was a detective in our Robbery Squad for many years before I climbed the ranks."

Driscoll reached out and shook his hand. "Well then, thanks for understanding."

"No problem. Nothing worse than having someone poke his nose in where it doesn't belong."

Driscoll smiled at Warner, then turned and hurried down the stairs, leaving the captain to clean up whatever mess the NYPD had created.

Chapter 29

As Driscoll walked back to his car, he was torn as to what to do. If he called Santangelo, that meant press, and nothing but interference from the top. If he didn't call, it would probably be the end of his career. As he reached for the door handle to the Chevy, in which Liz Butler and the suspect were seated, he decided he would rather go out a winner than to have that glory seeker foul things up and perhaps ruin the case.

He opened the cruiser's door, and Liz Butler stepped out of the car.

"I don't think he's our guy."

Driscoll had learned over the years that Butler's instincts were good, and he took her opinions seriously. "Why not?"

"He just doesn't feel right. He keeps insisting that it's his girlfriend's phone, and that all we have to do is call her. I don't think he even knows she's dead."

Driscoll could feel his prior exhilaration slipping away.

Margaret walked over to them. "He's got a bag full of Ecstasy, some dirty clothes, and two cans of beer in that sack," she said.

"Ecstasy?" said Driscoll.

"Yeah. You know, the clubgoers' sex drug. All the rage among the metrosexuals."

Driscoll scowled. "Liz, you and Luigi meet me back at the house. Margaret, you drive."

Driscoll knew that one of the best detective tricks was simply the employment of a long drive back to the squad room. People, even people in handcuffs, naturally wanted to talk during a long excursion. It always seemed more like a conversation than an interrogation.

As the car pulled onto Sunrise Highway, Driscoll spoke. "What's your name, son?"

"McGowan, Officer. Mike McGowan. Please call Amelia. It's her phone. I know I shouldn't have taken it, but I didn't think she'd call the cops on me. I only meant to borrow it. I was gonna bring it back."

"Why do you think she called us, Mike?"

"We had a fight. I wanted to go to the Hamptons for this major party, and she wouldn't go with me. I got mad and took the phone. I needed it to, you know, to keep in touch. I didn't think she'd flip out like this on me."

Driscoll could tell that Butler was right. This guy was no killer. He didn't have the hatred inside him to do what had been done to Amelia Stockard.

"What's with the pills, Mike?"

McGowan swallowed hard. "Look, I'm not going to lie to you. They're Ecstasy. I went to the Hamptons to score them. Amelia and I use them. They make you feel like you're flyin' while you're standing still. I had a chance to grab a hundred, and I did. That's why I needed the phone. You know, to make the connection. I'm sorry, but that's the truth. I'm very, very sorry." McGowan began to cry.

Margaret looked at Driscoll and shook her head. They both knew that Mike McGowan was no killer, and that their nightmare was far from over.

Driscoll reached for his cell phone and dialed the Command Center's number. Cedric Thomlinson came on the line. "Hey, Lieutenant. What's going on? Liz and Luigi just walked in, and they're not talking. We get him?"

"Nope. False alarm. Any press around?"

"A swarm of them. As usual, they're camped outside."

"OK. Here's what I want you to do. Get a couple of guys into one of the cars with the tinted windows. Have them pull up to the front door and put on a show. Have one of them sit in the backseat with his hands behind his back. When the press rush over to the car, I'll drive up to the rear door. Have Liz and Luigi meet me there. Call me on the cell when you're ready."

"You got it."

Margaret and Driscoll sat in silence, waiting for Cedric's call. Driscoll thought back to what an older detective had once told him. *Never get too high or too low on the job. Stay on an even keel. That way it can never get to you.*

The phone jingled. It was Thomlinson. "It's all set up," he said.

"Showtime, Cedric! Hit it."

The plan worked to perfection, and Butler and Vittaggio hustled the still-weeping Mike McGowan up the back stairs and into the Command Center.

Driscoll and Margaret walked into the Lieutenant's office and looked wearily at each other. "Thought we had him," she said.

"So did I."

"Now what?"

"Have Butler and Vittaggio take his statement. Take a couple of Polaroids of him, and have two guys drive out to the Hamptons and check out his alibi. If it checks out, have somebody useless around here process his arrest for the pills."

"Who's gonna break the news to him about Ms. Stockard?"

"Damn it! I forgot about that. Well, wait till his alibi checks out, and then have Liz do it. Tell her to be gentle." Driscoll headed for the door.

"Where are you going?"

"I'm going home. I need to recharge. We just took our best shot out there, and we crashed and burned. I need to think, I need to sleep, and I need to get the hell away from here. What about you?"

"I'll stick around and see that McGowan gets processed."

"OK, thanks."

"For what?"

"For being there. See you tomorrow."

With Margaret's eyes on him, Driscoll walked down the hallway and disappeared through the Command Center's door, leaving the case and his task force behind him.

Chapter 30

Driscoll pulled into the precinct parking lot the next day just before the sun came up. He had slept well the night before, and he felt invigorated. The disappointment he had experienced the day before had passed. He parked the cruiser, walked in through the back door, waved hello to the Sergeant on the desk, and bounded up the back staircase. He put the key in the lock and pulled the door open. It was just past six o'clock, and the Command Center was empty. It was a time he enjoyed. He surveyed the room and relaxed. All was quiet. Two hours from now the room would be humming with activity, and bedlam would be the order of the day. He cleaned out the coffeepot and carefully poured cool tap water into it. The aroma of fresh-brewed coffee soon filled the air and added to the pleasure of his solitude.

He walked over to the sign-in log and saw a note that Margaret had left him. He signed in at 0600 hours and picked up her note. The coffee was ready. He filled a cup, sat down at his desk, and began to read. There was something sensual about her handwriting, and he caught himself thinking about more than policework. He allowed himself the indulgence of picturing her making love to him, and the fantasy engulfed him. She was quite a woman. He took another sip of coffee and turned his attention to the note:

John,

McFeely and Johnson interviewed McPartland and the Stockard woman's cleaning lady. They struck out with both, adding nothing further to the investigation other than the fact that the Stockard woman was discreet. Mike McGowan's alibi checked out. I sent Dyer and Romanelli out to East Hampton, and at least a dozen people put McGowan there for the last few days. Seems he was a fixture at several beach bars and social events. I had Santos take the collar and book him on the drug possession. Liz broke the news about the Stockard woman, and he took it pretty hard. He didn't know she was pregnant. Apparently, they had met at a club in Manhattan and hit it off. He introduced her to Ecstasy, and they became lovers. Funny thing about the men's cologne. McGowan says that Stockard was so paranoid about being busted that she bought the cologne because she had read somewhere that the smell of cologne confused drug-sniffing dogs. Whenever they went out, she would wrap the pills in a cologne-soaked handkerchief and stuff it inside her purse.

We finished up at 5 A.M., so I told Butler and Vittaggio to come in for the 4 to 12. Cedric will be in at 8 to field any questions. I'll shoot for a 2 to 10 but I am pretty beat, and may not make it in till 4. See you then . . .
Margaret

PS. Here's something that'll make your day. Bellevue Hospital called. They're holding a homeless man there who claims to have seen some goings-on under the boardwalk in Rockaway. Looks like God closed one window while opening a door. M

Chapter 31

The derelict was wearing Bellevue's vomit-green hospital gown, which flapped open in the rear, revealing a bruised and lacerated patch of skin on his right buttock. His hair was matted, and his beard looked weedy and abandoned. As two old codgers played cards at a table near the nurse's station, the derelict watched the goings-on through the wire-meshed window of his cramped room.

"I gotta go pee," he muttered, venturing out into the corridor, heading for the communal lavatory across the hall. Just as the old-timer was pulling open the bathroom door, he heard his name spoken.

"Mr. Heath."

"I gotta go pee," he grumbled.

"I am Lieutenant Driscoll. We need to talk."

"Look fella, I got a quart of Glenlivet in my gut. I gotta flush it out."

"Glenlivet? That's fifty dollars a bottle!"

"I hit it big in Keno last night," the vagrant replied, smiling through missing teeth. "Can I go pee now?"

"All right. But make it quick." Driscoll leaned against the tiled wall and waited for the man.

The derelict reappeared. "Whoever cut these gowns got it all wrong. The fly belongs up front," he muttered.

"We'll use the office down the hall," said Driscoll. The Lieutenant ushered the derelict into a small room with a metal desk and two brown swivel chairs. Driscoll motioned for the man to take a seat. "Are you James Heath?" he asked.

"If you say so."

"Well, are you?"

"I'm told I am."

"Who tells you?"

"Everybody."

"Do you know why you're here, Mr. Heath?"

"No. Do you?"

"I ask the questions."

"You'll like my answers better if I get just a wee bit of Chivas."

"They don't serve alcohol here."

"Plum wine, perhaps?"

"That's alcohol."

"I'm awful thirsty."

"How about some mineral water?"

"I'll pass. Why'm I here?"

"That's what I asked you, Mr. Heath."

"I remember the ambulance. Those guys in the ambulance brought me here."

"You make your home under the boardwalk, is that correct?"

"What of it?"

"We found a blue-and-green plaid blanket under there. It belongs to you, right?"

"And I better get it back."

"You were screaming when they found you, Mr. Heath."

"I had . . . I had a bad dream," he mumbled through quivering lips.

"Tell me about your dream."

"It's personal." His face was now disfigured by dread.

"Mr. Heath, the ambulance attendant's report states that you were at the scene of a murder, one that was committed less than thirty feet away from where you were huddled."

"I didn't see nothin'!"

"What you saw could be important to the police."

"I was dreaming. . . . Wasn't I?"

"No, you were screaming when the police found you. It's possible that you saw something, something that scared the hell out of you."

"I wanna go! Now!" Heath yelled.

"Lower your voice. You don't want to spend the night in the lockup, do you?"

"Let me outta here!" Heath produced a corkscrew and pointed it menacingly at Driscoll.

"Put that thing down!"

"Open the fuckin' door!"

Exasperated, Driscoll leaned over the desk and forcibly grabbed the derelict by his throat. "Put it down on the desk, now."

The derelict growled.

"Now, I said." Driscoll applied more pressure to his hold.

Heath dropped the weapon.

"Tell me what you remember seeing that night," Driscoll ordered, picking up the corkscrew and placing it in his pocket.

"Why do we hafta go back there?"

"The sooner you talk, the sooner they let you out of here."

Heath's eyes bulged. His lips began to quiver again as he spoke. "He was down on his knees, the whole time. Like he was doin' somethin' holy. First he cut up the girl's body. I think she was already dead. Then he nailed her to the boardwalk. He kept hitting her with a ball-peen hammer, again, and again, and again."

"Who was the girl? How did she get there?"

"I couldn't help her, I really couldn't. He hit her so hard."

"Did you see the man's face? Can you describe him for me?"

"It may have been the dead of night, but living under the boards gives ya the eyes of a cat. I'm tellin' ya, I saw the guy."

"Could you identify him?"

"He was goin' at it real slow. Like he really got off on it."

"Did the killer see you?"

"No way."

The door opened, and a police sketch artist stepped into the room.

"I got here as soon as I could, Lieutenant. There was a tie-up on the Brooklyn Bridge. I hope I didn't keep you waiting."

"Your timing is excellent, Kelly. Mr. Heath here is about to describe our killer."

"I am?"

"Do you know what this is?" Driscoll asked, pointing to the artist's chalk in Officer Kelly Gilmore's fingers.

"I know nothin'."

"C'mon, you musta been a kid once. You musta played with crayons and colored chalk."

"I was born old."

"All kids enjoy playing with chalk, even old ones."

"So?"

"So, this nice lady came all the way in from Brooklyn to draw us a portrait on this here sketch pad. Why don't you just sit in this chair and start remembering?"

"She's a cutie," Heath snickered.

"That she is. And now she has some questions for you."

"But I ain't got nothin' more to say."

"How 'bout his hair?" Gilmore asked. "Was it curly? Straight? Long? Short?"

"Hair is hair. It was on top of his head."

"You gotta help me draw it. I wasn't there."

"I was there, lady, but it was dark."

"You mean his hair?"

"C'mon, lady. It was dark as a witch's ass."

Driscoll was growing impatient. He figured he'd try a different approach. "Drop it, Gilmore! This witness is a waste. We've got better things to do than stand around and listen to his arrogance. The guy didn't see anything. He's as blind as a maggot and even smells like one."

"Watch your tongue, Irishman," Heath sneered, casting a glare at Driscoll.

"I'm outa here!" Driscoll growled.

"Wait for me," Gilmore echoed, packing up her charcoal.

"*Ba dhuthchas riamh d'ar gcine chaidh gan iompail siar o imirt air!*" Heath shouted in Old Irish.

"What's he raving about?" asked Gilmore as she made her exit with Driscoll.

"Something from Ireland's national anthem," Driscoll answered, his voice carrying back into the room.

"Hey! I'm not done yet!" Heath bellowed. "Your guy is one of us!"

Was Driscoll being baited by an alcoholic vagrant, or did the man really have something to offer? The Lieutenant stepped back inside the room. "You better not be pullin' my chain," he warned.

"He's one of us," Heath sighed. "Shame on him. A man of Erin."

"What makes you so sure he's an Irishman?"

"I sure didn't see the blue of his eyes," Heath muttered, "but I can tell you by his Gaelic tongue that the fiend was born and bred in Sligo."

"Alcohol plays tricks on the mind, you know."

"My mind works just fine. I, too, was born and bred in Sligo."

In a flash, Driscoll realized he had stumbled upon his first substantial lead. Here in the confines of a psychiatric ward he had found the first witness to a psychotic killing. "Whadya friend from Sligo say?" he asked, cautiously.

"He was praying. Just kneeling there, praying."

"A priest?" Gilmore asked.

"Hell, no! He was prayin' in Old Irish over his kill."

"Heath, can you remember the prayer?" Driscoll urged.

"That I'll never forget."

The drunk assumed the killer's stance and moving slowly, as though he too enjoyed it, began hacking away at his invisible victim. *"Don ghrian agus don ghealach agus do na realtoga!"* he intoned.

Chapter 32

"*Don ghrian agus don ghealach agus do na realtoga,*" Seamus Tiernan, Chairman of Columbia University's Department of Celtic Studies, read. "To the sun and the moon and the stars, Lieutenant."

Busts of Celts and Britons, with shields and battle axes, stood vigil over the scholarly office.

"Druidic, fifth century A.D., a ceremonial incantation. Probably used for a sacrifice," Tiernan explained.

"Sheep and goats?" Driscoll asked.

"Roosters . . . and infants. True pagans. They believed they owned their children and could sacrifice them at will. Yes, Lieutenant, those were the dying gasps of heathenism in Northern Europe. Christianity saw that it didn't last much longer."

"Getting nostalgic?" Driscoll asked, an eyebrow raised.

"You've missed your calling, Lieutenant. It might have been the priesthood instead of the precinct."

Driscoll recognized the tone in his voice. He had

heard it many times before. It was the tone of someone who believed the police were a necessary evil. Someone to call when your car radio was stolen. It was a common affliction among the northeastern intelligentsia.

"Professor Tiernan, I have a few more questions."

"I'm sorry, Lieutenant, but I have papers to grade."

"Tell me, Professor, in your world are papers more important than human life?"

"That's your job Lieutenant, not mine."

"I wouldn't be here if I didn't think you could help me."

"All right, then. Fire away."

"Are these Druids still practicing? Perhaps in the tri-state area?"

Tiernan reached for his pipe and filled it with an aromatic mixture. A flame gushed from his Flaminaire as he fired the pipe's chimney. "They may be," Tiernan said cautiously.

"Maybe doesn't cut it. Are they or not?"

"I really do have work to do. Now, if you'll excuse me."

Driscoll reached in his pocket and pulled out several Polaroid crime-scene photos. "No. I won't excuse you," he barked. He threw the photos on Tiernan's desk. "There, Professor. That's his handiwork. Now, are you gonna help me?"

All of Tiernan's attitude abandoned him. He seemed to shrink before Driscoll's eyes. "Oh my God," he kept repeating. "Oh my God!"

"Well, Professor?"

"There is a secret society. They meet in a small town called Fremont Center in upstate New York. I visited them once in my fanatic days. Druids, with genealogy back to the Old Sod. But, I'm not sure if the society still exists." Tiernan was stammering.

"When was the last time you were there?"

"Christmas Day 1988. The winter equinox. Not since."

"Can you get me in?"

"I don't think so. Ever since I baptized my children, the society has shunned me."

An awkward silence settled between the pair.

"Lieutenant?" Tiernan managed, eyes fixed on the photos.

"Yes, Professor?"

"I'm not feeling well right now. Perhaps we can continue this discussion at another time. Say, dinner, at my house on Saturday?"

"Thank you, Professor," Driscoll said, wondering why Tiernan had made such a gesture. "I'd like to bring along a fellow detective. If that's OK with you."

"Please do. If you're wondering why the invite, my wife fancies herself a mystery writer. She would love to meet a pair of true-to-life homicide detectives."

"Then, Saturday it is," said Driscoll.

"May I ask one favor of you, Lieutenant?"

"Sure, Professor. What is it?"

"Leave the pictures at home."

Chapter 33

"Fate steps in, you know," Margaret managed as she sat in the passenger seat of Driscoll's Chevy. The pair were on their way to Professor Tiernan's house for dinner.

"And how's that?" said Driscoll.

"Correct me if I'm wrong, but as I recall, the last time we were together in this car we were talking about going out on a date." There. She'd said it. An inner voice whispered she was taking a risk, but that same inner voice was insisting she disregard all caution flags and put herself out there, regardless of how vulnerable it made her feel.

"So?"

"So? What is it we're doing right now?"

"I suggest you look at your watch. Our tour of duty began two hours ago. This 'date,' as you would have me call it, is part of an ongoing police investigation."

Had he made a mistake by inviting her to dinner? It was police business, but shouldn't he have known that Margaret would draw the wrong conclusion? And what was his own part in this? Was he unconsciously responding to Margaret's advances? And if so, was he being unfaithful to his wife? The thought tormented him. He had vowed to be true to Colette, through good times and bad, through sickness and good health. It was one thing to indulge in the fantasy of infidelity, but quite another to dance perilously close to the rim of its hedonistic lure. And that's what he was doing.

"You could have gone alone," Margaret said.

"True. I could have gone alone." *Hell! I should have gone alone.*

"But, you decided to ask me." Margaret twisted nervously in her seat. "And that makes it a date."

There was truth in what Margaret was saying, and Driscoll knew it. He had asked Margaret to accompany him to dinner because he had feelings for her. It being part of a police investigation helped Driscoll deal with his guilt. But his feelings for Margaret were genuine. Was he ready to share that with Margaret, or anyone else, for that matter? Hell, no! For now, he'd suffer in silence.

He stopped for a light on Bay Ridge Avenue and turned to face her. "We are two police officers investigating a series of brutal murders. We have been invited to dinner at the home of someone who may help us in our investigation. Whatever else you think this might be is in your very fertile imagination."

"Listen, I know you're my boss, and you're a married man. I know all of that. But I can't put aside these feelings I have for you as though they don't exist, and I know deep in your heart, neither can you."

"OK. Have it your way. But in the meantime, let's not let our feelings get in the way of our investigation. Can we agree on that?"

"Absolutely."

Chapter 34

The arches above the white door were more suited to a London town house than as the facade of an Irish college professor's residence.

The woman, framed in the illumination of the living room's torchère, was a diaphanous presence, with light hair and aquamarine eyes. She offered the Lieutenant her long artistic hand. "Eileen Tiernan," she murmured.

"I followed your husband's suggestion and invited Sergeant Margaret Aligante as my guest." Margaret's eyes were locked on Driscoll's as the pair were led inside the house.

"Are you the police?" a young child gushed, bursting into the room. "Will you take Timothy to jail?"

"This is Ryan," Mrs. Tiernan explained. "And Timothy is Ryan's brother. Timothy steals Ryan's toys."

Leprechaunlike, a second child's head popped out from behind a door frame, eyes wide open, staring at the intruders.

"And that's Timothy," said Mrs.Tiernan.

"You're goin' to jail. You're goin' to jail," Ryan sing-songed.

Timothy's head vanished.

"Hope you didn't run into any traffic," Seamus Tiernan declared as he entered the room, a Japanese chopping knife in hand.

"There's our man, Lieutenant. He's even got the murder weapon in hand," said Margaret with a grin.

"I confess, I showed those carrots no mercy. Perhaps a round of Jameson's before my arrest?"

"We mustn't deny the culprit his last request."

Tiernan dispensed the drinks.

Without warning, a winged thing swooped down, swallowed a beakful of Driscoll's whiskey, and perched itself atop a curtain rod, eyeing the guests.

"My bird loves to party," a newcomer said as she traipsed down the staircase. Entering the room, she beckoned the creature to sit on her shoulder. "Meet Chester. He's a red-billed toucan from eastern Colombia. And you must be Lieutenant Driscoll."

"I am."

Driscoll studied the young woman. She was wearing iridescent mascara, a sienna blush emphasizing her cheekbones, and burnt orange pigment on her lips. She sported a diminutive skirt that framed slender legs. Driscoll figured her for fourteen or fifteen. She certainly was sure of herself, and had a curious curl to her smile that said, "I'm here. I warrant attention." Despite himself, Driscoll was amused. He wondered what Margaret's impression was.

"Has anyone proofed Chester?" he asked.

The bird croaked at the sound of his name and launched an attack on Margaret's drink.

First mine, then Margaret's, Driscoll pondered. Was that some sort of sign? He was certain Margaret would think so.

"He's just warming up for his grand finale," his keeper boasted.

"Is he a song-and-dance man?" Margaret asked. "He looks a little like Jimmy Durante with that beak."

"Well, Chester here'll let you judge for yourself. And now, without further ado, may I present, direct from South America, for your entertainment pleasure, Chester, as W.C. Fields in zero gravity."

On cue, the bird fluttered cockeyed wings, let out a belch, and pirouetted in midair like a drunken sailor, finishing with a spiraling nosedive headlong into the shag carpet.

"Cut him off," hollered Driscoll.

The girl picked up the inebriated bird and cradled him in her pocket.

"I'm Moira," she announced. "Named after an Irish princess who fought valiantly against the Vikings. But, alas, I have been reduced by Mother to the menial task of research assistant, helping her write her great American detective novel about a psychopath who preys on nubile suburban teens."

"You're a writer?" Margaret said, turning to Mrs. Tiernan.

"Trying to be."

"Don't be deceived by the appearance of harmony that permeates this household, Lieutenant Driscoll. Demons fester in our midst," Moira cautioned.

"Moira!" her mother scolded.

"My whispery mother dreams the darndest things. Acts of carnage haunt her daydreams. She's a natural-born killer in a housewife's dress."

"Please excuse my daughter. She's actually fourteen, but I'm afraid she's never left her terrible twos."

"Chapter eighteen, page 192," Moira singsonged. "Mother likes to test her dialogue on unsuspecting guests."

"The Vikings didn't stand a chance," muttered Margaret.

"And you are?" Moira asked.

"Sergeant Margaret Marie Aligante," Driscoll answered.

"Such a long name," said Moira with a shrug.

"Sergeant Aligante, it is certainly a pleasure to have you grace our home," said Mrs. Tiernan.

"Please, call me Margaret."

"You've managed to thrill my mother, Sergeant Margaret Marie Aligante."

"Pay no attention to Moira. She delights in the resonance of her own voice," said Seamus Tiernan.

"Sergeant Margaret Marie Aligante, will you consider sponsoring me?"

"Your bird's the one who needs a sponsor. I suggest you try AA," Margaret replied, taking an instant dislike to the girl.

"I'm not talking about Chester, I'm talking about me," said Moira, sharply. "I'd like to become a police investigator."

"John Jay College of Criminal Justice may have what you're looking for," said Driscoll.

"College is for bookworms and preppies. I wanna be around cops. I need to feel the beat of police work."

"I know you officers have entered the electronic age. Unleash her on a computer, Lieutenant, and she'll have it doing cartwheels," her mother said.

"What do you know about the Pentium Pro XPS 200?" Driscoll asked Moira.

"Could teach it a trick or two."

"Can you now?" said Driscoll, suddenly seeing Nicole's smile in the girl's face.

The Lieutenant was drawn to the girl. The more he gazed at her, the more he saw Nicole, who was about Moira's age when she died. It pained him to look at the girl. So many memories flooded to consciousness. He wished he could slip off somewhere, someplace where he could be alone to resolve his anguish in private. At the moment, he felt like he was on a stage with a packed house staring him in the face.

"Lieutenant? Lieutenant, are you OK?"

"Yes, Moira. I'm fine," he managed.

"If you'll let me, I can provide a program that can safeguard your entire system from any kind of virus. It's a virtual vaccine for infected computers."

"We'd have to clear it with the Captain for security's sake," said Driscoll.

"Of course!" Moira raced out of the room. "Just give me a minute to get the CD."

"Higgins is not gonna like this," Margaret warned, lips to her glass, eyes peeking over its brim.

"Not to worry, whiz kids like Moira could probably teach Higgins a thing or two," Driscoll whispered. "And besides, what harm could she do? It's not like we're actually assigning her to the case. At best, we'll get a few lessons on how to use the computer to our advantage."

"What's next? Recruitment straight out of nursery?"

The remark made Driscoll grin.

Moira returned with the virus-seeking CD and slipped it into Driscoll's pocket. "Like a wonder drug," she said with a wink.

Mr. Tiernan then motioned for his guests to take their seats around a beautifully set table.

"The Erin Society was started by Sean McManus, an Irish coal miner from Pennsylvania, in 1952," Seamus Tiernan told Driscoll after hors d'oeuvres. "The New York chapter was established in the town of Hankins, in Sullivan County. There, McManus founded a seminary for the training of Druidic priests. But they have since gone underground."

"Why?" asked Driscoll.

"Theological differences."

"You said you had visited them. Did you attend their services?"

"If you ask me, the ASPCA should have gotten a call." Moira's voice echoed from the kitchen, where she had been beckoned to help her mother with the main course.

"How's that?" Driscoll called out.

"They built a wicker man, then filled it with live roosters and set it ablaze at dawn in honor of the rising sun. Weren't they sweethearts?"

"Moira tells it like it is," said Seamus Tiernan. "I took her on a trip upstate when she was eight."

"Next time, we go to Disney World," Moria hollered.

"I thought you told me you hadn't visited the site since '88," said Driscoll.

"I forgot the stopover with my daughter. That's a trip I regret. It was no place for a young girl."

"Perhaps it's time for another visit," Driscoll suggested.

The door to the kitchen swung open, and Moira appeared, holding a platter of barbecued chicken wings.

"Don't waste your time," she said.

"Why not?"

"Guys that get off on roasting roosters don't get off on murder."

A chill settled over the table.

"She even thinks like a cop," said her mother.

"Care for another assistant?" Moira asked with a smile.

"Oh, brother," Margaret moaned.

Chapter 35

Driscoll was seated behind his desk, poring over the photos of the remains of the latest victim. *How could one human being do this to another?* he pondered. *And what's with the sanitation dump site?*

Margaret stuck her head inside the door, interrupting his contemplation. "She's late," she said.

"Who?"

"The whiz kid."

"Who's watchin' the clock?"

"You said five P.M. Sharp! It's going on five-fifteen."

Driscoll gestured for Margaret to come in and take a seat beside his desk.

"You don't care for Little Miss Computer Brains, do you?"

"She's much too brassy for my liking. But I have a suspicion that you have somewhat of crush on the young girl."

"If truth be known, she makes me think of Nicole every time I see her."

Driscoll envisioned his daughter's smiling face. He remembered the warmth he felt whenever Nicole took hold of his hand. One such memory came racing to consciousness. Nicole was two, going on three. He and she were together in the playroom. "Daddy c'mere,"she beckoned, her little fingers entwined around his. "You get the wellwow ones," she instructed, holding a yellow block with the raised letter *T* on it. "Build dem, Daddy. Build dem." Driscoll got down on all fours and stacked *T* upon *S*, upon *E*, until the tiny tower of yellow blocks was complete. Nicole erected the blue ones. When the two columns were assembled, Nicole formed a tiny *O* with her lips, signaling Driscoll to blow the blocks down. How she giggled and grinned when Driscoll obliged.

"Just like you're doing now," said Margaret.

"What's that?"

"Nicole. You're thinking of Nicole." Her voice was sympathetic. "Your face always has that melancholy look when you're thinking of your daughter. Or didn't you know that?" Margaret watched as a tiny tear formed in the corner of Driscoll's eye. "It's very understandable," Margaret continued, her eyes drawn downward. "I only wish I had someone to blot out the nightmares of my past."

"You know I'm always here to listen."

"Forget I said it. I'm fine. Just a little distracted lately. That's all." Margaret squirmed in her seat like a school-girl. "Maybe it's the case with all its blood and gore. I don't know."

"Can I take a stab at it?"

"At what?"

"At what's got you distracted."

"Fire away, Mr. Freud."

"I think you're jealous."

"Jealous? Jealous of who?"

"Little Miss Computer Brains."

"Get real."

"No. I think that's it. Plain and simple. I saw the look on your face at that dinner table where Moira was fawning all over me. You're jealous of all the attention I give her."

"Yeah, like I'm gonna get jealous of a fourteen-year-old girl."

"Her age has nothing to do with it."

"What then?"

"You feel put out by my feelings for her, this transference that Moira brings out in me."

"You'd know more about these emotional issues than I would. I have to admit I'm in the dark when it comes to most psychological goings-on."

"I want you to know it doesn't take away from the feelings that I have for you." Oh, boy. Did he just say what he thought he said?

"Go on."

Trapped. Trapped by my own doing, and it's too late to do an about-face. "C'mon, Margaret. You know how I feel about you."

"I feel like I've just been asked to dance on a patch of thin ice. You have feelings for me?"

"Of course I do." He felt his face become flushed. His having feelings for Margaret had always raised guilt, but confessing to those feelings was something else. "I'm just not in a position where I can act on those feelings."

"But they're there?"

"Oh, they're there, all right." Driscoll's heart began to race as a stillness overtook the small room.

"Oh, boy. Where do we go from here?"

"You do understand my position. I mean, I'm still married to Colette."

"How do you manage to do it?"

"Do what?"

"Sit with those feelings, knowing how I feel about you."

A sad smile formed on Driscoll's face. He fought back the urge to hold her hand.

A knock sounded on Driscoll's door, interrupting their intimacy. Detective Thomlinson stuck his head inside, letting the tumult enter from the outer office of the Command Center.

"Somebody's birthday out there? What's all the hubbub?" said Driscoll.

"There's a teenage girl outside. Says she has an appointment with you, Lieutenant. She's dressed like a Times Square hooker! You'd better hurry. There's no tellin' what these johns'll do."

"You really know how to pick 'em," Margaret snickered as Driscoll darted for the door.

A huddle had formed in the squad room, encircling the young teen, who was clad in a flesh-toned tube top and black miniskirt. Driscoll elbowed his way in. The circle dispersed.

"Come with me!" Driscoll snapped, escorting Moira into his office and slamming the door.

"Why are you dressed like . . . like—?"

"Too flashy?"

"See if this fits," Margaret said, tossing Moira her jacket.

"I'm really sorry, Lieutenant. I didn't mean to upset you. I'll dress more appropriately next time."

"Next time? There'll be no next time."

"OK, I screwed up. But, can't I just have a go with my computer before I—"

"Ya got two minutes."

Moira sat down and opened her satellite-supported laptop, where her fleeting fingers danced across the keyboard. The screen sizzled with codes, numbers, logarithms, and equations. Within seconds, Moira had entered the nebulous zone of hacking.

"Lieutenant, did you know the FBI is also investigating these crimes?"

"They follow all serial cases," said Margaret.

"You tapped into the FBI's in-house files?" said Driscoll, incredulous.

"Impossible," said Margaret.

"No. Moria has accessed their private files. And, from the looks of it, they're keeping a very close eye on *our* investigation."

"Would you like a hard copy?" Moira asked. "I gotta act quickly before they're on to us."

"Go ahead."

"Done. We're out."

"Get away clean?" asked Margaret.

"Just like a bar of Ivory."

"I should report you for this," said Driscoll gravely.

"Sometimes I get carried away," Moira pouted. "I need a strong hand to keep me on the straight and narrow."

"Ain't that the truth?" said Margaret.

"Young lady, you really know your way around a keyboard." Driscoll grinned and shook the girl's hand.

"Thank you, Lieutenant. Just so you know my heart's

in the right place, tonight's demonstration is on the house. But next time it's gonna cost ya."

"How much?"

"Fifty dollars an hour. And I guarantee satisfaction."

"What're gonna do with all the dough?"

"Have you priced a motherboard lately?"

"Oh, John," Margaret groaned. "We've got a techno-geek on our hands."

"On that note, I'm outa here," said Moira. "Time for you two to hit the keys."

"What now?" asked Margaret.

"Your homework. I'm sure your crew of technicians have already scoured the Internet highways and byways, but it might be a good idea to do your own search. Your instincts may lead you to something they overlooked. It can't hurt. Remember, you guys will have to stay one step ahead of the G-men, or they'll be the ones cracking your case. Hasta la vista!" she added as she slipped out the door."

"So, where do we start?" Margaret asked.

"There's a great big World Wide Web out there, and you and I are gonna surf it."

"I'm no surfer, John. I don't even like getting my feet wet."

The door opened, and Moira stuck her head inside. "Don't waste your time in the FBI files, Lieutenant. They haven't a clue in the case."

The door slammed shut.

"Out of the mouths of babes," said Margaret.

Driscoll cleared his throat and turned his attention to Margaret. "You OK with all that we said earlier?" he asked.

"I'm fine. It's nice to know we share the same feel-ings."

"You understand that I can't act on those feelings, right?"

"Right."

"So can we put those feelings aside for a moment and get down to the business of catching this bastard?"

"You bet. But I'll need a little help getting started. I'm not that computer savvy."

"All right, then," Driscoll said, flexing his fingers over the keyboard. "Here at the Command Center we use Netscape as our Internet browser. That's that little icon on the screen with the ship's steering wheel. I'm clicking on it, see? Now we got search instruments: Lycos, Yahoo, Gopher, and lots more. We're gonna use them to look up everything we can find on every detail of the case. Now, type 'bones' in the search line . . . OK, now click 'Search' . . . That's it . . . There's your list of everything on the Internet dealing with bones. Just click the mouse on those topics you want to know more about. Keep going down the list. You find something that may be a lead, give me a holler. I'll be doing the same thing over here with 'Gaelic' . . . Ready?"

"Ready."

"Then let's start surfing."

Hours later they had downloaded volumes of data on bones, Gaelic, torture, sadism, and abductions, had printed reams of pages, and had amassed vast quantities of information. None of it pointed to any one suspect or in any particular direction. Their search was a strain on both the head and back.

Margaret pushed back her chair and glanced at the wall clock. It was 1:48 A.M.

"Jesus, I'm starving," she grumbled. "How 'bout Indonesian?"

Driscoll's stomach rebelled. "You want me to eat food where they load everything with chunky peanut butter? That's not for me. I'll pass."

"What then?" Margaret said, arms outstretched, caught in midyawn.

"You're the one who's hungry."

"Yeah. And you ain't helpin'. You're supposed to suggest the place." Margaret's head was cradled in her palms, her elbows on her knees. Her body signaled exhaustion.

"How 'bout my house? There's a new dish I've been dabbling with, and I've almost got it right." The notion brought a smile to Driscoll's face.

"You cook?" Margaret's blue eyes were riveted to his, and Driscoll wasn't immune to what those eyes conveyed. Her gaze spoke volumes, and those volumes begged for a romantic relationship with him. Driscoll wasn't blind to that, and he certainly wasn't blind to the woman's beauty and charm. There was no question about it. Margaret was a very desirable woman. This would be so much easier if he were single. He knew Colette would never awaken from her coma, so it could be argued that he was already single. The man trembled at the thought. Reason took hold. He was a married man. He'd have to maintain a platonic relationship with Margaret. But every instinct he had said he couldn't. What was he to do?

"I'm married to a French girl," he said lamely. "It was she who taught me to cook."

"I'm beginning to feel like the other woman."

"That's not fair. To me or to you."

He imagined his wedding band being fitted around his neck and tightened like a hangman's noose. His situation seemed hopeless.

"I'm too tired and too hungry to worry about what's fair. Tell me about this dish," Margaret said.

"*Saumon au vin blanc,*" Driscoll said.

"I love the sound of that. Tell you what, there's an all-night Food Emporium near my apartment with a great seafood selection. What say we raid the joint and head for my place, not yours?"

His imagined noose just got tighter.

"But it's almost 2:00 A.M.," he said.

"Whadya got against missing a little sleep?"

Driscoll hesitated, eyes fixed on Margaret.

"So what'll it be?" She reached for her purse and nervously withdrew her compact. The sheen of her lipstick had faded. On the verge of trembling, she applied a fresh layer.

"Why the hell not? Let's go."

Chapter 36

Pineapple Street was lined with quaint brownstones, with impatiens and geraniums adorning stoops and windows. The street was silent except for the whine of a stray cat.

Inside 124 Pineapple, the pair climbed the oak staircase to Apartment 2A. It was Driscoll's first visit to Margaret's place.

A clap of Margaret's hands turned on a ceiling-high row of track lighting that illuminated a fair-sized living room. Driscoll smiled, for he knew Margaret found solace in this living space, where a modular sofa encircled a traditional fireplace. In the center of the circle, a coffee table in glass and chrome stood on an earth-colored Oriental carpet. Driscoll eyed the high-tech entertainment center that supported a JVC stereo system, a Sony nineteen-inch color TV, and a stack of assorted CDs. Adorning the wall opposite the fireplace was an abstract painting in blue and green. Margaret had good taste.

That was evident, and what was comforting was that the furnishings made Driscoll feel at ease.

The dining room was adjacent to the living room, and boasted an oval-shaped white pine table with four American Colonial chairs. In the center of the table, a crystal vase held a bouquet of blue irises. Again, a very comfortable room.

"Welcome to my place."

"I like it. It suits you."

"I think the living room could use some dressing up."

"Looks fine to me."

"Really?"

"Really."

"Well, that just saved me $1,400 for the Henredon wall unit I had my eye on."

"You have quite the eye for interior design."

"You think so?"

"Yeah, I do."

"It's funny you should say that. Before I decided on police work, I took a couple of courses at Parsons."

"It shows."

"Let me have your topcoat," she said, helping Driscoll out of his Burberry. "Can I offer the chef a drink?"

"Scotch."

Driscoll stepped into the kitchen while still carrying the shopping bag crammed with food. A Jenn-Air gas range, set in a tiled island, took up the center of the room. Against the wall stood a Viking refrigerator with full-length steel doors. A battery of copper pots Driscoll recognized as Bourgeat hung from an overhead rack. Depression-era glass filled the windows of oak cabinets.

"Very impressive," he said, accepting a tumbler filled with whiskey.

"I had the place redone a couple of months ago. I'm glad you like it."

"I do."

When Driscoll entered the dining room, steaming dish in hand, Margaret had changed into a simple black dress, and her hair had been pulled back into a chignon. The table had been set for two, with Noritake china and Georg Jensen flatware. Two elongated candles were burning in Lalique holders.

"Now this is what I call two cops eating out," said Driscoll.

"I forgot the wine." Margaret hurried to the kitchen and returned with a bottle of Mondavi Fume Blanc.

Driscoll uncorked it and poured a generous portion into her glass. They ate and drank.

"How 'bout some music?" Margaret asked hesitantly when they had finished.

"Can't see the harm in that."

Johnny Mathis's "Chances Are" filled the room.

"Dance with me," she heard herself say. Was it her talking, or the wine?

Driscoll looked at her, startled.

"What's the matter? Something wrong with two cops dancing to a little mood music?" Margaret felt as though she were stuttering.

A soft breeze blew, extinguishing one of the candles as Mathis crooned.

Driscoll found himself in Margaret's arms, swaying languorously to the vocalist's lyrics, enjoying the intimate company of a woman, a vivacious, fun-loving woman. The scent of her perfume enveloped the pair as they danced. It was the scent of early spring, and Driscoll found it to be subtle and intoxicating. His heart was beating rhythmically. He felt electrified, thrilled to be alive. As he closed his eyes, he felt Margaret's warm cheek brush against his. It was pure delight.

Another gust of wind extinguished the remaining candle. The starry night's sky illuminated the room through an overhead skylight. Their two shadows melted into one.

"Maybe it's time to clap your hands again," said Driscoll.

"Let's not."

Their dancing continued. She felt warm in his arms.

"I'm going to kiss you," she breathed. And then, pressing her lips against his, she lingered at the edge of his tongue.

He did not resist. Her tongue was inviting, her lips moist. He withdrew slowly. Her lips found his again. This time she was more daring, more exploratory.

"What say we sit this one out," she murmured.

"It's getting awfully late."

"Please. Just sit with me."

A lassitude enveloped him. It had been years since he'd been kissed so ardently. For years he had not felt the alchemy of intertwining tongues. When she offered him her lips for the third time, he surrendered.

A ringing in the darkness interrupted them. He froze.

"What is it?" she whispered.

"My cellular. It's in my coat."

"Don't, John. Don't."

Driscoll rushed to the closet, grabbed his phone, and flipped it open.

"Yes, Lucinda . . . Have you called 911? . . . I'll be right there!"

"What is it?" Margaret asked, alarmed.

"It's my wife. She stopped breathing."

Chapter 37

"She stopped breathing," Driscoll sighed, "but the CPR unit brought her back. They got there just before I did. I could have lost her, Elizabeth. The call arrived when I was kissing my assistant. Imagine that. I'm kissing Margaret, feeling emotions I forgot I had, and the cellular starts ringing. It was three o'clock in the morning! I should have been home in bed, not out getting it on with another woman."

"Is three o'clock after your curfew?"

Doctor Elizabeth Fahey was Driscoll's psychotherapist. She had nursed Driscoll's soul through his near collapse at the loss of his daughter and the onset of his wife's coma.

"Curfew. What curfew? I'm not a teenager, for Christ's sake!"

"Well, you're the one out necking at three o'clock in the morning."

"She stopped breathing. I'm out gallivanting, and she stops breathing."

"Let's not even think about the shape you'd be in if the two of you had had sex."

Driscoll looked at her. "You're really off to the races now."

"Tell me you don't see the message here."

"So, this is all about guilt?"

"Irish Catholic guilt."

Driscoll slouched back in his chair. "I know I'm gonna sound like a broken record, but I still don't think you understand how much I miss my wife. She was my first love, remember, the first woman in my life. I adored her. Everything about her. I still carry her in my thoughts everywhere I go. Just the other day the phone rang. This woman with a French accent was looking for some guy named Claude. A wrong number. It sounded just like her. I hung up the phone and cried. Then I remembered she's not dead. She's just in the other room."

His eyes moistened. "Like we discussed from the onset, it's like I'm married, but I'm not married. I have Colette at home, but I live alone. I see her every day, but she doesn't see me. She doesn't even know I'm there! We both know this is not grounds for an annulment. Not if you're a Catholic. Married for life am I. Do I like it? Can't say that I do. Can I do anything about it? Damned if I can. What's down the road for me is one lonely day after another. There certainly can't be any future with Margaret."

"There's not even a present. Tell me more about this woman."

"She's beautiful."

"And you're a handsome man. That can account for

the physical attraction. But tell me more. What's she all about?"

"She comes from an Italian-American background. Her father, the bastard, was a cop. She followed in his footsteps."

"Why did you call him a bastard?"

Driscoll sat back in his chair, thoughtful. His eyes drifted toward the floor.

"Margaret didn't exactly have what you'd call a happy childhood," he said.

"Who does?" Tell me about hers."

Driscoll felt a pang of guilt. Should he reveal a confidence that Margaret admitted to him over a couple of beers? He scanned Fahey's face. This was his therapist, for God's sake.

"She was sexually abused as a child."

"By whom? The bastard father?"

Driscoll nodded. "Then when Margaret was seventeen, the son of a bitch drank himself into a stupor and took his head off with his service revolver. If you ask me, the parasite had it coming."

"Well, that explains a lot of things. Is she in therapy?"

"She was when she was a teen. I don't think that continued, though."

"The human mind is a very protective device. Often victims like Margaret are able to block out the memory of their abuse, or at least the emotions she was feeling at the time of her abuse. But what she'd likely to be left with is an anxiety disorder with both an attraction and a distrust of men, on an unconscious level, of course. Her father killing himself doesn't help. It raises abandonment issues. How long have you two been working together?"

"Four years."

"I'm willing to bet this is the first time you two are tracking down a serial killer of women."

"It is."

"Whether they block out their emotions or not, incest victims never fully recover. The earlier the age, the more severe the psychological trauma. A trauma that unconsciously determines their every move. Right on through adulthood. It's probably why she became a cop."

"What's this serial killer got to do with it?"

"This isn't your run-of-the-mill serial killer. He's not using a shotgun to take out his victims. He's boning them, dissecting their flesh. This is a very intimate method of murder. The intimate slaughter of women. Much like her own intimate slaughter."

"So you're saying there's a connection."

"Absolutely. She relives her destruction at every crime scene. Unconsciously, what resonates in her is fear. A child's fear. Remember, it's why she became a cop. And to this frightened cop, you represent the knight that is out to slay the dragon, this butcher of women. And in so doing, you'd be avenging her own desecration."

"Her fear is what attracts her to me?"

"You are the way out of her nightmare. In you, she's seeking a father imago."

"You mean some sort of replacement father figure?"

"No. An imago. It's a clinical term. Suffice it to say, Margaret, the little girl, is looking to you for protection, all on an unconscious level, of course. Margaret the adult then translates that urgent need into something else. Something more grown-up, the best example being a relationship. It's what two adults have when they're attracted to each other, for whatever the reason. That's how her conscious mind reconciles her feelings toward you."

"So her feelings aren't real."

"There as real as these four walls, but they stem from her childhood. Her unconscious primal fear."

Driscoll's eyes widened. He then shook his head.

"You gotta be right, Elizabeth. I've been working with her for four years, but she's only shown an interest in me since the onset of this investigation."

"She can't help herself. It's a form of self-preservation rooted deep within her psyche."

"So, the child in her is looking to me for protection and the adult is looking for a relationship."

"You got it."

"But I'm a married man!"

"You really like to beat that drum, don't you? Tell me something. Do you honestly believe Colette would want you to spend the rest of your life alone?"

Driscoll looked plaintively at Fahey. He always felt like he was doing something wrong when asked to consider what Colette's wishes might have been.

"The other night with Margaret, she had on this Johnny Mathis song, "Chances Are." Was she trying to tell me something?"

"You're the detective. What do you think?"

"Could be."

"Could be? Does she have to wave a checkered flag?"

"But I shouldn't even be in the race."

"You, or the Irish Catholic altar boy that lives inside you?"

"Come on."

Fahey hummed "Chances Are."

Driscoll crossed his arms as though he had made a decision. "Checkered flag or no checkered flag, Margaret's gonna be real disappointed."

"Like she isn't already?"

Driscoll sighed heavily.

"You know, Elizabeth, I can only admit this to you, but sometimes I wish Colette had died in that terrible accident. Does that make me a bad person?"

"No, John. It makes you human."

Driscoll toyed with his wedding band and remembered the notion he had of it being a hangman's noose. He had to admit that the feelings he had for Margaret were as real as the feelings he had for Colette. That truth was undeniable and inescapable. Sure, the feelings were different. Hell, the women were different. Though he wished he could, he couldn't turn back the hands of time. He had crossed the line. He had acted on his feelings. Should he face the gallows for such an offense? All he did was kiss another woman. But it wasn't just another woman, it was clearly a woman he had feelings for. While still married to Colette! He knew Elizabeth was right. This was all about guilt.

"If you don't mind, I'd like to change the subject," he said.

"Does it have to do with the case you're working on?"

"There you go, reading my mind again."

"You want a therapist's view on what makes him tick. No?"

"Exactly. Like I explained briefly on the phone, the guy is dissecting them and stealing their bones. What I didn't say is that he's taking their heads, hands, and feet, too. I wanna know why."

"How does he leave what's left of the bodies?"

"He nailed one to a boardwalk in Rockaway Beach. Another we found in an abandoned boathouse in Prospect Park. The third we recovered from the Canarsie Sanitation Dump. The last victim had been eviscerated and stuffed in a trash bag."

"Why do I get the feeling your guy's just warming up?"

"That's what I'm afraid of."

"Your guy despises flesh. Feminine flesh. I'd say his crimes are not sexually motivated, not in the usual sense. He's collecting something he needs and wants, and in each woman he goes for something hard and imperishable in their softness. Their bones. He's a skilled cutter?"

"The guy knows his anatomy. Whadya figure his motive to be?"

"Did Genghis Khan need a motive to build mountains from human skulls? What you could have here is a display of an archaic war rite, where women are his quarry. He guts them and takes their skeletons as hostages. What he does with the head, hands, and feet puzzles me. But there's a good possibility this savage has a war room, an intimate museum filled with the souvenirs of his expeditions. That's where he'd store his human medals. You've got to find that treasure chamber, that gallery where he showcases his loot."

"This sounds like Anthropology 101."

"Sure it does. He's got the mores of his Neanderthal ancestors."

"So I should be looking for some guy covered in animal skin, wielding a stone ax?"

"More chance he'll be wearing Armani."

"Then I'll have to strike at the beast behind the broad lapel."

"Make it a sure strike."

"Is he curable?"

"The prognosis is not in his favor."

"Then I have no choice. I'll have to take him down."

"That'd be my advice."

Driscoll looked haunted. "Is my hour up?" he asked.

"Twenty minutes ago."

"Thanks for the extra time," he said as he stood up. "As always, I feel better after seeing you."

"Give some more thought to what I suggested about Colette's wishes. The doctors are unanimous about her condition, aren't they? She's never coming out of the coma."

Driscoll's eyes were fixed in a blank stare.

Elizabeth continued, "But you don't believe them, do you?"

"What are you getting at?"

"You haven't given up on that fantasy, have you? You think she's gonna get up from that bed and brew you some French Roast coffee. Tell me the truth. You're just waiting for that day, aren't you?"

"You don't give up. Do you?" Driscoll said, smiling harshly.

"What kind of a therapist would I be if I did?"

Chapter 38

Margaret and Driscoll were once again seated before the NYPD computer monitors inside Driscoll's office at the Command Center. They were going through the motions of searching the Internet, but their thoughts were elsewhere. And so were their voices. Their awkward silence was interrupted only by the pecking of keys.

Thomlinson entered. A glaring look from Margaret told him he'd stepped into a minefield.

"Catch you guys later," he said, ducking out the door.

Margaret lifted her fingers from the keyboard and did a one-eighty in her swivel chair. "I think we need to talk about it," she said. "Ignoring it isn't gonna make it go away."

"You're right. We do need to talk about it."

"I'm not sorry it happened. Are you?" *Please say you're not.*

"I can't say that I'm sorry. But I gotta be honest with you, I am filled with guilt."

"That's a good sign. It means you have a conscience. But you shouldn't be too hard on yourself. You were only acting on true feelings. Right?"

"Yes, I was acting on true feelings, but I shouldn't have had those feelings. I'm a married man."

That she didn't need to be reminded of. "Feelings are feelings. They're neither good nor bad. They're just feelings. You shouldn't beat yourself up over having them."

Driscoll fingered his wedding band. "It's one thing to have the feelings. But it's a whole other ball game when you act on them."

Time to muster some courage, she thought as her heart pounded inside her chest. "I'm about to say something, John, that'll have you thinking."

"Go ahead."

"Colette would understand."

A quizzical look filled Driscoll's face. "You're the second female inside of two days to say that."

"Well, I'm not gonna ask who the other bright visionary is, but take it from me, given the circumstances, your wife would understand."

"Part of me is beginning to believe that, but the larger part is calling for harsh punishment."

"Penance? You want penance? You're being much too hard on yourself."

"I need some space, an emotional rest so I can sort things out. For now, let's just try to get on with our lives and focus our energies back on the case."

"OK, we will. But, you don't have to beat yourself up. Trust me. I know I'm right about how Colette would feel." *At least I hope so*, her inner voice said as her mind raced.

"Space. Just a little space. OK?"

"You got it."

The telephone chimed and the Lieutenant answered it. "Driscoll here."

"I gotta talk to you." Moira's voice was filled with apprehension.

"So, talk."

"Not on the phone. I don't trust AT&T."

"Moira, you caught me at a bad time."

"They make an awesome bacon cheeseburger at the Empress Diner."

"What is it you want?"

"I told you, I won't discuss it on the phone."

"Then come to my office."

"Your office is like Grand Central Station at rush hour. It's no place for conversation."

"E-mail me." Driscoll cradled the phone under his chin and threw both hands in the air.

"Just give me ten minutes. The Empress Diner."

"You've got five. And it better be worth it."

Chapter 39

The waitress sneered at Driscoll as he slid into the booth across from the teenage girl.

She really did resemble Nicole. The more he saw of the girl, the more he was reminded of his daughter. The likeness was uncanny. "Here I am," he said. "What is it you wanted to tell me?"

"I know," she whispered, sipping a cherry coke.

"You know what?"

"I know how he picks them."

"You know how who picks them?"

"The killer. I designed a program and analyzed the data."

"What data?"

"From your files."

"Goddamn it, Moira! Those files are police property!"

"Did you know all of your victims were members of an online service?"

"Yeah. So what? So is half the country."

"I think your guy is luring the women through the Internet," she said, knowing the gurgling sound of her straw irritated him. "I could hook up with him."

"Hook up with him! Moira, if you're right and he is luring his victims through the Internet, do you really think hooking up with him would be a wise thing to do? Hell, I wouldn't send my best undercover into that lion's den without plenty of backup."

"I take my assignment seriously. I'll do what needs to be done."

"Assignment! What assignment?"

"Unofficial agent investigating case number 29AW16."

"Oh, brother."

"Maybe he flirts with them in a chat room, but I doubt it. My guess is, he's planted some goody on a bulletin board. He'd have thousands of chicks, worldwide, checking him out."

"A global serial killer? That would be a stretch. I think you're getting in a little too deep."

"Since the killings are local, we can start with city ads. My program'll sniff out the ferret. I've narrowed the list of ads down to 1,876. That's where you come in."

"How's that?"

"You can have the Task Force continue the search."

The girl might be on to something. It wouldn't be the first time a criminal used the Internet as his playing field. And if Moira was right, it would be a very deadly field. This was no place for a fourteen-year-old. Driscoll knew what he needed to do. He needed to protect the girl. "Moira, I want you off this case."

"You're not gonna make Captain without me."

"I'll look into the possibilities your theory raises. But we're dealing with a vicious murderer. The last thing I want you to do is to try and hook up with him. If he turns out to be our killer, you'd be putting yourself in grave danger."

"I know the highways and byways of the Internet better than anyone. I'm tellin' ya, I can hook up with him."

"And I forbid it. It'd be no place for a fourteen-year-old girl."

"That's it. Isn't it?

"What's it?"

"You don't trust me just 'cause I'm a kid. You grown-ups are all alike. Afraid to admit that a kid might know more than they do."

"Granted, you dazzle me with your computer expertise. But I can't allow you to put yourself at risk."

"I'm sure I'm right about this one. All the dead women were members of an online service."

"But not the same online service."

"That wouldn't matter. They'd all have access to the World Wide Web."

"I promise you, I'll look into it. But, while I'm doing that, I want you to steer clear of any inclination you have to hook up with the guy."

"OK," she said begrudgingly, sliding out of the booth.

"And Moira."

"Yes?"

"Stay out of those police files. If I catch you nosing around in there again, I'll lock you up."

The Lieutenant sat back in the empty booth and thought about the exchange. Could Moira be right? He grabbed his cellular and punched in the number to his office. When Margaret answered, he said, "Find out what you can about each victim's online service."

"Is this you talking, Lieutenant? Or the whiz kid?"

"Moira thinks our killer may be luring his victims through the Internet."

"It wouldn't be the first time. You think she's on to something?"

"She raised the possibility. We'd be foolish to ignore it."

"I'll get on it right away."

Chapter 40

Driscoll eyed the wooden crucifix that was affixed to the far wall inside the dimly lit parlor of St. Mary's Star of the Sea rectory. His palms were sweating, and he thought he could hear his heart beating. But Elizabeth Fahey was right. What was weighing heavily on his mind was guilt. Irish Catholic guilt. And who better to speak to about such guilt than an Irish Catholic priest? That being the case, Driscoll had asked around. Liz Butler lived in Rockaway. She was a devout Catholic and had told Driscoll her pastor was a with-it kind of guy. Driscoll had placed a call to her church's rectory and arranged a meeting with Father Sean McMahon.

The Lieutenant stood up as the priest entered the room. McMahon was a young priest with a ruddy complexion that suited his round Irish face. Driscoll figured him to be somewhere in his thirties.

"Good afternoon, Lieutenant. Welcome to St. Mary's,"

Father McMahon said, motioning for Driscoll to take a seat beside an ornately carved mahogany desk.

"Thank you for seeing me on such short notice."

"You're welcome."

"I gotta tell ya, Father, it's been ages since I've been inside a rectory, and years since I've been to church."

McMahon smiled. "I'm glad you've returned."

"I'd like to get right to the point, if you'll let me. I feel like my insides are about to explode."

"Our cleaning lady wouldn't like that."

Driscoll liked that the man had a sense of humor. "I wanna talk to you about certain feelings of guilt I'm having. My wife, Colette, was involved in an automobile accident six years ago. Our daughter, Nicole, was killed in the accident, and my wife was left comatose. According to her doctors she'll never regain consciousness."

"I'm so sorry to hear that."

"I've remained faithful to my wife, Father. That is, up until recently." Driscoll studied the priest's face for any sign of condemnation. Finding none, he continued. "I've become friendly with a woman that I work with. Her name is Margaret. She's a good woman who understands my circumstances. The thing is, I have feelings for her. Romantic feelings. The other night we had dinner together at her place. One thing led to another, and I found myself in her arms, kissing her. I haven't kissed a woman in six years. I gotta tell ya Father, I liked it."

"Were you raised Catholic, Lieutenant?"

"Yes. Catholic grammar school. Catholic high school. I even did a stint as an altar boy for four years. Back in those days, the Mass was in Latin."

"So I've been told."

"Father, I guess I'm here for absolution. Absolution for a sin I'm yet to commit. Does that make sense?"

"And what sin is that?"

"Breaking my wedding vows. Cheating on my wife."

"You've already made up your mind you're going to pursue this relationship?"

"That's where the guilt comes in. I realize that Colette is never coming back to life, life as we know it, but a voice inside me is demanding that I stay faithful to her, regardless of her physical condition."

"You said before her doctors all agree that she will never regain consciousness. Right?"

"Right."

"Aside from how you perceive the Catholic Church would look at your circumstances, what advice would your wife give you, if she could?"

"Colette was my best friend. I'm beginning to believe she would understand. Am I just looking to sidestep my vows here?"

"I think the answer to that question lies within you. You've got to live with yourself. But, let me say this. Jesus Christ, who walked this earth as a human being, chose twelve apostles, not one. And his love for each one of them was immeasurable."

"Are you condoning a relationship with this other woman?"

"It wouldn't mean you stopped loving your wife. It's important you realize that." McMahon leaned his small frame across the top of the desk and let his eyes fall level with Driscoll's. "You said before Colette was your best friend."

"That's right."

"Well, then, I'd say it's time you had a conversation with your best friend."

Chapter 41

Driscoll approached the house. He felt like his knees were going to collapse. He steadied himself, and as he reached for the brass doorknob, he felt his stomach curdle. Like a schoolboy late for class, he guiltily turned the knob and stepped inside. The whirring sounds of his wife's life-support system, which before had gone unnoticed, clamored in his ears.

"Are you OK, Lieutenant? You look like you're gonna throw up." It was Colette's nurse, Lucinda.

Driscoll forced a smile. "I'll live," he said as his eyes fell upon Colette's ashen face. "Would you excuse us, Lucinda? I need some time with my wife."

"You got it," the nurse replied, then quickly disappeared as the Lieutenant straddled a bedside chair.

Behind him, an orchestra of high-tech medical gadgetry played their monotonous and repetitive symphony. Before him lay his wife, his beautiful and loving wife. How could he love again? How could he run the risk? He often felt it was his doing, somehow, that brought about his wife's fate. Punishment for some un-confessed dereliction, perhaps. Would he then imperil Margaret? Would she fall victim to his ill fortune?

Driscoll took hold of his wife's hand. How lifeless her skin felt. Tears blossomed as he fingered the wedding band that encircled her finger. He opened the drawer to her night table and reached for the emollient Thomlinson had given him, then applied the lotion to her hands and arms, the same hands and arms that had held him lovingly through the years. *In sickness and in health*, a tiny voice sounded. He grimaced. What was he about to do? How could he trample on his wedding vows? He played back the message Father McMahon so reverently had given him. Christ had chosen twelve apostles, not one.

"I met someone," he murmured as his heart pounded in his chest. "Her name is Margaret." His admission was greeted with silence.

He leaned in and planted a kiss on his wife's fore-head while pushing away two strands of errant hair from her face. "I met her on the job. She and I are working together on a case. She's a caring woman who would like to further our relationship."

Driscoll stood up and walked over to the wall unit, which contained a small wine rack and an assortment of liquors. He poured himself two fingers of Tullamore Dew and returned to his wife's bedside, slowly sipping the whiskey, hoping the spirits would give him the courage to tell her what he knew needed to be said. Hell, he'd bite the bullet. "She would like to further our relationship," he said. "And so would I."

Again his disclosure was greeted by silence. He had half expected his wife to sit upright and scold him, take him to task for such a selfish transgression. Driscoll had hoped, on some level, that the admission would bring her to consciousness, allow her to break free from the forceful grip that held her so unmercifully. Of course, it did not.

Driscoll leaned forward and held his head in his hand. He thought of the once-vibrant Colette, a wonderful and doting woman who would change heaven and earth for him.

An epiphany unfolded. It was a vision of Colette, his loving wife, who smiled and took hold of his hand. *You poor soul,* he heard her say. *You poor troubled soul. It's all right, my dear. I know you love me, and I know you always will. But, it's time you moved on. Beyond my illness. Beyond your worries. It's time for you, my darling, to live among the living.*

He felt a rush, not unlike the surge of adrenaline he felt when he apprehended a criminal. Then a calmness settled over him. He had thought his guilt would cripple him, but it did not. Relief. That's what he felt. He knew in his heart she understood.

Chapter 42

The five-year-old boy stuck his head out the Maxima's rear passenger-side window. "Whirr! Whirr!" he intoned, mimicking the sound of the emergency vehicle sirens that could be heard in the distance.

The boy's mother veered the sedan off onto East Fifty-seventh Street. She'd have to travel four blocks to Mill Avenue to avoid the traffic jam, but the detour would be worth it.

A beep erupted, startling her. "What was that? Robbie, did you unfasten your seat belt?"

"No, Mom."

The boy stuck his hand in the pocket of his jacket and produced a telephone pager.

"Where'd that come from?" his mother asked, craning her neck.

"I found it."

"You found it? Where?"

"At the mall. In the store with the candy."

"Sweet Delights?"

"Uh-huh."

"But that was last week."

The boy shrugged.

A phone number showed on the device. She used her cell phone to punch in the number.

"Hello?" It was a male voice.

"Hi! Did you just beep someone?"

"Ah! I see you found my pager. I've been trying the number for days."

"Well, my son found it."

"Thank God! Where are you?"

"On the Belt Parkway. Why don't you give me your address? I'd be happy to drop it in the mail."

"Are you near Exit 10? We could meet at The Lobster Trap. It's a great new eatery on Emmons Avenue. I can retrieve the pager and thank you personally."

"That's the sweetest offer I've had in weeks. But I really can't. I teach violin, and my class is giving a recital on Sunday. I'll be tied up with practice tonight, tomorrow, and into Sunday morning. I'm on my way now to drop my son off at his grandmother's."

"Oh, a single parent?"

"Well, yes."

"That makes two of us. C'mon, let's not snub fate."

"This is starting to feel like a date."

"No, just gratitude."

"Well, I suppose it'd be all right. I'll only have time for a cocktail, though. And I'll have to drop Robbie off first."

"OK. Let's say we meet in an hour."

"That's sounds about right. How will I recognize you?"

"I'll be the man with a red amaryllis next to his drink at the bar."

Apprehension and a strange sense of curiosity flooded her. She hadn't asked to meet this man, and yet they had a date. She turned to look at her son. The child was asleep. She breathed a sigh of relief that he hadn't heard the longing in his mother's voice.

Chapter 43

The drive to Sheepshead Bay was a sluggish one. There was construction on the Belt Parkway at Ocean Avenue. Workers in overalls and hard hats were plugging potholes that the snows of last winter had carved into the asphalt.

She veered the Maxima off at Knapp Street and, turning right, headed for Emmons Avenue. Pulling up in front of a parking meter, she turned off the engine. She could feel the hammering of her heart. Flipping down the visor, she checked her eye makeup and took a deep breath.

When she entered The Lobster Trap, she was struck by the din of a hundred conversations in progress. She was momentarily disoriented but recovered as her eyes searched the bar for the telltale flower. There was no amaryllis on the bar. Was she too early? The grandfather clock at the end of the bar said otherwise. Maybe she should go back to the car, wait fifteen or twenty minutes, and return to the bar appropriately late, or perhaps she should make herself comfortable and order a glass of Chablis. *Could he have been detained?* she wondered. Maybe that glass of wine would settle her nerves, after all. She stepped up to the bar and ordered her drink.

The bartender smiled as he poured the wine into a stemmed crystal glass. She felt as if her femininity were exposed to the world. She hadn't been out to meet a man in eight years.

She glanced at her watch. What was keeping him? As she watched the second hand sweep past the twelve on the face of her Timex, a thought occurred. How much time was left on that meter? She believed there was a two-hour limit. Or was it one?

With purse in hand, she headed for the revolving door. As soon as she stepped out onto the street, she spotted him. He was standing there, facing the restaurant, a strikingly dressed man holding an amaryllis.

"Hello," she said as her heart raced.

Chapter 44

She stared at him, shock and bewilderment still ablaze in her eyes. The rope singed swollen flesh at her wrists and ankles, worsened by her futile attempts to loosen the restraints that held fast to the wooden chair.

Colm heard her mutter something through the plumbing tape. It was unintelligible, but her eyes flashed a threat. How audacious some of them remained, even at the end, he thought.

"You would have been a gracious dinner guest," he said. "Unfortunately, given the circumstances, I thought it best to wait outside. It wouldn't have been wise to have us seen together, now, would it?"

Vengeful eyes stared back at him.

"I knew it was only a matter of time before you'd come out. Thank goodness you were alone. I wasn't sure what I'd do if you had brought company." He pulled up a chair and took a seat across from her. "I hadn't planned this ending, you know. I kept thinking it might be OK to simply recover the beeper and be done with it. I even considered the thought of actually keeping my promise and sharing a meal with you. But my resolve dissipated and a more familiar yearning kicked in . . . pure rapture. You're sure to rival some of my most cherished trophies."

Realization settled, in her dilated pupils as she watched him nonchalantly reach for the blade.

Chapter 45

"OK, here's what we've got," said Margaret, her voice strong, her eyes focused on Driscoll's, giving the Lieutenant the sense that she was OK with how things were. "Deirdre McCabe was hooked up at America Online. We got zip on Monique Beauford, our drifter. And the tea heiress, well, we're not sure what she used, although the whiz kid claims she had an account with Juno. The folks over at Juno list an A. Stockard on their books. But, their Internet service is free, so—"

"So they have nothing more than an A. Stockard. No billing address. No phone number."

"You got it."

"Juno. Netscape. I tell you, it's all Greek to me. Moira even *thinks* in another language."

"You've gotta realize that these kids are miles ahead on the information superhighway."

What was Margaret up to? Driscoll wondered. She

sounded like she had become a fan of the technogeek. *She's just being contrary,* he surmised.

"The Internet is the tool of tomorrow," Margaret continued.

"And possibly a killing field today."

"I've been doing a little research. Thought I'd sharpen my skills."

"And what did you discover?"

"Did you know that the Internet got its start as a project of the Defense Department? They had urged certain universities to link their computers in the name of scientific exploration. The idea caught on, and before anyone realized it, everybody, scholar, peddler and soothsayer alike, was linked. They're predicting 400 million cybersites by the next millennium."

"And to think I thought George Orwell was a dreamer. Four hundred million sites?" Driscoll wondered. Then after a pause, he asked, "Could Moira be right about the killer luring his victims through the Internet?"

"She thinks she is."

"OK, I promised her I'd look into her theory, so let's pull the computers available to the McCabe and Stockard women and have the guys over at the Computer Investigation & Tech Unit see if they can match up any common Web sites, e-mail messages, or instant messages. If they can establish any sort of common link or IP address, then we may have something to run with."

"I'll call Lieutenant White over there. He has a thing for me. He'll see to it they get on it right away."

The desk phone purred. The Lieutenant grabbed it. "Driscoll, here . . . Uh-huh . . . We'll be right there."

Margaret stared at him, her face a question mark.

"Victim number four's a floater. She just washed ashore under the Brooklyn Bridge. Let's go."

From the right lane of the bridge, Driscoll could make out a cluster of emergency vehicles on the span's Brooklyn side.

He exited at Court Street and circled around to the waterfront. A yellow police ribbon marked the zone closed to the public. Brooklynites watched uniformed police officers and plainclothes detectives explore the area. Driscoll and Margaret flashed their shields and stepped under the ribbon, and onto the sandy shore.

The bridge, colossal in its architecture and straddling the river in its massive concrete and brick pontoons, cast an ominous shadow over the crime scene.

"What a dreary place to die," Margaret muttered.

"Awesome, is more like it," Driscoll said, assessing the bridge's huge expansion cables.

"I think they're waiting for us." Margaret gestured to the Forensics Team, the local precinct's squad detectives, and the members of the Harbor Patrol that were gathered around the victim's boneless remains. The headless corpse lay three feet from the shoreline. The hands and feet were missing as well.

An older detective walked over to where they were standing. Driscoll recognized him, but couldn't remember his name.

"Chief of Ds called. Says we should turn this one over to you, Lieutenant."

"What have we got?" Driscoll asked, approaching the human wreckage.

"Two strollers discovered the floater a little after ten this morning. They're back at the house now, but they really didn't see anything. Guzman is taking their statements. I'll have the DD5s hand-delivered to your office as soon as they're typed. Other than that, there's not much to go on. From the looks of it, she wasn't killed here. And the fact that she's bloated up like that says she's been in the water for some time."

Driscoll hunched over the flotsam. He scanned the body and the immediate area for a driver's license or some other form of ID. There was none to be found. But his eye detected something. There appeared to be some sort of marking on the victim's right arm.

"What's that?" he asked.

"What's what?" the older detective responded.

"Get the ME over here, and the Crime-Scene guy with his camera," Driscoll ordered.

The Lieutenant knew not to touch the body. Floaters were delicate, and if not handled correctly would either explode in your face from all the gasses built up inside, or fall apart like tenderized meat. Better to let the experts handle the corpse. The cops in the Harbor Patrol were good at it, but the ME was better.

"Yes, Lieutenant?" It was Jasper Eliot, the Medical Examiner's assistant.

"You see something? Right there on the forearm? Looks like a tattoo or something? Can you make it out?"

Eliot gingerly moved the remains of the body to expose the forearm. "This, Lieutenant?"

"Yeah, that's it. Crime Scene, get a closeup of that. I want it blown up and at my office in an hour."

The Forensics photographer took several shots from different angles. When he was finished, Driscoll leaned in to get a closer look. "Son of a bitch." he grumbled.

Driscoll knew in an instant what he was looking at. This psycho liked to ID his victims, and this poor woman's ID was etched into the skin of her forearm. It was a barely readable inscription, in black ink:

L t w For t r M m ry

1041944

"Margaret, our killer is playing with us. He left us a clue. He wants us to decipher its meaning."

"Looks like a tattoo to me. With some of the letters rubbed off."

"What do you think? Should we send this down to Quantico? Maybe their Hieroglyphics Unit can tell us what it means."

"I don't know, John. Santangelo will have your head if he finds out you invited the FBI into the case."

"I know, but how many more women have to die just because he's too proud to ask for help?"

"Good point."

"OK, see what you can do to decipher it yourself, but, as soon as the photographs come in, express mail a set down to Quantico. Who do we know that works with the Feds?"

"Cedric knows a guy on the Joint Drug Task Force."

"Good. Have Cedric get a hold of his buddy and ask him to make a call for us. See if Hieroglyphics can work on this and keep it between us."

"Will do."

"All right. Call everybody over here."

Margaret rounded up the precinct detectives, the Harbor Patrol, and the Crime-Scene investigators. Once everyone was gathered in one place, Driscoll said, "Listen up, everybody. The first thing I want to know is where this body came from. Then, how did it get here? Harbor Patrol, contact the Coast Guard. Have them check their high- and low-tide charts and consider the currents. See if they can determine where she may have been placed in the water. At least have them give you an educated guess. "Crime Scene, wait here until the tide goes out. Then I want you to collect every scrap of paper, every bottle cap, and every speck of trash that's left on the beach, and process it. Maybe we'll get lucky."

Driscoll turned to the senior detective. "You and your squad, go with the body to the morgue. I want the autopsy done today. Make sure that everything is done right and that nothing is overlooked. Let me know what the autopsy reveals. If there was water in her lungs, I want to know about it. That sick bastard may have watched her drown before he cut her open. Or he might have dissected her first and dumped her from some boat. See what's in her stomach. Maybe that'll lead us somewhere. I want the whole ball of wax. Got it?"

"Yes, Lieutenant. I'll call you as soon as it's done."

"That'd be good. Thanks for your help."

Driscoll's face turned somber as his eyes caught sight of the Forensic Team bagging the remains of the fourth female victim. "We gotta catch this guy, Margaret. He's beginning to tread on my dreams."

Chapter 46

Margaret hurried into Driscoll's office to report her findings. She had stolen Quantico's thunder. She had broken the code herself.

"I've got the missing letters," she said, authoritatively. "ES, E, GE, HE, E, and O. The full inscription reads: "Lest We Forget Her Memory, 1041944. Our "Jane Doe" is Jewish. I traced her through the Holocaust Survivors' Bureau using the number. It's a date. Not only do they maintain records of the survivors, but they also reveal a wealth of information about their descendants."

"The autopsy of her remains says she's too young to be a Holocaust victim, herself," said Driscoll.

"But her grandmother wasn't. Florence Tischman died at Auschwitz, October 4, 1944." Margaret gave Driscoll photocopies of the documents she had gathered at the Holocaust Survivors' Bureau.

"And, she had a child," Driscoll surmised.

"Maxine. Born in 1942. The camp was liberated by

the Red Army. The Red Cross inherited the babies. Maxine arrived in New York in 1946, as a ward of the Jewish Rescue Mission. She was later adopted by a family in Brooklyn, where she lived for the rest of her life. In 1964, Maxine Cooperman gave birth to a daughter, Sarah. She's our victim."

"Why the tattoo?"

"We'd need to ask her that one. My guess would be strong allegiance to family."

"The poor woman. Her mother escapes the Gestapo, but Sarah can't manage to dodge our murderous madman."

"Sarah had a child. A young boy."

"Where's the father?"

"Works as a banker. In Tel Aviv."

"And the boy?"

"Sarah's mother-in-law, Anita Benjamin, had called in a missing person. She's sure to have some information on the boy, and hopefully some knowledge of Sarah's last known whereabouts."

"You'll be following up with her?"

"My next order of business."

"Margaret, you beat the Feds at their own game. How does it feel?"

"Great!"

"While we're on the subject of feelings, are you OK with how things are? Between us, I mean?"

"I should be asking you that question. You're the one who's bearing all the emotional stress. Stress you don't need to carry, I might add. I do have one question, though." There was that rapid heartbeat again.

"Fire away."

"Have you given any more thought to what I said about Colette's take on this?"

"You mean about me seeing other women?"

"This woman!"

The notion blindsided Driscoll. She certainly got right to the heart of the matter. He had to admire her directness. "What we shared the other night was wonderful. I forgot I could feel so good. The truth is, I do have strong feelings for you. I'd be lying if I said I didn't. But, I still need more time to think things over."

Margaret gazed into the Lieutenant's eyes. "John, I appreciate your being frank with me. I really didn't know what to think. You've seemed so distant lately. I thought you had some regret over what happened between us. I'm happy to hear you don't." A smile erupted on Margaret's face. She took Driscoll's hand. "Take all the time you need to sort things out. I'm not going anywhere."

It was Driscoll's turn to smile.

Chapter 47

"Mrs. Benjamin, I have questions, disturbing questions, and I regret that I must ask them," said Margaret as she returned the older woman's gaze. There was a sadness to the woman's eyes, a sadness that went beyond the present circumstances.

They were sitting in Mrs. Benjamin's finely upholstered living room. It was quiet and heavily furnished, with thick velvet drapery. Votive candles burned on a table.

"I want to help where I can," said Mrs. Benjamin. "Sarah would have wanted it that way."

The response put Margaret at ease. There was no pretense about the woman. And it was apparent that she and the victim shared a loving relationship.

"Did your daughter-in-law tell you where she was going Friday night?"

"To her recital hall. Sarah taught violin. Her class was giving a recital on Sunday. They were to play Beethoven.

It was going to be a working weekend filled with practice, late Friday through Sunday. That's why she dropped Robbie off. She was going to pick him up after the show on Sunday. When she didn't, I called the hall. She had never shown up! I got frantic. I knew something had happened. But no one could ever imagine . . ." Her voice cracked.

Margaret fought back the urge to take the woman's hand. She had interviewed hundreds, if not thousands, of grieving relatives in her career. The nurturing urge was always there. She was proud of it, but she was always able to remain objective and professional by curtailing it. "I'm sorry I have to ask this next question."

"Go on. I want to help where I can."

"How was Sarah's relationship with her estranged husband, your son?"

"My son was a scoundrel."

The answer surprised Margaret. She thought it refreshing to interview someone who displayed a frankness and willingness to be so open with someone she had never met. A smile formed on Margaret's lips as Mrs. Benjamin continued. "Sarah never stopped loving him, though. Even after the divorce. He was the only man she ever loved. She was hoping for a reconciliation."

"Did you know much about her social life?"

"She was dedicated to her music. That much I know."

Suddenly, a sobbing child darted into the room and threw himself into the older woman's arms.

"My grandson Robbie is practically an orphan," said Mrs. Benjamin, cradling the crying boy.

The young boy stole a look at Margaret.

"Robbie, where did your mommy go after she dropped you off?" asked Margaret.

The boy buried his head in his grandmother's arms.

Margaret produced her police shield and held it out to the boy. He raised his head again.

"Can you find the Indian on my badge?" she asked.

Moist eyes searched the shield. A tiny finger pointed out the Manhattan Indian.

"Would you like to wear my badge?"

The boy nodded his head.

"I appoint you Deputy Robbie Benjamin," Margaret announced, pinning the shield to the boy's shirt.

Mrs. Benjamin smiled.

"Am I a real policeman?" the boy mumbled, tugging on Margaret's sleeve.

"Yes. It's official now."

"Can I tell my friends?"

"Sure."

"Do I get a gun?"

"What for?"

"I'm gonna shoot the bad guys."

"Well, Officer Benjamin, I'll see what I can do."

"A beeper, too?"

"A beeper?"

"A blue one."

"Why blue?"

"Like the one I found."

"Where'd you find it?"

"At the mall. It beeps when someone wants to talk to you, like the guy who beeped us in the car."

"What guy?" Margaret felt a rush of excitement.

"The guy Mommy talked to."

"Mommy talked to a guy?"

Margaret and Mrs. Benjamin exchanged glances.

"Mommy made a phone call from the car on her fold-up phone."

"Do you remember what Mommy said on the phone?" said Margaret.

The boy shrugged.

"Where's the beeper now?"

"Mommy took it when she called the guy from the car."

"Mrs. Benjamin, did Sarah have a cell phone?"

"Yes."

"I'll need the number."

"Certainly. It's 917-288-1274."

Chapter 48

Driscoll listened intently to Margaret's voice as it crackled through the speaker of his car phone.

"Cellular One shows Sarah Benjamin's last outgoing call lasted nine minutes. The call was to a pay phone on the first floor of the Kings Plaza Shopping Mall in Brooklyn."

"Dead end," muttered Driscoll. He made a left turn off of Eighth Avenue and pulled to the curb in front of 411 Garfield Place.

Mrs. Benjamin's residence was as Margaret had reported, an unassuming brownstone on a street of ordinary attached houses. He climbed the steps leading to a gothic oak door. It was ajar, letting out fragments of conversation from the inner rooms.

He stepped into the vestibule. Men and women, dressed in mourning attire, stood in small groups, talking softly. It felt to Driscoll as though the house were overheated. He took off his Burberry and hung it on an elaborate Victorian coatrack.

"You must be Lieutenant Driscoll," a voice said. "I'm Anita Benjamin."

"I'm very sorry for your loss."

"It's comforting to have you among us." Mrs. Benjamin ushered Driscoll into a room crowded with visitors.

Driscoll recalled the Irish wakes he had attended. In this house, there was no coffin, no viewing of the departed. Instead, platters of food crammed an elongated mahogany table.

"I'd like to meet your son," said Driscoll.

"That's him, the scoundrel, over there with the brunette."

Driscoll walked toward Isaac Benjamin. "Mr. Benjamin, I am Lieutenant Driscoll, and I would like to talk to you."

A cloud of darkness crowded Benjamin's eyes as he studied Driscoll. The brunette excused herself and disappeared. Benjamin spoke. "I caught the look on my mother's face when she pointed me out. I'm really not the bad guy she makes me out to be. Let's just say we each handle the loss of a loved one in different fashions."

"I understand."

"Why don't we move into the study? We can continue our conversation in there."

Driscoll followed Benjamin into a small room where a simple pine desk supported a laptop computer and a cluster of bills.

"The papers say Sarah was the target of a serial killer. Is that true?"

"It's a strong possibility. How long have you and she been divorced?"

"Goin' on three years."

"And when was the last time you saw her?"

"I'm a banker. An international banker. I was in Tel Aviv when she was killed, if that's what you're getting at."

"And you saw her for the last time, when?"

"When the divorce became final. Three years ago. And if you're gonna ask me the usual questions, you may as well forget about it."

"And what are the usual questions?"

"Did I know of anyone who may have wanted to harm Sarah? Was I aware of any strange telephone calls? Trouble at work? And on and on."

"I take it you didn't know much about Sarah's life since the divorce."

"I didn't know much about Sarah's life before the divorce! That's why we're divorced."

Silence settled between the two men. It was Benjamin who broke it.

"Was she mangled like they're saying on the news?"

"It was a very brutal slaying. For the most part, the newscasters have it right."

"They're saying her body washed up under the Brooklyn Bridge."

"That's right."

"That part's ironic."

"Why's that."

"Fourth of July, 1989, our first date. We watched the fireworks from a sailboat as it made its way under that bridge."

The thought rocketed to Driscoll's consciousness.

Did the killer know that? Was that why he dumped the Benjamin woman in the waters under the bridge? Was there some sort of distorted significance to the drop site?

Chapter 49

The Sixty-first Precinct located Sarah Benjamin's car. It was collecting parking tickets at an expired meter on Emmons Avenue and East Twenty-first Street," Margaret reported as she sat beside Driscoll's desk. "That's Restaurant Row. I'm running her photo by every hostess and waiter. Maybe we'll get lucky. And since the last call she made from her car was to a telephone inside the shopping mall, I checked the incident reports at the mall for that day. They logged in two arrests for shoplifting, and nothing more."

"That's dead end number seventeen and eighteen. But who's counting?" Driscoll grumbled. "Do me a favor, call your buddy, White, over at the Computer Investigation & Tech Unit. See what they've got on the two victims' computers. They seem to be taking their sweet time. I thought you said White had a thing for you."

"Speaking of computers, your postman's ringing."

"My what?"

"Your computer. You have e-mail."

Driscoll rolled his chair over to the monitor and typed in his password. His correspondence flashed on the amber screen.

It's me, Moira. I've been burning the midnight oil. Peel open your sun-soaked eyes and see what I see. It's all about first dating. That's what the drop sites have in common. They're where the women first encountered their first love. Did you know that Amelia Stockard once dated Newark's Commissioner of Sanitation? That explains the sanitation dump. And now, hold your breath, Lieutenant, 'cause . . .

I've made contact with him!

Shocked? Bewildered? Awed? You should be. Surprise! Your killer's got a name. It's Godsend. And check out the ad he's placed on a bulletin board:

WOMEN OF GOTHAM,
WANT TO REKINDLE YOUR FIRST LOVE?

Where is he? Your Romeo? Your Lancelot? The one who first taught your heart to skip a beat? YOUR FIRST LOVE! LE GRAND AMOUR! Gone now but never forgotten, and I can arrange the meet. Just imagine that. For the modest initiation fee of just $99.95, you're on your way. Don't let this opportunity pass you by. And more importantly, act today!

Could she be right? thought Driscoll. Had this precocious teen really unearthed the murderer? Was this what the victims had in common? Had they all been lured to their deaths by some fiendish Internet psycho, only to have their bodies recovered at the site where they had once rendezvoused with a first love? Moira's pace was astounding. And if on target, so was her find.

He reached for the desk phone and pounded in her number. Moria answered on the first ring, and once Driscoll greeted her, continued to show off what she had learned. "Deirdre McCabe's screen name was DeeDee22 at America Online. Monique went by Candy-Ass at Netscape. And the tea heiress picked Chamomile33 at Juno. The Benjamin woman was out of the pattern. She has no online service. She never went near a computer, but I'll bet the waters under the Brooklyn Bridge have some significance."

"More than you know, Moira. You've beaten our technicians at their own game. How'd you get this?"

"Women are savers. They save their love letters. I downloaded their e-mail and retrieved all of their correspondence with Godsend."

"So let's see. You burglarized the hard drives of the victims' computers, stole their passwords, and downloaded their correspondence. Do I have it right?"

"You really live up to your name, Detective."

"I want all that stolen data in my office. Within the hour!"

"I already sifted through it. It doesn't reveal the killer's identity."

"OK. You arranged this exchange. Suppose you tell me the next step."

"I wanna be the one to collar him."

"What!"

"I wanna nab the bad guy."

"Moira, need I remind you you're barely fourteen?"

"There you go again with the age bit."

"What you did was illegal."

"I did it to help you. Take the present, will ya?"

An awareness struck Driscoll. This young girl, who had shown up the Department's technical experts, was putting herself in harm's way. She was delusional in thinking she could apprehend the killer. But, there seemed to be no stopping her. Was he to blame? Was he so blinded by the memory of his daughter Nicole that he overlooked the caution flags and invited Moira into the chase?

"Lieutenant, go back to your screen. Check out my response to Godsend's ad—"

"Oh, Jesus!"

Dear Godsend,

Your ad sounds soooo . . . tempting. Are you for real? I mean, really track down my first love? I'd just die to know what became of Donny Tesorio. You bet I'm interested. What's next? Light the way.

Signed,
Excited

Bet you're riveted to the screen now, Lieutenant. Wait! There's more. Feast your eyes on our demon's reply.

Dear Excited,

Not only will I deliver Donny Dearest, but, for the unfathomable fee of just $249 (minus your $99.95 initiation fee), I'll guarantee an experience of a lifetime. If you're still "excited," I can send you a questionnaire.

Godsend

Dear Godsend,

A query at the tip of my tongue, O valiant prospector. Surely gold isn't your only reward in your mission to reunite ancient lovers? What fuels this passion? Answer my question and put my soul to rest.

Excited

Dear Excited,

Rest in peace, my child. I once loved a sister, a comrade at heart, a first love, and prime mover of my soul. Departed to other climes, never to return.

Godsend

Godsend,

Saddened am I. Rush me the questionnaire.

Excited

NAME   AGE
ADDRESS
Married? Yes.....No.....
Happily? Yes.....No.....
How do you rate it?
    Poor.....Fair.....Satisfactory.....Excellent.....
Going steady? Yes.....No.....
How do you rate it?
    Poor.....Fair.....Satisfactory.....Excellent.....
How often do you think of your first love?
    Once a night.....
    Once a week.....
    Once a month.....
Why do you want to hook up with your first love?
    A journey down memory lane.....
    Revisit my first kiss.....
    Reminiscences of our first intimacy.....
    All of the above.....
*** After reviewing your application, I'll ask you to scan me a photo of yourself, Excited, along with Donny's. It will help me find your first love. And you'll let me know exactly where you were when you celebrated your first date.

Lieutenant, he had their photographs. That's how he stalked them. He knew where they spent their first date. That's where he dumped them. Now, feast your eyes on *my* application:

NAME   Catherine Palmer   AGE.....A woman never tells
ADDRESS.....278 Carroll Street. Brooklyn, New York
Married? Yes.....No (X).....
Happily? Yes.....No.....

How do you rate it?
    Poor.....Fair.....Satisfactory.....Excellent.....
Going steady? Yes.....No..... (SORT OF)
How do you rate it?
    Poor.....Fair (X). Satisfactory.....Excellent.....
How often do you think of your first love?
    Once a night.....YOU BET!
    Once a week.....
    Once a month.....
Why do you want to hook up with your first love?
    A journey down memory lane.....
    Revisit my first kiss.....
    Reminiscences of our first intimacy.....
    All of the above.....XXX It's been almost nine
    years since our last kiss.

Stay awake, Lieutenant!

Dear Catherine,

It's soooo faaaabulous to know you, darling. Your reason for rekindling your first love is inspiring. I was touched. What a torch! Requests like yours are a thrill. Makes me glad I chose genealogy as my hobby. Next, give me the scoop on Donny. I want the low-down on the scrumptious hunk of burning flesh with the killer lips. Answer me this: Where did you and your lover-boy spend your first date? And now is the time to scan me his photo. Include some candid snapshots of your lovely face as well. For it'll then be time to let the show begin. Remember, it's magic. Keep your eye on the hat, young lady. Abra cadabra!

                                 Godsend

"I have Lieutenant White from Technical Support on the other line. The kid's right. The victim's computers show correspondence with Godsend," Margaret whispered.

"Wait, there's more," said Driscoll.

Catherine Dearest,

Merci for the lurid details about you and the Donster. I'm tracking the hare as we speak. And thank you so much for the pix. Oh, that Donny, what shoulders, what deltoids, what lips! Oh, mon dieu! And your face. Eat your heart out, Julia Roberts. Speaking of his killer lips, are you getting yours geared up for that Kodak moment? It's just around the corner. Stay tuned.

Is mise le meas,
Godsend

"*Is mise le meas!* That's Old Irish! Moira, get in here! Now!" he barked into the phone.

There was no one on the other end of the line.

"Moira? Moira? She's gone."

"She's off-line too. But, wait, she left you a message."

Driscoll and Margaret peered back into the screen.

Gotta run. I work better under open skies. He's trying to reach me now. Maybe we'll catch a break. Remember, Lieutenant, the drop sites. They're all part of his game. Don't overlook the drop sites. Therein lies the link.

Back on the job,

Moira

"Can you believe this kid?" Driscoll hit the phone's redial button. After four rings, Seamus Tiernan's recorded voice sounded in his ear.

"Hi! You've reached the Tiernans. Sorry no one is available . . ."

Driscoll hung up.

"My God! What if . . ." Driscoll's face drained of all color. "Margaret, could she be serious about trying to collar him?"

"With her, anything's possible."

"I've got to stop her." He reached for his Burberry and headed for the door.

Chapter 50

The electronically amplified voice of Detective Vince Viallo still echoed in Margaret's ear. He had reached her on her cruiser's car phone to inform her that a bartender at The Lobster Trap had ID'd the photo of the Benjamin woman. She had come in to the restaurant alone, ordered a drink, and left alone. Disgruntled, Margaret pulled the Plymouth to the curb in front of the One Stop Pharmacy and got out. She made her way into the drugstore, a vast space flooded with white fluorescent lights. Approaching the store's counter, she spotted the store's proprietor, Gerard McCabe, who was offering a selection of condoms to a perplexed teen.

"So, what'll it be? Ribbed? Lubricated? Or do you want the ones with the little catchall pouch at the end?" McCabe asked.

"I just want . . . uhh . . . uhh . . ." the disoriented youth stuttered.

"Look kid, you're nowhere near a decision. Do me a

favor. Come back and see me after you've started to shave."

The youth scrambled toward the exit and vanished as McCabe turned his attention to Margaret.

"They're gettin' younger and younger every year," he sighed. "Tell me you're the bearer of good news on the investigation."

She wished she was. She knew it would be of some comfort to this grieving husband. But the investigation, thus far, had produced more questions than answers. And here she was, about to ask another one.

"This may seem like an odd question, Mr. McCabe, but where did you and your wife go on your first date?"

"You're right. That is an odd question. But our first date was no secret. We had dinner in New York City and visited the Empire State Building."

"You and your wife ever go to Prospect Park?"

"No, not together. Why do you ask?"

"We're working on a theory."

"Does it have something to do with why you found her body in the park?"

"In part."

"Well, we were never there together, that's for sure. Listen, my mother-in-law dropped off a box of my wife's stuff. From when she was a kid. She thought I should have it. I'm not ready to open it, though. Maybe you'd like to go through it?"

Margaret nodded.

McCabe sauntered into the storage room and returned with a cardboard box. He handed it to Margaret.

"Maybe it'll help," he said.

The box was crammed with memories of a young girl's adolescence. Class pictures, two teddy bears, several folded sheets of looseleaf containing handwritten notes between best friends, a pair of soccer trophies, her high-school ring. Margaret picked up an embossed notebook and leafed through it.

It's about her first love, she noted, excited by her find. A Caribbean man . . . parents didn't approve . . . had to hide their love away. Look at this, she wrote a poem:

Our special time hovers,
Be still my pounding heart.
Soon to rendezvous as lovers,
Entwined forever, not to part.

Passion beckons to the lake.
By cascading water,
My heart, my soul, to take
Amidst sweet laughter.

The boatkeeper's made departure.
The swans and clouds are at rest.
Let us treasure the rapture
Of our borrowed love nest.

I'll bet my next promotion that love nest is the Swan Boat House in Prospect Park, Margaret thought. She grabbed her mobile phone and dialed Driscoll's cellular number.

"Driscoll here."

"Any luck finding Moira?" she asked.

"None. I've been sitting on the Tiernan house all morning. The place was empty until Mrs. Tiernan came home with her groceries. I told her I was trying to reach her daughter and I think I managed to keep my anxiety in check. She told me Moira doesn't have any close friends. She's likely to be alone. Just her and her god-damn satellite computer off somewhere in cyberspace. She could be anywhere. I alerted the local precinct. Cedric is informing the Task Force, and every other precinct in a twenty-five-mile radius. She has me very worried."

"I can hear it in your voice."

"My Nicole had her moments. But this kid is something else."

"She must open old wounds. I'm very sorry."

"Thank you. So what did your visit with McCabe produce?"

Margaret told him of her discovery.

"The whiz kid strikes again. She was right about the Benjamin woman, and that poem makes her right about Deirdre McCabe. Margaret, I want you to get back to that body piercer on Houston. See if he further corroborates Moira's theory about the drop sites. I want to know if he has any idea why Monique Beauford's body was found nailed to a boardwalk in Rockaway Beach."

Chapter 51

Margaret pried open the aluminum door to Lester Gallows's trailer.

"Oh Jeez! You're back?" said Gallows, as Margaret marched herself into his emporium.

"I wanna hear it again," she said.

"You're like a fly on shit."

"Let's hear it. Tell me about the last time you saw Monique."

"What's to tell?"

"You got it on with her. Right?"

"I already told you that."

"What else can you tell me about her?"

"The bitch was kinky."

"What's kinky?"

"Her pussy was laced with silicone."

"Implants?"

"No. Beach sand. The slut pulls out this pouch. I figure she's goin' for a condom. Instead she pours out a handful of sand. She rubbed it in before we screwed. It was like fucking sandpaper. My cock was in heaven!"

"She tell you why she got off on sand?"

"Told me the first time she got laid was under the boardwalk."

Margaret grabbed her cell phone and quickly relayed the information to Driscoll.

"That's another special drop site," Driscoll's voice reverberated in Margaret's ear. "We've got the boathouse in Prospect Park, the water under the Brooklyn Bridge, and now the boardwalk. Moira's batting a thousand."

Chapter 52

Driscoll was mindful of what Moira had said in her last communication: that she worked better under open skies. But it had begun to rain. And on rainy days, Mrs. Tiernan had told Driscoll, Moira liked to frequent any one of a half-dozen coffee shops in the area surrounding her home. There, she could sit uninterrupted for hours, while she pounded away on her laptop.

Over the last two hours Driscoll had personally visited all of the neighborhood's coffee shops but had failed to find Moira, and none of the shop's employees remembered seeing a young girl that fit Moira's description. He left his card with each store manager in case the girl stopped in. Seated behind the wheel of his idling automobile, he watched the rain collect on the Chevy's windshield. He grabbed his cell phone and placed yet another call to the Tiernan household.

When Seamus Tiernan's answering machine kicked in, he disconnected the call. Disheartened, he returned to his office, where he discovered he had e-mail. Pulling up a chair, he focused his eyes on the computer's amber screen and grew sick with worry as he read the following volley of electronic communications:

Catherine,

I'm mystified! I'm baffled! I'm stumped! I'm striking out on my search for candied-lipped Donny. What, has Don Juan mastered the cloak of invisibility, or had he never had an identity? I'd loathe to think that you made him up. That wouldn't be fair play. Would it?

Godsend

Godsend,

You must be a joker. Made him up? That's ludicrous! Could it be you're not the magician you claim to be? I suggest you get a new wand. Donato Tesorio was! And I predict, is! I suggest you give it another shot. Your best shot!

Catherine

Catherine,

No. Your Donny was never spawned, except in your twisted imagination. I charge you with three counts of Cyber-fraud. First: Fabricating an identity. Second: Criminal trespass of the Internet highways, with intent to misrepresent. Third: Downright bad netiquette. I swear, by the power of the gods Ram and Pixel, I will drag you in chains to the ecumenic council of mighty Magellan On-Line. There you will be stripped of your hard drive, chained to your joystick, and burned. May they impound your modem for all eternity, you cyber-sinner, you.

Godsend

Godsend,

Let's cut the doo-doo. I know who thou art. Nailing the bitch to the boardwalk was a coup. *Nine Inch Nails* wailed for you that night. What a romantic. You have such a way with women. Exalt, oh shadow of the night! It is I, and I alone, who knows your lair. And while New York's Finest unravel the puzzle, I, the cybermole, will burrow close to your wormy heart. In the Internet inferno, Dante has programmed a new circle for the likes of you. Your gigabyte brain will fry for all eternity.

Catherine

Catherine,

A villain thou art. You've cost me much insomnia, you mite on the back of a giant tyrannosaurus. Demons of earth, awaken! I am forced now to hunt you in cyberspace, for all eternity. Tell me, oh Enlightened One, how did you find me? Answer that and I will make you rich like Croesus.

Godsend

Godsend,

I am the pathfinder, Shiva's third eye. I scuba the currents of the Net like a Maui native on Hawaiian breakers. Tell me, do the bones make good bouil-lon, or do you bury them like feral dogs?

Catherine

Chapter 53

Behind the Statue of Liberty, the setting sun was gilding the sky, igniting a conflagration of primary colors that painted the Manhattan skyline in scarlet and gold. But this vista was lost on the solitary figure seated on a wooden bench on the upper deck of the South Street Seaport, staring at the screen of his Lynksys wireless-powered laptop.

"Do you bury them like feral dogs?"

The words loomed on the screen, taunting him. Never had an insult cut so deep. Colm slammed closed the laptop, flung the computer into the water that bordered the Seaport, and marched toward the parking lot where he had left the van.

Her last message had dismantled him. He felt like tracked prey. He thought about his pursuer, this woman who had navigated the Internet in search of his bait. The fact that she had found it infuriated him, for her intrusion had now made it necessary for him to find another lure.

He stopped. A smile slowly emerged on his face. *He* had not been found. She had only found Godsend, who was now resting thirty feet below the surface of the East River. His only inconvenience would be having to find some other way to select and attract future collectibles. The realization consoled him, but when he finally reached home, he was tired and listless. Inside the house, he collapsed on the living-room sofa, where he soon began obsessing over the loss of his last quarry. The pleasure of the Benjamin woman had not alleviated the pain of losing the young girl at the mall.

There was solace under the house. With his trophies, he would find consolation. He made his way down to the cellar. As his eyes adjusted to the darkness, he heard his mother's voice. "The young honey got away from you at the mall, didn't she? And now ya got another filly onto ya. A computer-literate filly, no less. You cyber-ghoul, you! Can't you do anything right?"

"Whatcha gonna do now?" nagged his father.

"You've made a mess of it for sure," his mother scolded. "The police'll be all over you soon."

"And I'll find a way to be all over them!" he screamed. "Now, shut up, both of you!"

The cellar became silent again. He eyed his parents' skeletal jaws for any sign of movement. They didn't budge.

Chapter 54

After dismissing a young patient who had been nearly paralyzed as a result of a motor-vehicle accident, Doctor Colm Pierce picked up the next case from a pile of folders on his desk. It was that of a gerontological patient, an eighty-eight-year-old woman with an injured coccyx. Pierce felt sorry for the poor soul. She was without family and relied heavily on her city-appointed caretaker. What brought a smile to the woman's face was that Pierce insisted he would personally escort her from the waiting room to his office every time she came in to see him.

Cheerfully, he stepped outside and walked down the narrow corridor. The hospital's loud speaker crackled. "Trauma team, report to Pediatric ICU, Stat!" There was a shuffle of feet. A member of the trauma team rushed past him, heading for the bay of elevators. It was Doctor Stephen Astin.

"Steve, we gotta talk," Pierce called out.

"Not now, Colm. I'm on my way to a Code Blue." Astin stepped inside the elevator and hit the sixth-floor button.

Just as the elevator's doors were closing, Pierce slipped inside. "Need I remind you you're into me for nineteen grand?" he said to Astin.

"Like you'd let me forget."

"Your third installment was due a month ago, so why haven't you answered my e-mail?"

"Night Rider is running tomorrow night at Belmont. He's got five grand of our cash running with him. It's a sure thing. Money in the bank."

"That's what you said the last time."

"C'mon, kid, you don't need the money. Why ya houndin' me?"

"Whether I need the money or not is none of your fucking business. It was a loan. Not a grant."

"Don't hand me that shit."

"What shit? I did it to help you."

"No, you didn't. You did it to see me strung out. It gives you a charge. Admit it."

The doors of the elevator opened, ushering the two angry men into the pediatric intensive care unit, where they were greeted by Doctor George Galina and Susan Dupree, the ICU nurse.

"It's the Parsons girl," Nurse Dupree announced. "It's the damndest thing. She wakes up screaming her head off. You'd think those punctured lungs were down for the count, but no."

"Wha'd she say?" asked Astin.

"I couldn't understand a thing."

The trauma team geared into action, and within seconds, Clarissa's body was punctured, injected, and palpated, sending each of her monitoring units into an electronic frenzy.

"She's flatlining!" Doctor Galina hollered.

Astin grabbed hold of two electric defibrillator paddles. "Clear!" he shouted, electrocuting the girl's heart after Susan Dupree lay bare the girl's chest.

Clarissa's body jerked, and her chest muscles tightened as waves of electricity riddled her nervous system. Tendons contracted and released. The heart convulsed, fluttered, and finally kicked in, forcing blood to vital arteries.

"Set up a drip of dopamine HC1 and titrate. Stat!" Galina ordered. "A push of epinephrine. Now!"

The needle entered the ravine between Clarissa's breasts, punctured her cardiac muscles, and delivered the stimulant, making the heart beat faster. As freshly oxygenated blood rushed to Clarissa's brain, it slowly recovered from its torpor. Her eyelids quivered, then opened. Her ears intercepted muffled sounds.

What was happening to her? Who were these masked men? She felt like carrion being plucked by ravenous beaks. Tears flooded her eyes, fogging her field of vision.

Suddenly, the face of the man who molested her came rocketing into sight. With it came the memory of his lecherous pursuit. The uninvited images filled the girl with dread, stirring a feeling of horror. Her fright quickly exploded into panic, propelling her into a full-blown cardiac arrest.

"She's leaving us!" Galina hollered.

"Clear!" barked Astin, grabbing the defibrillator paddles again and jabbing them brusquely against the girl's chest.

Two hundred joules coursed through Clarissa, jolting her small frame. Inert, her body endured another discharge of electrocution, and another, and another.

"My God, we've lost her," Doctor Astin sighed.

"What the hell went wrong?" Pierce protested, praying she didn't miraculously regain consciousness.

"Sometimes God has other plans."

"Not while I'm around." Pierce picked up the defibrillator paddles and, like a cymbalist clanging his brass instruments, he pummeled the girl's chest again and again.

Clarissa's body quaked under the assaults, only to return to the listlessness of death.

"Doctor, she's dead!" Nurse Dupree screamed.

"Have you lost all faith?" Pierce bellowed, about to go in for yet another assault. But Doctor Astin grabbed hold of his arms.

"Enough!"

With a feigned look of defeat filling his face, Pierce dropped both hands and stared down at the girl's inert frame.

"Kids these days. Some of them just don't want to be saved."

Chapter 55

"INTER-NET"

That was the headline plastered across the morning edition of the *New York Post*. The article itself, which spanned two pages, indicated that the crazed killer who had been holding the city hostage was luring his victims through the Internet. The *Post* credited sources close to the investigation for the information. The story prompted one particular call to the Task Force tip line. It was from a Cathy Spenser, who claimed to be with Clarissa Parsons the day she was hit by the car at the Kings Plaza Shopping Mall. She said Clarissa was at the mall to meet someone she had corresponded with over the Internet. Margaret was assigned to talk to the girl.

Behind the wheel of her Plymouth, Margaret headed over the Brooklyn Bridge, allotting Howard Stern his three minutes before his raunchiness became just intolerable. She surfed the car's radio waves, searching for an easy-listening station, preferably the hits of the forties.

The voice of WNYB's news anchorman, Paul Waters, startled her. "It's a very sad day for District Attorney Jack Parsons and family as they bury their only daughter in the family mausoleum at Long Island's Pinelawn Cemetery. It was only eight short weeks ago that Jack Parsons won a stunning victory over Donald Fruman of Brooklyn, capturing Manhattan's coveted DA seat. Undisclosed sources inform us that a serious investigation has been launched into the circumstances surrounding the young girl's death. Now this . . . Need guns? Need ammo? We got plenty. Come to Al's Sporting Goods on Route 25 in East Islip. We stock—"

Margaret hit the radio's off button, silencing the barker's assault, and fought the Flatbush Avenue rush-hour traffic. The Plymouth's speedometer registered fifteen miles per hour. But she knew that was about ten miles over her actual speed. She finally made her way to Bergen Street, where she broke from the string of endless vehicles and made a left turn.

"444" was etched across the third step of the first four-story brownstone on the block. A girl was sitting to the left of the numerals. With its clean facade and recently painted ironwork, the house was an anomaly against the decay of a neighborhood trapped between tenement wars and regentrification.

"Detective Aligante?" the girl asked timidly as Margaret got out of her car.

"You Cathy Spenser?"

The young girl nodded, bewilderment flooding her deep-set eyes.

"Let's go inside," Margaret suggested.

"There's a coffee shop around the corner. Can we go there instead? I've become a prisoner of my room."

Margaret assented, and they walked in silence on uneven pavement. Inside the shop, they found a booth away from the window and the blinding morning sunshine.

"I knew something bad would happen. I knew it the moment she told me she was meeting some stranger at the mall," the Spenser girl said.

"Why is that?" asked Margaret, feeling a strong sense of compassion for the girl. She was at such an impressionable age. It was a pity to see her tormented by disturbing circumstances surrounding the death of a friend. And who was this stranger the Parsons girl was to meet? Could the man have been the killer?

"Look, I know you're a cop and everything, but . . . you got a cigarette? I'm sorta bent out of shape."

"They don't allow smoking in here."

"I need a rush. I'd die for a Camel."

"That's a smelly animal. Not worth the effort."

The girl chuckled.

When the waitress appeared, they both ordered Coke.

"What did you mean when you said you knew something bad would happen?" Margaret asked.

"It did, didn't it?" Tears collected in the girl's eyes. "The cops wanted to know what Clarissa was doing at the mall. I said she was meeting some guy and she got stood up."

"What guy?"

Cathy's eyes drifted. "Clarissa, she was into this game."

"What kind'a game?" Margaret felt her heart race.

"I don't know exactly . . . something about this guy . . . She was supposed to meet him for the first time at the mall, but he was a no-show. I bumped into her at Aubrey's Bookstore, and then we went over to Sweet Delights. The cashier there had a surprise for the both of us. Real nerdy type, ya know? Anyway, we're just about to leave when he hands us both a bag of fruit drops. Says we won the prizes."

"Prizes?"

"Miss Sweet Delight and Miss Perfect Confection. I was Confection!"

Margaret smiled. Teens these days. "What happened after that?"

"We left the sweet shop and split up. I was gonna do some shopping. I needed boots. Clarissa was going home to see if the guy had left her any messages."

"Messages?"

"On her e-mail. The guy called himself Godsend."

Chapter 56

"Our guy is playing with fire. The DA's daughter?" said Margaret incredulously into the car phone as she headed north on Flatbush Avenue. "The Spenser girl says Clarissa was supposed to meet a guy at the mall. He seemed to be a no-show. But how's this for a scenario? After the Spenser girl and Clarissa split up, Clarissa does meet with Godsend. He attacks her and tries to drag her into his vehicle."

Driscoll figured out the next step. "But she gets away and, in her panic, runs headlong into the path of the oncoming station wagon. It's been known to happen before. Look at that hate crime in Howard Beach where a gang of whites, brandishing baseball bats, chased down a black youth. The kid ran directly into traffic on the Belt Parkway and was hit and killed by a speeding automobile. That's a very viable theory, Margaret. Where are you headed now?"

"Over to St. Vincent's to speak with a Doctor Stephen Astin, Clarissa's lead physician. Any word from Moira?"

"None yet. Listen, keep me in the loop if anything else looks even remotely related to our bone thief."

"You got it."

Margaret parked the Plymouth on West Eleventh Street and sauntered toward the stately hospital's visitor's entrance. She flashed her shield at the uniformed security officer, who directed her to a bank of elevators that would carry her to the third floor. Inside the elevator, Margaret checked her watch. She'd be right on time for her meeting with Doctor Astin. At the third floor, the elevator doors opened. Margaret stepped off and headed down the corridor in search of room 335, the doctor's office. Finding it, she stepped inside. A nattily dressed gentleman who spoke in a soft, effeminate voice was conversing with a strikingly handsome man clad in a dark blue suit that would have rivaled any one of Lieutenant Driscoll's. Hickey Freeman or Hart Schaffner & Marx came to mind. Margaret read the handsome man's nameplate: COLM F. PIERCE, M.D., CHIEF OF RADIOLOGY. The softspoken gent told Doctor Pierce he would relay his message to Doctor Astin word for word, then turned his attention to Margaret.

"You must be Sergeant Aligante," he said.

"Yes. I have an appointment with Doctor Astin."

"I know. I'm Bartholomew Wiggins, Doctor Astin's assistant. He told me to expect you. And you're right on time," he noted, checking his watch. "The good doctor offers his apologies, though. He was called into surgery not ten minutes ago."

"Oh, I see."

"You may wait for him here if you'd like, or, if you wish, you can visit Chez Francois. That's our cafeteria."

"I could use a bite to eat."

"It's well worth the trip," said Doctor Pierce. "The place is on a par with Four Seasons," he added, dead-pan. "Their tuna melt has just become the eighth cardinal sin. Would you like company?" he added, mindful of his promise to his badgering parents concerning the police; instead of them being all over him, he'd find a way to be all over them. He'd begin by turning on the charm.

Margaret hesitated, casting a curious stare at Pierce, who returned the stare with a smile.

"Why not?" she said daringly. "Lead the way."

"I recommend the meat loaf du jour," the counter-man said to Margaret.

"Howard, this lady deserves your tuna melt," said Pierce. "It's actually my recipe. I like to give Howard the credit," he whispered to Margaret as he selected an apple from a display of fresh fruit.

"Let me guess. You moonlight as the hospital's nutritionist," said Margaret.

"No. The position was filled. I had to settle for radiology."

"Maybe you should put your name on the list. You never know when there might be an opening."

The suggestion brought a smile to Pierce's lips. But he soon got back to business. "So you're the police officer making inquiry into the death of the Parsons girl?"

"In fact, I am," she said, helping herself to a cup of coffee. "How did you know that?"

"Hospitals are like small towns, where news travels at lightning speed. Put it on my account, Howard," he said, gesturing to the attendant.

"Does the radiology department buy lunch for all the visitors?"

"My horoscope suggested I make a new friend."

"Let me guess, Sagittarius?" Margaret ventured.

"Perish the thought! I'm the model Aquarian."

Pierce escorted Margaret to a corner table, where a window overlooked the city's skyline.

"I've never met a radiologist before. Tell me, are you all such food connoisseurs?" asked Margaret.

"No. Just me," he said.

Margaret bit into her sandwich, amused. It was an generous fusion of tuna, mayonnaise, and Jarlsberg cheese.

"Well?" Pierce asked.

"For a hospital cafeteria, not bad. I'll give it a six."

"We haven't discussed dessert. At La Patisserie. Over on Twenty-third?"

"Tell me, do you hit on all the visitors?"

"Can't fault a guy for following his horoscope. Libra? Right? Let's see if the stars will make an exception for you today." He walked over to a newspaper rack, returned with a *New York Post*, and turned to the horoscope page. He read aloud, "Throw caution to the wind. You deserve a break. There's always time to get back to your responsible life. Indulge yourself and enjoy invitations that might arise."

"Does it really say that?"

"You disbeliever." He handed her the paper.

There it was, in black and white, but how did he guess my sign? she wondered.

"But I am sympathetic, for as a true Catholic, and I

assume you are, what with a saint's name and all, this must be heresy," he said.

"I'll burn in hell for sure, and all my bones will be scattered."

"Oh, what a loss."

Chapter 57

Godsend may be safe. But, was *he?* Just how tenacious was this computer-savvy intruder? There was much to do to cover his tracks.

Catherine,

You have located me in the infernal web. Hail to you, the champion! You have ferreted me out of my dingy warren. I am now out in the light. And for you and you alone, will make myself visible. You among mortals will be privy to the face that has done the dastardly deeds. Before the Centurions in Blue handcuff my spirit and parade me in chains along my Via Dolorosa to some downtown precinct and then to some court of law, where I will be crucified for all my victims' parents to see, I will manifest myself to you, and you alone, my dear one. I will appear at exactly 10:00 A.M. tomorrow at Toys R Us near the Kings Plaza Shopping Mall in Brooklyn. I will be in aisle three, Magicians' Supplies. I'll be holding a wand in my hand. I will appear to you, the Victor, only for an instant, but long enough. I trust you are a lady of character, ruled by an exacting code of chivalry. I expect you to be honorable in your dedication and not alert the civil authorities as to our secret rendezvous. If you fulfill this first obligation, in due time I will surrender myself to you, and the city will lionize you for your great deed. You will make history as the insightful beauty who tamed the savage beast.

Godsend

The phone rang on Driscoll's desk and the Lieutenant picked it up. It was Moira.

"Where on earth have you been? I've been scouring the city for you."

"Been doing my job. You're gonna love the progress I've made on the case. Check your computer, Lieutenant. You've got mail."

Driscoll positioned himself in front of his monitor and hit the e-mail icon. "Catherine's" latest communication from Godsend filled the screen. A surge of adrenaline flooded through Driscoll's body as he read the killer's latest message.

"Where are you?"

"Home. Don't you wanna hear my plan on how I'm gonna capture the bad guy?"

"Moira, if you think for one minute—"

"What? You think I should just ignore his offer?"

"On the contrary, I think his instructions are to be followed exactly. But it won't be you following them."

Chapter 58

Driscoll's voice filled the room. "Listen up, everybody. This may be our one good shot at this guy, and I don't want any screwups." He moved toward the easel that had been placed in the middle of the Command Center.

"This is a plan of the Toys R Us parking lot. There are two ways in and out. I want each entrance covered by two cars. I'll be in the TARU van with Danny O'Brien. Sergeant Aligante, and Detectives Butler and Vittaggio will be inside the store. Danny's hooked up a pole camera so that he and I can see everyone who goes in or out. I'll be in radio contact with the three officers inside the store and will give them a heads-up when anybody goes in we think looks good. I borrowed encrypted radios from Technical Services so that if this guy's got a scanner, he can't pick us up. We take him outside the store. Is that clear? I want everybody in this room to understand that. The last thing we need is to have some civilian or Toys R Us employee get hurt. Also, I decided against letting the Toys R Us people know what we're doing. They might inadvertently give it away and spook the guy. We take him as he goes through the exit doors. Coming out. You got that, coming out! Sergeant Aligante, Liz, and Luigi will approach from the rear, and Danny will be up front with me. Cars two and three will pull up in front of the store, and cars four and five will block the exits from the parking lot. Once he's taken down, I'll ride back to the house with him along with Sergeant Aligante and Liz. Everybody else will meet back here. OK? Any questions? Good. We've all done this a hundred times before. Everybody knows what's expected of them. Cedric will hold down the office. See Sergeant Aligante for your assignments. Liz, Luigi, over here."

Both detectives walked over to Driscoll.

"When you guys get inside, grab a baby stroller and throw a couple of packs of Pampers in it. It'll look more natural if you have something to push around. Besides, you never know, Luigi, you may get lucky some day."

Liz laughed, and Vittaggio looked embarrassed.

"Seriously, I put you two inside because I trust you the most. Keep your eyes open and use your heads."

"Will do," said Butler. Vittaggio was still trying to recover.

Driscoll wished them luck.

"Margaret," he yelled. "When you're finished . . ." He pointed to the inside of his office.

Margaret finished giving out the assignments and walked in to meet with Driscoll.

"Yes?"

"What do you think? Will he show?"

"My woman's intuition says yes. It's obvious the guy

likes to play games, and Moira's set the game ball in motion."

"Think we'll be able to spot him?"

"I think he'll give himself away. He'll be a lone male, waiting in aisle three for Moira."

"That's why I want you in there."

"I know. I'll know him when I see him. I'll *feel* him."

"All right, but remember, stick to the plan. We take him as he comes out."

"Yes, Lieutenant," she said mockingly.

"I want you to be careful. This guy's no joker."

"I know. I've seen his work." Her tone turned serious.

"OK, then. Let's rock."

Driscoll stood up from behind his desk, and he and Margaret walked out of the Command Center together.

"Hold on a sec." Driscoll ducked back inside the squad room. "Cedric?"

"Over here, Lieutenant."

"Call the Division dispatcher and have them keep all radio cars away from the shopping center. I don't want some nosy cops snooping around and scaring him off."

"You got it. Anything else?"

"Yeah. Here's a radio. I want you to monitor what's going on out there. If anything goes wrong, you can switch to Division and get us help right away."

"Good thinking, Lieutenant. I am, as always, ever-vigilant."

"Thanks, Cedric. Wish us luck."

"Lieutenant, when you're as good as you are, you don't need luck."

"Never hurts, though," said Driscoll and in a flash, he was gone.

Chapter 59

Driscoll and Danny circled the Toys R Us parking lot just to make certain everything was as Driscoll had planned. Finding everyone in position, Driscoll had Danny guide the TARU van into an empty parking space some sixty feet from the store's main entrance. Driscoll picked up the encrypted receiver. "Radio check," he barked.

One by one the units responded. Now the waiting game began.

"Danny, is the pole camera working?"

"Perfectly, Lieutenant. We've got a clear view of the store's only entrance."

"OK, then. Let's settle in. It may be a long wait."

Moments later, another van slid slowly into a parking space in the Voyager Boatyard and Marina. It sat across Flatbush Avenue, some 300 yards from the Toys R Us parking lot. Using a pair of Tasco high-powered binoculars, its driver took note of the Chevy sedan that was sitting close to the lot's west exit. Under the car sat a pool of water, condensation from a running air conditioner. On the ground, just under the driver's door, was a pile of cigarette butts. Inside the car two middle-aged men dressed in suits occupied the front seats. On the Chevy's dashboard were two Styrofoam coffee cups and what looked to be a folded newspaper. A grin formed on the driver's face. "Let the wait be on," he muttered.

For the next four hours the entourage of police personnel fought boredom. It was one-thirty in the afternoon when Driscoll depressed the speed-dial button on his handheld radio.

"Margaret. Anything? Anything at all?"

"Nothing. I guess my woman's intuition was out to lunch."

"Liz, what about you?"

"Besides aching feet and a deep hatred for pushing a baby stroller, nothing. I counted four customers in the last hour, none fitting the profile of our guy. Four customers! How does this place stay in business?"

"OK, then. That's it. The guy's a no-show. Margaret, Liz, Luigi, you can come out now. You guys in cars one, two, and three get something to eat. Meet me back at the Command Center in an hour. Car four, you're to hang on a minute until I make sure everyone has a ride back."

"Ten-four," the radio crackled.

"Danny, I've got to stretch my legs." Driscoll slid open the van's passenger door, stepped outside, and watched as his three detectives exited the store. He walked over to the weary cops. "We gave it our best shot," he said. "I guess luck wasn't with us today. Luigi, Liz, you guys got a ride back?"

"We came with Sergeant Aligante," said Detective Vittaggio.

"Here. Take my keys." Margaret said. "I'll ride back in the van with Danny and the Lieutenant." She handed Luigi her keys.

Driscoll went to say something further when he caught a glimpse of a familiar figure. "Goddamn it, Moira. What the hell are you doing here? I thought I made it clear I didn't want you within a hundred miles of this place. How did you get here?"

"I took the bus."

"You took the bus." Driscoll was ready to explode. He turned his attention to his two detectives, Butler and Vittaggio, "You guys can go. Grab a bite to eat and meet me back at the house." The two cops did an about-face and walked away. "Now, young lady—"

The crackling of the radio interrupted his tirade. It was car number four.

"Lieutenant, are we good to go?"

"Bring the car over here," he said.

As the car pulled up in front of Driscoll, he grabbed Moira by both shoulders, opened the sedan's rear door, and pushed her inside.

"Take this young lady home," he ordered.

"Will do," said the detective seated behind the wheel.

Driscoll and Margaret watched as the unmarked police sedan pulled away.

"I'm gonna kill her. What if he had shown up and somehow grabbed her?"

"Let's be thankful he didn't."

Driscoll slowly shook his head.

"I'm hungry," said Margaret. "And my feet are killing me. Let's go sit down somewhere and eat."

The pair climbed in behind Danny. As they made their left turn out of the parking lot, neither of them noticed the slow-moving van that had pulled up behind car number four.

Chapter 60

It had been hours since the failed attempted capture at Toys R Us. A frightening thought occurred to Driscoll. What if the killer could track down Moira through her computer? He reached for his desk phone and punched in Thomlinson's extension.

"Cedric, contact the Tiernans and arrange to pick up Moira and bring her in. I have some technical questions for the little miss."

"Consider it done."

Meanwhile, on the other part of town, Pierce sat patiently behind the wheel of his van. He stretched his back and narrowed his eyes to tiny slits. Waiting was not a favorite pastime. His mind hit upon the details of the day's activity. The siege at the toy store. The interminable wait. The arrival of the girl, and his following the unmarked police car to her home, outside of which he now sat. It was a quiet, tree-lined street, and his van was not out of place parked where it was, behind a Volkswagen beetle.

Cedric pulled a set of keys from the pegboard, signed out using the log, and walked down the back steps of the station. He began to look for unmarked department auto number 238. The car could be parked anywhere. There were two things detectives never did. One was to put gas in the car, and the second was to leave a note with the keys indicating where the car was parked.

Thomlinson walked north on Yellowstone Boulevard, searching for the car. As he walked he noticed a line outside a local bodega. Curiosity got the better of him, and he made his way over to the store to see what was going on.

"What's up?" he asked the last man on line.

"Two hundred fifty-two million dollars is what's up, my brother."

Of course! The Mega Millions lottery, he thought. One of the biggest payoffs in history, and he'd almost walked right by it. He took his place in line, figuring Driscoll wouldn't mind. Hell, if he won, he might give Driscoll a million or two. It was the Lieutenant who had stood by him when all the others had turned their backs on him.

As the line slowly shuffled toward the store's counter, Thomlinson began to dream about what he would do with all that money. It would mean a new life for him. He could finally go home. For good. Home, where it was warm. Home, where he could escape New York City and its cold, relentless winters. He had always longed for the sun and the glistening sand of his native Trinidadian beaches.

It would also take him away from all the stares, the whispers, and the looks. Away from the accusing eyes and the contempt that was directed toward him. Hell, the city could keep its pension. As a big winner he would walk into the Commissioner's office, throw his shield on the desk, and, without a word, turn and walk out the door. It was every cop's fantasy. So, why not his?

The line moved forward slowly, and it was twenty minutes before he got to play his numbers. He shoved the tickets into his shirt pocket and resumed his search for the car.

The car was parked in a bus stop 200 feet from the bodega. He got in, started her up, and turned on the radio. Bob Marley's "I Shot the Sheriff" blared from twin speakers. *That's it. It must be a sign,* he thought to himself. *Yes, Mr. Lottery Director, I'll take the full cash payout, no installments for me, thank you.*

As he pulled away from the curb, three uniformed cops stopped to stare at the crazy detective who was singing at the top of his lungs.

Chapter 61

Moira slammed the door behind her, bound down the steps, and ran past the hedges onto the sidewalk. She looked up and down the street, but didn't see the car she was expecting. She paced back and forth. Her thoughts were of Driscoll. He had yelled at her in front of his men and had embarrassed her. And now he needed her help again. *This time, it's gonna cost him big time,* she thought.

Pierce couldn't believe his luck. There she was, right out in the open. He could tell by her actions that she was waiting for a ride. But from whom? Caution flags unfurled in Pierce's brain. After a couple of minutes of hesitation, he seized the moment and acted.

He waited until she turned her back on him and then eased the van out of its parking spot and slowly made his way down the street. As he pulled up next to Moira, he rolled down the window and smiled. He would follow her lead.

"Driscoll send you?" she asked, visibly puzzled.

"That he did. Hop in."

"I was expecting Cedric."

"He got called away, so they sent me instead."

He was a nice-looking man in a tailored suit. Moira decided he looked the part and got in.

"I'm Detective Sweeney," Pierce said, as he stuck out his hand.

"Moira," said the girl as she shook it.

Pierce eased the van away from the curb and stopped at the corner. He turned to face his prize. "Moira, I dropped my cell phone, and I think it slid behind your seat. Could you reach around and grab it for me?"

"Sure," said Moira, bending her body away from Pierce.

With a rag soaked in Halothane, Pierce smothered the girl's face. Moira quickly succumbed to the powerful elixir, and a gleeful Colm Pierce now had a new toy to play with.

Chapter 62

By the time Thomlinson got to Moira's house, the girl was nowhere to be found. He rang Moira's bell. Her mother told him the last time she saw her daughter was when she was pacing the sidewalk waiting for her ride. That was twenty minutes ago.

Thomlinson used the car's police radio to contact Driscoll. "Lieutenant, I'm outside Moira's house, but the girl's not here. Her mother says she was waiting outside the house for me. She call you?"

"No. I haven't heard a word from her." A feeling of dread came over Driscoll. "Cedric, start knocking on doors and see if anyone saw her in the last half hour or so. Get back to me, pronto."

"OK. Anything else?"

"Yeah. What the hell took you so long? It's a half hour ride, and it took you close to an hour."

"I hit construction on the Belt. It was backed up solid," Thomlinson lied.

"OK. Start knocking on doors and get back to me."

Within ten minutes Thomlinson was back on the phone to Driscoll. "Lieutenant?"

"What have you got?"

"A lady down the street saw Moira get into a van and leave about a half hour ago. She says she wasn't really paying attention, but she's sure it was a van. Nothing else. Just a van. She doesn't even remember what color it was."

Driscoll felt sick in the pit of his stomach. *He has her.* His policeman's instinct told him so.

"Detective Thomlinson, get your ass back here now!" Driscoll hung up without another word.

As he drove back toward the precinct, Cedric pondered his fate. He was far too good a detective not to know the girl was in danger. For the second time in his life, his mistake had put another human being in harm's way. He retrieved the Lotto tickets from his shirt pocket, ripped them in half, and tossed them out the window. There would be no warm winter back home, no early resignation, and no escape from his fellow officers' looks of disdain.

He saw the sign for KELLY'S BAR up ahead. Veering the car toward the curb, he pulled into a spot out front. Stepping out of the car, he opened the wide oak door and slipped inside. Wordlessly, Detective Second Grade Cedric Thomlinson stepped out of the light and into the shadows that were his past.

Chapter 63

Twice that night, Driscoll's sleep was shattered by the whine of distant sirens. Each time he had dashed to the window, only to stare at a deserted shoreline. Sleep starved, he pondered what Margaret had reported to him concerning the DA's daughter. She had interviewed Doctors Astin, Galina, and Pierce, along with the ICU nurse, Susan Dupree. What Driscoll found curious was that Nurse Dupree had indicated that Doctor Pierce, a radiologist, had tried repeatedly to revive Clarissa using defibrillator paddles. Now what was a radiologist doing in a pediatric ICU with defibrillator paddles? Margaret further reported that all three doctors were at the girl's side when she suffered a massive heart attack and died, despite the extreme measures exercised to bring her back. Had the cardiac arrest been a result of the injuries she had sustained? None of the physicians believed so. Her autopsy indicated no link as well. So why the heart failure? And what about the conversation she had had with Godsend over the Internet? Where did that fit in?

Driscoll had dozed off with the TV on, tuned to New York 1, an all-news channel. His eyes became fixed to the screen as Aaron Miesner announced breaking news: "This morning, at 4:32 A.M., security officers at Pinelawn Cemetery reported that a mausoleum had been desecrated, and a body interred in its white marble chamber had been mutilated. The butchered remains have been identified as those of Clarissa Parsons, the daughter of Manhattan's District Attorney, Jack Parsons—"

The telephone rang. Driscoll answered it. The DA's voice roared in his ear.

"Jesus Christ, John. If you can't defend the dead, what am I paying you for?"

A beep interrupted the verbal assault.

"Jack, that's call-waiting. It's gotta be someone from the squad. I gotta put you on hold."

"Don't you—"

Driscoll cut off Parsons and depressed the "talk" button. It was Thomlinson.

"The motherfucker mutilated the girl's body, and now Parsons is on the warpath. He went up one side of me and down the other. Called me an incompetent drunk! Said I was the reason for the fuckup. And now he's after you. I tried to head him off, but he's bearing teeth."

"I know. I got him frothing at the bit on the other line."

"There's more. The son of a bitch has got Moira! We just got word by e-mail."

"Read it to me!"

Centurions in Blue,

Hail to you all with the thankless task of apprehending us lower demons. Your sweet lamb is now in the wolf's den. I relish the thought of the nearing orgy. Such fresh flesh, inviting canine claws. Such unblemished skin soon to be lacerated by bestial talons. Such delicate bones holding such moist meat. Moira is her name.

Adieu

Chapter 64

When Moira came to, her palms and ankles were nailed to a pine chair. The slightest stir delivered infinite suffering. Perfect stillness temporarily kept the agony at bay. The nails had lacerated cartilage and tendons, perforated muscle tissue, and pulverized her bones. She had ceased screaming long ago. Now, no sounds could escape her mouth, sealed as it was with plumbing tape. No tears could secrete from her eyelids—they were clamped together with globs of Krazy Glue.

"I knew you'd come," the voice lumbered. "The certainty never wavered. Curiosity is such a stimulating elixir, don't you think? I also knew you'd be naive. It's quite amazing how both traits coexist so comfortably within one's mind."

He had an educated voice. The realization struck Moira as odd.

Someone moved what she thought to be a metal

chair. She imagined her torturer shifting his weight as he sat there, watching her.

"I knew you had to be young. And my guess was right. Only a youthful mind would waste its precious resources trying to catch a demon like me. That's because the young believe in Satan and all his minions and the power of the magician's wand. Therein lies my realm, dear one. My element. It's funny. But, somehow I knew sooner or later a heroine dressed in Buster Browns and a double A bra, barely past the onset of menstruation, would come traipsing into my lair. Yes, curiosity is a dreadful yet divine commodity, don't you think? I had a hunch it was you when I saw you approach that group of detectives. I was at a safe distance, watching your every move through my field glasses. And such a legion of policemen they had brought with them. My, oh my! Of course, I wasn't playing by the rules. Not being there in aisle three wasn't quite fair, but sometimes we demons lie. But then, so did you. Your Donny was a fraud. Remember?"

She heard the creaking sound. He had moved again.

"At first, I thought your makeup a bit excessive for your seraphic face. I wondered about that. And that brown suede miniskirt? 'Heavens,' I cried. 'That's how she's dressed for our date?' In case you were wondering, my plan was a simple one. I simply followed as the policemen took you home. They left. You eventually came out. And now you're here."

The chair creaked again. She heard the sound of his footsteps.

Chapter 65

The decoy police sedan worked very well, parked beside the row of hedges lining the shoulder of the Palisades Interstate Parkway. Inspector Tom Mueller at Highway Patrol 17 may have been short staffed, but he believed it was senseless to let an extra police vehicle sit dormant in the precinct's garage. He ordered the marked cruiser to be situated at a strategic location along the Parkway. It was unmanned, but a speeding motorist wouldn't be able to tell; the motorist would slow down at the first sighting of the highly visible dark blue vehicle with its colorful array of emergency lights.

It was nearing 10:00 P.M., time to retrieve the decoy, when Highway Patrol Officer Bill Simmon's patrol car #643 pulled in behind the parked cruiser. Officer John Masterson, his partner, stepped out onto the shoulder of the road. Three steps from the decoy's door, he unfastened the safety on his 9-mm automatic. He had realized the vehicle was occupied.

A girl's body leaned against the passenger door. The smell of regurgitation and human excrement singed Officer Masterson's sinuses. His flashlight illuminated blotches of dried blood staining the girl's blouse and miniskirt.

"You'd better forget the card game, partner," he grumbled. "We're gonna have one helluva night."

Chapter 66

Colm had never boned dead virginal flesh before. The audacity of the feat intoxicated him. To celebrate Clarissa's desecration, he visited his wine cellar and lingered before the bins. He finally selected a 1975 Chateau Latour.

Whispers of adulation, murmurs of delight oozed through the concrete flooring. Soon he would join the cheering party gathered beneath him with his prize. He would rattle Clarissa in the face of his parents. How dare they think she would have gotten away? But for now, he would savor his trophy in seclusion.

When he had had his fill of the wine, he descended to the lower level to meet with his tenants. At first, they could not contain their exaltation. But at the sight of the new skeleton, the assembly became silent, resenting that their cramped quarters would be shared by yet another.

Clutching the child's bones, Colm eyed the shelves

for a suitable place to deposit them. He would need time to build her showcase. The residents groaned in unison. He understood their grievance. It was crowded enough already without another relic. He would renovate the atelier, he thought. It would add another one thousand square feet to their catacomb. It meant he would have to cease his killings, for the time being, but he could resume his sport once the expansion was underway.

Maybe he would apply to the New York State Council for the Arts for a grant to back the project. After all, these were former residents of New York City, now inhabiting Nassau County. It would be a form of income-maintenance subsidy to guarantee proper lodging for these former taxpaying members of the community. He filed the thought for consideration at a later date.

The ground suddenly shimmied, followed by stillness. A second tremor was more pronounced. It displaced a clavicle, which tumbled from its shelf and shattered on the terra-cotta-tiled floor.

Earthquake! he thought. He wedged himself into the lift.

Reaching the ground floor, he bolted out of the house, expecting an apocalyptic landscape of shattered houses and burning cars. But the street was intact. A diesel breeze fumigated the thoroughfare; smoke billowed from a bulldozer with a spider arm, its jackhammer pulverizing the asphalt. Huge steel pipes lay nearby, awaiting installation.

Colm envisioned the bulldozer causing the walls of his precious trophy room to cave in, entombing his possessions in mountains of rubble. Then a worse fear crept into his consciousness. What if the vibrations didn't bury his guests? What if it unearthed them?

Chapter 67

A grief-stricken Eileen Tiernan straddled the chair, hugging her son, Timothy, close to her bosom. Ryan was clamped to her leg. Her husband sat at her side. They all glanced up as Driscoll and Margaret stepped into the pediatric ward's corridor.

"They won't let us see our daughter," said Seamus Tiernan.

Driscoll walked over to the policeman stationed at the door to room 732. "What gives, officer?"

"I got my orders from Captain Hollis, Lieutenant. No one's to be let inside. And he means no one."

"They'll be with me."

"I'd like to accommodate you—"

"Then let us in."

"But I've got my orders."

"You just got new ones."

The officer stared hopelessly at Driscoll. "I'll have to check. Give me a minute."

Driscoll shrugged, and the officer walked down the corridor to a wall phone.

"Margaret, why don't you accompany these folks to the cafeteria?" Driscoll suggested. "It may take a few minutes to reconcile the situation."

"We're not going anywhere until we see our daughter," said Mr. Tiernan.

"How about I take the kids for a soda?" said Margaret.

"I wanna see Moira," said Timothy, red faced.

"They'll wait right here with us," said Mrs. Tiernan.

The policeman returned and spoke to Driscoll. "I'm sorry sir, the Captain's orders don't apply to you." He opened the door to let the Lieutenant in.

"They're coming with me," Driscoll announced as he ushered the family inside. Then the Lieutenant's eyes widened. Moira's body was completely encased in plaster, the shell strategically punctured by catheters and tubes to allow for respiration and feeding. There were two slits for the eyes and two apertures for the nostrils.

All heads turned as Doctor Stephen Astin came into the room to check on his young patient. "Her bones were fragmented, some of them pulverized," he reported.

Mrs. Tiernan's face drained of all color. She stood frozen, staring at the plaster cocoon that contained Moira.

"How could someone do such a thing to our little girl?" Mr. Tiernan asked. "He's crushed our Moira. Do you know what it feels like to see your only daughter shattered, Lieutenant?"

"More than you know."

The Lieutenant's eyes were brimming with tears. Not since Nicole's death had he felt so heartbroken. And why not? Hadn't Moira become his daughter in Nicole's absence? He cast a look at the girl, this madman's latest victim. And as his eyes took in the living and breathing plaster mummy that Moira had become, his rage was set aflame. The son of a bitch had made it personal. And by doing so, he had signed his own death certificate.

As Driscoll stepped away from Moira's bedside, his eyes met those of the Tiernan family. It pained him to witness the emotional damage that had been inflicted upon them.

Their daughter had been savagely brutalized, and Driscoll knew why. This heartless assault was a message. The killer could have murdered the girl and boned her like all the others. But he didn't. He chose to let Moira live, a cripple for life. She would be an ever-present reminder to Driscoll of his meddling. He was telling the Lieutenant to back off. Like hell he would! If it took assigning legions of policemen, Driscoll would track down this bastard and dole out vengeance.

As Driscoll scanned the room, a feeling of claustrophobia overtook him. He fought the urge to pound the walls, send a quake throughout the building, wake up the dying, call attention to the living. For he knew Moira lay somewhere between the two. Why, he asked himself, had the women closest to his soul met with tragedy at such an early age? His mind began to race. He found himself inside the Plymouth Voyager that carried Colette and his daughter on that ill-fated day in May. He imagined throwing his body over Nicole's as the gasoline tanker collided with the family van. Was that some sort of silent death wish? Was that what was going on inside his guilt-ridden head? Here, now, was Moira, another daughter in his charge. He should have stopped her from the start. What was he thinking? How could he have allowed her to step into the path of a murderer? It was because of him that Moira was so horribly victimized. He was certain of that. That reality would follow him to his grave.

He approached Moira and gently placed his hand on her plaster-encased shoulder. "I'm sorry," he said. "I hope you'll forgive me. I know I'll never forgive myself."

Chapter 68

"What'd he do?" the rookie patrolman asked.

Richie Winslow, the veteran detective, shot a disdainful glance at the prisoner in the holding cell.

"This here's a vandal," said Winslow.

"He looks a little old to be a graffiti artist. What'd he vandalize?"

"Our friend here got a yen for earth-moving equipment. He poured a pint of maple syrup into the diesel fuel tank of a bulldozer. Speaking directly to the prisoner, he asked, "Now whad'ya go and do that for?"

Colm winced. He felt caged, ensnared inside the Old Brookville Police Department's holding cell. "How long will I be held here?"

"As long as it takes!"

The phone purred on Winslow's desk. He spoke briefly, then turned to his prisoner.

"Your medical degree just bought you a desk appearance ticket."

"Does that mean you're letting me go?"

"For now. Tomorrow, you've got an 8:00 A.M. appointment with a man in a black gown. And you'd better have lost your taste for pancakes."

Chapter 69

Driscoll kept being hammered by the DA, the Mayor, and the Police Commissioner. He felt as though his head were a drum and everyone from the Mayor on down were pounding away with their drumsticks. He couldn't stop his mind from racing. Moira's circumstances kept coming to the forefront of his thoughts. Burdened with guilt, he summoned Margaret and Thomlinson to his office for a brainstorming session. He needed to get his mind back on the case and to restore his sanity.

"Cedric, are you all right? You look a little pale."

Driscoll knew. Thomlinson was sure of it. He'd wait until the case was resolved to deal with it. "A little touch of the flu," he said.

Driscoll shot him a look. A look that said "we should talk." The moment passed in silence. It was Driscoll who broke it. "Have the tech wizards figured out the password to Moira's hard drive yet?"

"Fraid not," said Margaret.

"They're being overpaid."

"What is it with the bones?" she asked.

"That's the sixty-four-thousand-dollar question."

"And our guy takes the whole lot. What the hell does he do with them?"

"Maybe he's rebuilding his ladies from the inside out," said Thomlinson. "Sorta like the serial killer in *Silence of the Lambs*. Remember? The guy was sewing together pieces of flesh he had carved from the bodies of his victims."

Margaret poured herself a cup of coffee. "Flesh on top of bone. Now there's a thought. Maybe our guy reads the Old Testament."

"I'm listening," said Driscoll.

" 'And I will lay sinews upon you and will bring up flesh upon you and cover you with skin.' Ezekiel. Chapter 37, verse 6," she said.

Driscoll was astounded that Margaret was so familiar with liturgical verse. He looked at her and smiled. "Lord knows he wouldn't be the first Bible-savvy predator."

"In Kings, they actually talk about bones being stolen," said Thomlinson.

Driscoll was impressed. "You guys might really be on to something."

"So, we'll add that to the profile. Our guy may be driven by particular scenes from the Bible," said Thomlinson.

"We could use a bone specialist," said Driscoll. "Margaret, aren't you dating a bone man?"

"One date. Lunch in a hospital cafeteria. I'd hardly call that dating."

"But you did say he had suggested dessert somewhere

else. He's opened the door for you. Why don't you give the good doctor a call and ask him out to dinner. That wouldn't be out of the ordinary. This is the twenty-first century, remember?"

"But, he's no osteopath. His specialty is X-rays."

"Close enough."

"Does that give me a green light to discuss the case?" she asked.

"Not in any great detail. Just pick his brain a little. Keep in mind that this man, a radiologist, was in St. Vincent's pediatric ICU using defibrillator paddles on the DA's daughter. That's got odd written all over it. I say we keep a watchful eye on the guy."

"Will do," said Margaret as she swept passed Driscoll and made her exit. Thomlinson lingered behind.

"You think it's coincidence that brought Doctor Pierce and Margaret together, Cedric?" Driscoll asked.

"As opposed to—?"

"Suppose the guy's got his own reasons for staying close to a police investigation."

Chapter 70

A dockhand cast the line, and the ferry pulled away from its berth, foaming the water with its propellers. The sun had begun its incendiary descent against the Manhattan skyline, igniting it in flamboyant amber. The fifteen-minute crossing would land Doctor Pierce and Margaret at the foot of Battery Park just steps away from the restaurant she had chosen. Pierce had suggested the island-hopping cruise to set the mood.

A soulful instrumental version of "The Nearness of You" serenaded the passengers. A bearded black man, his upturned hat at his feet, was making magic with his reed.

"There's nothing like a saxophone at twilight to take the edge off the day," said Pierce.

Margaret studied Pierce's face. She thought he resembled a dark-haired Donald McDonough, a friend she had made at the Police Academy during the onset of her career. The notion brought back a blizzard of memories: cramming for tests, overcrowded study halls, repetitive on-site procedural drills, and fun weekend partying. Back then, Amstel Light was her drink of choice. As she continued her study of Pierce's features, she asked herself the question Driscoll had pondered. What would a radiologist be doing in the pediatric ICU at the bedside of a comatose patient? And why was he using defibrillator paddles?

"Margaret? Are you all right? You look as though you're in a trance."

She answered him with a smile. "I'm fine," she said. "You resemble a friend I haven't seen in years."

"Each face has a dozen lookalikes that span the globe. How would you handle that particular happenstance in a police lineup?"

"Number 4, step forward . . . no, number 3 . . . make that number 7 . . . or is it number 10?"

The pair shared a laugh as a humid breeze entangled Margaret's hair, spilling strands of it into her eyes. She sipped champagne from a paper cup.

"We mustn't let the harbormaster know we smuggled our own Veuve Clicquot on board," Pierce laughed. "The Captain will have us walk the plank."

From Amstel Light to Veuve Clicquot. If only McDonough could see me now.

"Champagne's the perfect accompaniment for night sailing. Don't ya think?" said Pierce.

"I'll say." She took another sip.

"Those monks at the Benedictine Abbey of Hautvillers deserve a debt of gratitude for discovering this wondrous concoction."

"I'll be sure to drop them a line."

"You know, they buried their deceased brethren alongside casks of wine."

"To continue the party?"

"For all eternity. And did you know that the Pharaohs were buried with their beer?"

"I had no idea. Hey, Colm, you're a walking encyclopedia when it comes to booze!"

"I should be. I own a winery."

"Really? Where?"

"On the North Fork of Long Island. Maybe someday we'll go there."

Margaret was enjoying Pierce's company. She found him to be intelligent, good looking, charming, and delightfully mysterious. To top it off, he had a pair of soulful blue eyes that a woman could get lost in. But the question kept gnawing at her. *Why the defibrillator paddles?* She was determined to seek an answer at dinner.

"Ever been to the catacombs in Rome?" Pierce asked.

"Back in high school. I don't think I could have endured them, though, without some help from a bottle of Chianti Ruffino," Margaret mused. "When in Rome—"

"Been there, done that. With pictures!"

"Pictures?"

"Used an infrared camera," he boasted. "Don't forget, I have an anatomist's interest in bones."

"Bones, hmm."

"Incredible substances. As hard as granite, lighter than wood, and very much alive. Bones are made to withstand mountains of stress. They don't rust, they are non-corrosive, and they are edible. A true miracle of evolution!"

The Harbor Club boasted a spectacular view of downtown Manhattan. The pair chose a table near a bay window overlooking the Wall Street skyline. The waiter made his approach. "And now for tonight's specials..." Margaret and Pierce sat through the interminable oration. "May I suggest starting with a cocktail?" the waiter finished.

Margaret ordered the house Chardonnay, while Pierce chose the Merlot.

The waiter returned with their selections, took their dinner order, and quickly disappeared.

A gust of laughter erupted at an adjacent table. Margaret pricked her ears to steal fragments of the conversation between the two women. They spoke in a foreign tongue that had a Slavic ring to it.

"They sound like they're enjoying themselves," she whispered to Pierce.

"Scandalous stuff. The one in the blue dress caught her husband with their nanny... in the playpen, of all places."

"That's so sad. Why are they laughing?"

"Three million dollars! That was the divorce settlement!"

"Wow, I'd laugh too," Margaret said, sipping her Chardonnay.

Pierce was bilingual. Margaret wondered what other languages he'd mastered.

The waiter arrived with their hors d'oeuvres.

"*Coquelet poule au poivre,* for madam. *Escargot* for monsieur.*" The waiter delivered his lines like the unemployed actor he was.

"You don't mind if I use my fingers?" asked Margaret.

"All the better," Pierce answered, taking a sip of his wine.

The pair exchanged smiles.

"So, Margaret, I know so little about you. I know

you're a policewoman, but what exactly does that entail?"

"I catch the bad guys," she said, dismantling her Cornish hen.

"Is that so?" he said, staring intensely at her meticulous dissection of the bird.

"And I'm good at it."

"Oh, I have no doubt about that."

"New York City Police Sergeant Margaret Aligante at your service."

"Well protected am I. Sounds like an exciting job. Any interesting cases of late?"

She was mindful of Driscoll's instructions. She shouldn't discuss the case in detail. But she saw no harm in letting the man know she was part of the Task Force.

"Actually, there is one. You must have read about it in the papers."

"I don't read the papers. I get all my news through the Internet. Let me guess . . . the child abuse of the six-year-old in Greenpoint?"

"I investigate homicide."

"Don't tell me you're on the case involving the madman who's killing all those women and stealing their bones?"

"I'm part of the team."

"I'm impressed. What's his fascination with bones?"

"You're the radiologist, you tell me."

"I've read all there is to read about the case through the Internet. But none of the articles tells you very much."

"Wow, you're really following the case."

"Well, like you said, I am a radiologist."

"And what do you think?"

"I think it's too gruesome to talk about over *coquelet poule au poivre.*"

"Nothing gets in the way of my appetite."

The waiter reappeared with their rack of lamb à la Berrichonne, for two. He gracefully sliced a portion of the meat and placed it on Margaret's plate. He then uncorked a bottle of Charmes-Chambertin and filled two glasses.

The pair ate silently, savoring the rich bouquet of spices mingling with the gamey lamb.

"I guess you're really not supposed to talk about the investigation," Pierce said.

Margaret, caught with her mouth full, moaned a languorous "no."

"Even if I can help?"

Margaret stared intently at Pierce. She was here to pick his brain a little, and he had just given her an opening.

"We are quite curious as to what he does with the bones."

"My guess would be he collects them as trophies. Reminders of his conquests."

"He takes their heads, hands, and feet, too."

"He must be trying to hide their identities. He wouldn't want the police to ID them from their fingerprints or dental records . . . But wait a minute. The reports say you've been able to ID them."

"True."

"Then I'm at a loss. Why would he need their head, hands, and feet? Unless he's trying to complete their skeletons. If that's what he's after, he'd surely need the skull, the metatarsus, a full set of phalanges, and the rest of the tiny bones that make up the hands and the feet."

"That makes sense," said Margaret. Is this guy stating the obvious, or am I being played, she asked herself. She was not one to be toyed with. Neither as a woman nor as a detective.

"Perhaps it's not a murderer you're after. He could be a simple thief. A bone thief."

"Try telling that to the victims' families."

"That's one part of your job I don't envy."

"I'm sure in your line of work, there comes a time when you need to give a patient's family bad news."

"On occasion."

Margaret took a sip of her wine and gazed at Pierce. It was time to tie up some loose ends.

"There's one question in the investigation that remains unanswered, Colm, and it involves you."

"Me?"

"Why were you in the pediatric ICU using defibrillator paddles on the Parsons girl?"

A broad grin erupted on Pierce's face. "I was wondering when someone was going to ask me that question."

"Well, here I am. Your dinner date, and I'm asking."

Margaret watched as Pierce dabbed at his lips with his dinner napkin before answering the question. Not much to read in that gesture. The man had a poker face.

"Doctor Astin and I were riding the elevator together," said Pierce. "He was responding to a Code Blue in the pediatric ICU."

"The Parsons girl."

"Right. The two of us were in a fiery discussion about an irrelevant matter. When the doors of the elevator opened, we continued our heated discussion, and before we knew it we were both standing at the bedside of the Parsons girl. And as to why I was using the defibrillator paddles, I was using them in an attempt to save the poor girl's life."

"Would a radiologist do that?" She didn't think it likely.

"This radiologist would."

Silence settled between the pair. After a moment had passed, Pierce took hold of Margaret's hand. "When I became a physician, I took an oath. I swore I would do everything in my power to safeguard life. My actions that day were obligatory. I was there. The girl had suffered a heart attack. Doctor Astin had attempted to revive her using the defibrillator paddles, but had failed. When he gave up hope, I grabbed hold of the paddles and used them myself. Unfortunately, our efforts failed to bring her back to life, and the young girl was pronounced dead. I had to use the paddles, Margaret. I had sworn an oath."

Margaret leaned back in her chair and pushed her plate forward. It could have happened as he said, but a radiologist using defibrillator paddles? That she didn't buy. There was something wrong with that. It aroused suspicion. She became mindful of Driscoll's sixth sense. And that meant she would use caution when dealing with this man.

As the busboy cleared their table, Margaret's eyes remained fixed on Pierce. She had her work cut out for her. It remained to be seen whether she was dining with a charmer, or with the devil himself.

Chapter 71

Margaret found Driscoll inside his office, slumped in his chair. He had been battling influenza. Shattered by the intensity of its symptoms, he had teetered near the brink of exhaustion until antibiotics broke his fever. Though fatigued, he was now able to move about without waves of vertigo.

"You look terrible. Shouldn't you be home in bed?"

"There'll be time enough to sleep when we have our madman in custody. Speaking of our madman, how was your dinner date?"

"He took me to the Harbor Club."

"Top shelf. Was he able to shed any light on our investigation?"

Margaret seemed lost in thought. Her answers to Driscoll were hesitant. "He thinks the reason our killer is collecting bones is to erect their skeletons. That's why he takes the head, hands, and feet."

"Don't you find it a little curious that he has that insight? I'm telling you, Margaret, I'm really beginning to like this guy for the killings."

"Smug."

"What's that?"

"That's the feeling I had about him the other night. The word escaped me at the time. The guy is intelligent, charming, and smug. He has a certain air about him. You know what I mean?" Margaret settled back in her chair. "The son of a bitch might be playing me. Fuck. If he is, I'll kill the bastard myself."

"Since you started seeing him, the killings have stopped. So I want that to continue. But promise me this—you'll be careful and always on your guard."

"Fuck! He might be playing with me. Fuck!"

"Careful, and on your guard."

"Yeah, yeah, yeah. Don't worry. Careful and on my guard. If he could play me, the least I should do is return the favor. I'm good at schmoozing, ya know. And that's what the good doctor will get. My best schmooze."

"Margaret, I want to change gears here for a minute. I want to talk about us."

That caught her attention. A grin creased her face; her eyes widened. "Go ahead, lover boy. Gimme whatcha got." *Hey! I'm getting good at this*, she thought.

"The last time we talked, I told you I needed more time to think about our relationship. Remember?"

"Like it was yesterday."

"I think it's time to make some time for us."

"Whoa. Talk about changing gears." Margaret's grin blossomed into a smile. "You really know how to get a girl's attention." Margaret's heart was in her throat. *Don't screw this up*, she thought. "John, you took my breath away. You're sure about this? Right? I mean, you've thought it all through?"

"I'm ready. That is if you are?"

"Ready, willing, and able. Are you kidding? I've been dreaming of this day for God knows how long."

"I want us to be discreet. These guys we work with can be clowns sometimes. You don't have a problem with us being discreet, do you?"

"Discreet, that street, whatever you want. I'm just so happy I could explode. Can you tell?"

"You do look happy. I gotta tell ya that."

Driscoll reached across his desk and took hold of Margaret's hand. A sheepish smile sprouted on his face. "We can make this work. I know we can."

"I like that word."

"Which one?"

"We."

Chapter 72

Driscoll was pleased that Seamus Tiernan had succeeded in transferring Moira to her own room at home. He saw it as a sign of hope. Attended by a registered nurse, the young girl lay without her cocoon, surrounded by stuffed polar bears, Beanie Babies and a Britney Spears poster with five darts radiating out from the center of the pop star's face. Inert in her own bed, her bruised body was connected to a cluster of instruments that included a pulse oximeter, a suction machine, and a home-care ventilator. Her vital signs were being recorded around the clock as zigzagging lines on amber screens, attesting to the vibrancy of her organs. But the Lieutenant was anxious because her brain still showed as a flat line.

Driscoll, who visited the young girl regularly, stood at Moira's bedside, listening to the thud of an artificial respirator and the purr of a dialysis machine. The sounds were all too familiar. That realization saddened him. He gazed at the machinery. All the monitors were working properly, keeping his star witness alive, though mute. He had the impulse to shake the girl, provoke her with a well-turned phrase, irritate her, deride her to get some reaction, and in so doing, reignite her adolescent fury, which had so attracted him.

He scanned the room. The shelves were overcrowded with books and mementos, decorative boxes, and a huge collection of teddy bears. Nicole had been a collector too. She had collected miniature dollhouses from around the world. She had played with those houses like an anthropologist would, learning how certain architecture fit a particular type of terrain, like how terra-cotta roofing was favored in hot and sultry climates. She was amazed to discover how the Tuaregs in the Sahara lived in clay houses and kept their living space cool with damp mud.

On a trip to Dublin, Driscoll had happened upon a store that flaunted an Irish village in its window: twenty-one houses, one church, one firehouse, one movie theater, and six pubs. He had purchased the entire ensemble and brought it back to Nicole.

"My God!" she said. "What do you have in the box? Is it a life-sized teddy bear?"

"No. Something much better."

His daughter had been breathless after she opened her gift: she realized she owned her own town. She had arranged all the houses on her hook rug, with the church in the center, and then stood up triumphantly and told her father he'd been elected mayor.

Driscoll had bowed from the waist, accepting the distinction. "My first directive as mayor," he had said, "is to impose a curfew of 9:00 P.M. for the entire town. And that includes you, little girl."

The memory saddened him. He closed his eyes and envisioned Nicole's face: her rosy red cheeks in winter, the way her little round chin protruded, the softness of her blue eyes, the way his heart would melt when she smiled that crooked little smile at him, her gentle laughter. He missed his daughter. He missed his wife. And now he missed Moira.

A gurgling sound from the dialysis machine brought Driscoll back to the present, to a present where he could find no forgiveness for his part in Moira's fate. He should have cut her off from the word go. How could he have been so blind to the danger she was putting herself in? This young girl whose body had been inhumanely brutalized had him to thank for it. It was as though he wielded the weaponry himself. Guilt haunted him day and night. Were he Seamus or Eileen Tiernan, he would have come gunning for Driscoll, armed with a bazooka. Driscoll, to this day, couldn't understand their passivity. He was guilt ridden for them as well. The suffering his mismanagement brought about was inexcusable. As he stared down at Moira's fractured body he made a silent and solemn vow. He would track down this killer and stop at nothing until he is dead or captured. The killer had now made it very personal. Driscoll was after him with a vengeance.

Overcome with the same feeling of helplessness he had when he sat beside Colette, Driscoll's gaze fell away from Moira and drifted to row after row of hardcover and paperback books that filled the shelves on the far wall. There were titles like *Visual Basic Web Data Base*, *C++ Builder*, and *Intermediate MFC*. There were also boxes of diskettes, CD-ROMs, electronic gadgets, and PC peripherals.

Were his eyes deceiving him or was that an IBM

Thinkpad laptop wedged between two hardcover dictionaries of Delphi Components and Cobal II? My God! She said she worked better under open skies. Of course. She'd need a laptop. And here it was! The police had been scouring the wrong computer. It wouldn't be her desktop she'd be using—it'd be the laptop. Why hadn't that registered before?

He retrieved the computer and switched it on.

Jesus! She's got more programs here than the National Security Agency, thought Driscoll. He kissed the girl's forehead, placed the laptop under his arm, said goodbye to Moira's nurse, and proceeded down the stairs. While the team at Technical Services worked on Moira's desktop, he and Margaret would have a go at the laptop.

Chapter 73

"God, what I wouldn't give for her password!" said Driscoll.

"Gotta be a doozy."

Driscoll and Margaret had been sitting at his desk for what seemed like hours, fixed on the translucent surface of the laptop's screen. They had tried, unsuccessfully, every probable and wildly improbable password gleaned from Moira's biography. Her date of birth. The date in reverse. Kate Leone, her first grade teacher, followed by every other teacher she had ever had. Her favorite Baskin-Robbins flavor, Muddy Road. Her loyalty to her favorite Jell-O, Raspberry. Citre-Shine, her preferred shampoo. Lafeber's, the only brand of seed her bird, Chester, would peck at. Vassarette, her brand of panties. And 34B, her bra size. And to frustrate them even further, each time Driscoll typed in a password, the image of Moira's face flashed on the screen with a finger to her lips, while the teen's recorded voice jeered through the laptop's tiny speakers: "Not that one, silly. Read my lips!"

"If I hear that little voice or see that smirking face one more time, I'm gonna scream," said Margaret.

"She ever mention a boyfriend?" Driscoll asked.

"Just type D-R-I-S-C-O-L-L."

"Cute."

"I mean it. Give it a try."

"Don't be ridiculous."

"Here . . . let me do it." She typed in the Lieutenant's name.

"Not that one, silly. Read my lips!"

"What's your middle name?"

"Give me a break!"

"I know . . . William."

"Not that one, silly. Read my lips!"

"I think it's time for a break," Margaret grumbled, rummaging through her purse, searching for her compact. Finding it, she applied a fresh layer of lipstick.

"Margaret, I could kiss you! That's gotta be it. She wasn't shushing me then, and she's not shushing us now. Don't you get it? She's *pointing* to her lips! Get Eileen Tiernan on the phone. I gotta have the name of Moira's lipstick."

Chapter 74

Driscoll palmed the open tube of lipstick.

"It smells fruity," he said as he sniffed it.

He turned the cylinder bottom side up only to find an illegible fingerworn product label.

"According to Product Marketing Research there are 2,691 different lipsticks being sold nationally," said Margaret. "In New York City alone there are over 1,300 labels."

"You have any idea where your daughter shopped for her makeup?" Driscoll asked Eileen Tiernan who was sitting rigidly in the chair next to Driscoll's desk.

"Probably at the Queens Mall. That's where Moira bought everything."

"Worth a trip," said Margaret.

Their trek to the mall led them in and out of CVS, Revco, Bath & Body Works, Essentials Plus, Nature's

Element, J.C. Penney, Claire's, and Rite Aid. None of the retailers could identify the lipstick.

"Teenagers are like pack animals," said Driscoll as he stood with Margaret in the center of the mall. "They hang out in specific spots, shop the same stores, and buy the same stuff. Maybe we missed a store."

An outburst of laughter erupted from a group of adolescents spilling out of Candyland, a sweets boutique. Driscoll and Margaret looked at each other. "Gimme the tube," said Margaret. "They'll think you're a dirty old man." With tube in hand, she headed toward the teens.

"Can any of you girls help me? There's twenty bucks in it for anyone who can ID this lipstick."

"Twenty bucks! Give it here," said an acned brunette.

Margaret complied.

"Yeah! I know this one. It's one of those fruit smears." She handed the tube back to Margaret. "Go ahead. Taste it."

"You mean it's edible?"

"That's why they call 'em Fruit Licks."

"Where can I buy it?"

"Cute Cuts. It's a hair boutique right here in the mall."

"Point the way, and the twenty is yours."

"It's on level two. Right next to the Gap. Ya can't miss it."

Driscoll and Margaret made their way up the escalator and into the haircutting salon.

"Do you have an appointment?" a bleached-blond receptionist asked.

"Do I need one?" said Driscoll, flashing his shield.

"What's this?" Margaret asked, handing the woman the lipstick.

The woman eyed the cosmetic and gave it back to

Margaret. "That's a Fruit Lick. That one's called Mango Madness. They're mostly for teens. With your complexion, I recommend Summer's Dawn—"

"We can't thank you enough," said Driscoll as he and Margaret headed for the door.

Chapter 75

"Well, Lieutenant, are you ready to do a little dancing with me?" asked Margaret.

Driscoll gave her a curious look.

"On the keyboard, John. On the keyboard."

"Cute," Driscoll said with a grin as he began to type the name of the lipstick into Moira's laptop computer. A chime sounded. MANGOMADNE was as far as he got.

"Too many letters," Margaret muttered.

"I'll try breaking it down."

He typed. MANGO.

"Not that one, silly. Read my lips!"

He tried MANGOMAD.

"Not that one, silly. Read my lips!"

MADMANGO.

"Not that one, silly. Read my lips!"

MADMAN

"Not that one, silly. Read my lips!"

Margaret seized the computer and brought her face eye to eye with Moira's. "The game's over, sister. Talk to me." When she didn't get a response, she sighed and tried, MANMADE.

"Not that one, silly. Read my lips!"

MANMAD, she typed. "That's just what you are, Moira."

The sound of a muted trumpet emanated through the laptop's tiny speakers. "Aha! You found the lipstick. No keeping you out now. Kudos to you."

Margaret smiled triumphantly as Moira's digital face quickly faded into oblivion. "We're in!"

It took Driscoll and Margaret a little more than thirty minutes to deduce how Godsend had spun his webs on the bulletin boards of every online service on the Internet. Moira's Received Mail and Outgoing Mail folders contained every correspondence between herself and her abductor, as well as all the correspondence she had hacked from each of the victims. It all supported her theory about how the madman had lured his prey.

"That son of a bitch," Driscoll seethed. "Moira had him dead in his tracks from the start."

"And since she unmasked him, you can bet Godsend has vanished into cyberspace."

"No wonder the killings have stopped. But who's to say everyone he lured got snuffed?" Driscoll picked up the desk phone and punched in Thomlinson's extension.

"Thomlinson here."

"Cedric, you online?"

"Can be in a minute. What's up?"

"I want you to post a message on every online service's bulletin board."

"Will do. Whad'll I say?"

"Anyone having had bad karma with Godsend is to contact me. Include my e-mail address."

Driscoll and Margaret stared at the laptop's luminous screen. Their eyes focused on the two words Godsend had used to sign off with on his last correspondence with Moira: *Leigheas Duine.*

"It's Old Irish," said Driscoll.

"What does it mean?"

"Medicine Man."

Chapter 76

It had only been twenty-four hours since Thomlinson placed Driscoll's message in cyberspace. It was yet to prompt a response, but the Lieutenant remained hopeful. He picked up his desk phone and summoned Margaret and Thomlinson to his office. Within thirty seconds the two officers came in and took their seats. The Lieutenant was all business.

"Margaret, your friend has a record."

"My friend?"

"Doctor Pierce. They caught him trying to take out a bulldozer."

Driscoll handed Margaret the rap sheet. It read:

21st May 2004. Pierce, Colm F. Arrested 2100 hours by P.O. Jack McGuinness of Old Brookville P.D. Witness did observe defendant pour maple syrup into the diesel fuel tank of a bulldozer.

"What the hell is that all about?" Margaret asked.

"He called the DEP to complain about the bulldozer making too much noise. They've got him on tape."

Driscoll handed Thomlinson the DEP report.

"There's more to his story." Driscoll was filled with excitement. He felt he was closing in. When he spoke, it was with conviction. "I don't think it's a coincidence that he works in the hospital where the Parsons girl died. I checked the logs. He called it quits at three o'clock the day Clarissa was hit by the car, and failed to respond to his medical beeper all afternoon." Driscoll paused and took note of Thomlinson's reaction. He'd seen that look before. It was the look a good cop gets when he was on the tail of the right suspect. "Again, why does he, a radiologist, show up later at her bedside? With defibrillator paddles, no less?" Driscoll believed Pierce had his own agenda. The defibrillator paddles were somehow part of that agenda, and Driscoll was determined to find out what the connection was. "I'm convinced the guy needs a thorough background check, and that's what I intend to give him. Cedric, while I'm at it, I want you to keep an eye on that Internet mail. Margaret, you're to keep a close leash on the doctor." Driscoll said a silent prayer. This was Margaret now, dancing with the devil. "Continue to date the man as though nothing was up. Remember, the killings have stopped since you started seeing him. Let's see if there's a correlation. But be on your guard. He just might be our Medicine Man."

Chapter 77

"Cedric, hold the fort," Driscoll said into his car phone as he drove along Interstate 91. "I just left Fremont Center, where Professor Tiernan last encountered his secret Druidic society. But they've closed up shop. No one there has heard from them in years. Another dead end. If anyone's looking for me, I'm heading for Vermont. That's where Pierce received his first license to drive. And get this. It's the first record of any kind for the guy. It's almost as though he didn't exist until he received his driver's license. The address on the license put him in Windsor County, in a town called Hortonville. I'm heading there now to speak to a Cyrus Karp. He's the town's sheriff."

Later, when Driscoll and Karp met, Karp got down to business quickly. He asked, "Lieutenant, did you say 1172 Mackmore Lane?"

"That's the address I got from Vermont's Department of Motor Vehicles, Sheriff."

"Please call me Cyrus. Folks looking to spend the night in jail can call me Sheriff."

"OK, Cyrus, why did the woman at Motor Vehicles suggest I call you?"

"Why, you were plumb lucky, son. You see, that woman is Emma Machleit. And when she heard some big-city police detective was asking about a license that had as its address the old place on Mackmore, she thought it best to refer you to me."

"Is the house haunted?" Driscoll asked curiously.

"It ought to be. 'Cept there ain't no house to haunt."

"You mean, the address is a phony?"

"Nope. The address is for real, only the house that used to be there, ain't. What year did you say that driver's license was from?"

"1984," answered Driscoll.

"Well, the last house that had that address burned down in '68. A young girl and her parents burned to death in the blaze. C'mon, I'll take ya there."

Karp and Driscoll walked to what once was 1172 Mackmore Lane. The vacant lot, stretching between two Victorian homes, was a field of weeds.

"The townies, they won't go near it," said Karp. "They swear the lot's haunted."

"Did you know the residents?" asked Driscoll.

"No. Only the stories."

"And what do they say?"

"That the occupants of that house were into pain," Karp said, his eyes fixed just above the tufts of wild weeds. "Lots and lots of pain."

"You said a young girl and her parents were lost in the fire. Were there any survivors?"

"A young boy."

"What became of him?"

"Last I heard, he was adopted by the well-to-do Pierce family in Manchester."

"I don't mean any disrespect, Cyrus, but, how is it you know that?"

"Cause Hortonville's a small town, where everybody knows everyone else's business."

Chapter 78

Driscoll veered the Chevy into the driveway of Edgar and Charlotte Pierce's estate in Manchester. Japanese pine trees dotted the lawn. Sculptured bushes bordered fields of red calla lilies in flamboyant bloom. Two bronze Siamese lions stood guard in front of a portal of carved wood.

"You must be Lieutenant Driscoll." A Chinese valet ushered Driscoll into a vast reception room. "May I offer you some green tea?" he asked.

"Coffee, please."

The valet vanished, leaving Driscoll alone. He felt as though he had entered a gallery in some museum. On one wall, a painted Japanese screen depicted soldiers in armor, brandishing swords, decapitating a row of human heads emerging from the sand. Many heads had already been severed, their blood dyeing the earth. The spectacle was watched by a bearded man in pink robes who reclined on a sedan chair. *That must be the Emperor,*

Driscoll surmised, and wondered why he had ordered such a bloodbath.

"There sits Zheng, a passionate sort of fellow," said a voice behind him.

He turned to find a silverhaired woman in a long, fluid dress sashaying toward him. "The chap beheaded thousands of freethinkers."

"Your interior decorator has some sense of the macabre," said Driscoll, shaking her hand.

"Oh, no, Lieutenant. My decorator, Gustave D'Ambroise, protested at first, but how could I resist Premier Lin Piao? He insisted I display it. Regrettably, we women are at the mercy of powerful men. Well, in any event, I'm Charlotte. You said on the phone you wanted to talk about Colm."

"That's right. I do."

Charlotte Pierce motioned for Driscoll to take a seat on an upholstered sofa.

"Shall we start with when we adopted him?" she asked, seating herself on a high-backed chair.

"That'd be fine"

"We couldn't legally adopt him until he left Wellmore."

"Wellmore? A boarding school?"

"Oh no. It's sort of a rest home for children, an enchanting place. My husband contributed largely to its continuance."

"A psychiatric residence."

"Yes, a child's amusement park, if you will."

"Why was Colm committed there?"

"You haven't read the police report?"

"I didn't know there was one."

"He played with matches, the poor boy. He was fascinated with fire. Torched his house, I'm afraid. But he

wasn't known as Colm Pierce then. I can understand
why you weren't aware of the police report."

"What was he known as?"

"Colm O'Dwyer."

Driscoll made a note of the name. He now understood why he could find no records of Pierce before he
received his driver's license.

"Were there any casualties?" Driscoll asked.

"His parents, and possibly a sister. It still isn't clear
what happened to her. Colm managed to escape the
flames by burrowing himself in the cellar."

"Did he ever confess to his crime?"

"He was . . . catatonic. I believe that's what they call
it. Doctor Hudson, the neurologist at Wellmore, was
quite certain the fire's excessive heat brought on the
condition. But a year later, he was back to normal, having recovered most of his memory. The fire was not
part of his recollections, though. He went on to redeem
himself marvelously during his stay at Wellmore,
putting all the errors of his youth behind him. We're
very proud of his cure. He was released to our custody
ten years later because of his admirable behavior and a
true sense of moral conscience."

"Why did you adopt him?"

"On Tuesdays, back then, I volunteered my services
at Wellmore, helping the nursing staff. I just fell in love
with the child."

"Did your husband share your love?"

"Absolutely. Edgar and I had lost a son, so Colm was
welcomed in our home. Edgar spoiled him lavishly. It
was my husband who introduced him to the finer things
in life."

"I'd like to meet your husband."

"I'm afraid Edgar can't receive you. He suffers from Alzheimer's."

"I'm very sorry."

"Edgar has lost his ability to speak intelligently, but there is one word that he voices repeatedly, and that's 'Colm.' "

The valet entered with coffee service.

"Will you stay for lunch, Lieutenant?"

"Certainly, and after that I thought I'd visit Wellmore."

"I'm afraid it's past visiting hours."

"In the middle of the day?"

She ignored the question. Instead, she reached for Driscoll's hand and squeezed it tightly. "This house feels like a mausoleum at times. I do crave companionship, and I appreciate your visit, but for the life of me I can't figure out why it is you're here."

Driscoll searched her face. It was sharp and angular and full of power. It expressed a tenacity he had rarely witnessed in a woman. He wondered what secrets she was hiding. Being mother to the boy, she must have known his every inclination.

"A patient died under your son's care," he said flatly, watching her every move.

"If this is about malpractice, we will compensate generously."

A supportive mother? Or was there something else behind the gesture? "It's about homicide."

"And you think my son is involved in such an affair?"

"That's what I'm trying to rule out."

"Thank goodness! And are you any closer to finding the culprit?"

"We're clueless," he lied.

"I find your sincerity jarring. Who was it that was murdered?"

"A young girl."

Charlotte reached for a cigarette from an antique box and lit it. Her face showed no emotion.

"Her parents have influence," said Driscoll.

"Obviously."

As the two proceeded down the long corridor to lunch, Charlotte Pierce, her arm entwined in Driscoll's, whispered, "Be on your guard, the patients aren't the only crazies at Wellmore. If I were you, I'd avoid the place."

"Your concern is noted," said Driscoll.

Chapter 79

Driscoll thought Wellmore looked more like a golf resort than a psychiatric facility. A guard escorted him to the administrator's office, where he was greeted by a man casually dressed in Levi's and a Hawaiian shirt. A mane of blonde hair cascaded down to his shoulders.

"Are you Courtney's dad?" the man asked.

"No."

"Strange. You look just like Courtney."

The door opened and a jovial woman entered, wheeling a computer monitor atop a utility table.

"May I help you?"

"I'm Lieutenant Driscoll."

"Ah, yes, from New York. I'm Sarah Abbott. I see you've met Gunther Etteridge. He's one of our residents."

"Why don't you read him my goddamn file, while you're telling him everything about me?" said Etteridge.

"I do apologize," said Ms. Abbott. "I'll get Mr. Lazarus, Lieutenant."

The facility's administrator was a man with a massive bald head and a Prussian mustache. "What is it I can do for you?" he asked.

"I have some questions regarding one of your former patients, one Colm Pierce."

"Ah! Young Colm, our star graduate."

"I'd like to have a look at his records."

The two men eyed each other. "Tell me Lieutenant, why the curiosity in young Colm?"

"We're questioning a casualty at his hospital."

"Malpractice is an insurance matter."

"When it involves the daughter of a city official, everybody gets involved. I was hoping I could count on your cooperation."

"How so?"

"I'd appreciate a tour of the place, and a look at Pierce's records."

"Out of the question." Lazarus crossed his arms across his chest. "You must be familiar with doctor-patient confidentiality."

"What is it you're trying to conceal?"

Driscoll took an instant dislike to the man. He didn't appreciate his obstinance. Was Lazarus intentionally withholding information that would shed some light on the investigation? That would be a criminal act in itself. Or was the man simply being contrary? Driven by a larger-than-life ego, perhaps.

"Shattered lives and broken spirits crouch behind these walls, Lieutenant. Souls injured by the world you come from."

"I'm only trying to conduct a routine inquiry."

"Well, if you drove all the way from New York seeking a psychological profile of young Colm, I hope you took the scenic route."

"You're telling me I'm not gonna get a look at those records?"

"You know the rules . . . We psychiatrists are like priests, we swear an oath of confidentiality. Only a court order will pry open those files."

"I'd hate to have to use a political pass key," Driscoll countered, realizing he didn't have sufficient grounds for a warrant.

Lazarus responded with a grin, as though he realized Driscoll was bluffing. "Enjoy the rest of your day, Lieutenant," was all he said as he turned and left the room.

Chapter 80

Driscoll had anticipated the outcome, but his exchange with Lazarus had enhanced his own intuition concerning the mental state of Doctor Pierce.

He strolled the grounds of the palatial estate, sensing answers shielded behind its walls. A winding path led to a miniature lake carpeted with water lilies. It was an enchanting spot, a painting by Monet come to life, and he sat on a bench to enjoy it. He felt a presence behind him. He turned around and saw it was Gunther Etteridge.

"I used to come here with Colm," Etteridge said. "Did you know dragonflies have to molt five times in their lifetime, or they'll die?"

The man seemed harmless, a simpleton of sorts. He sported a tight-lipped smile that hid crooked teeth. Driscoll guessed him to be about the same age as Pierce, and that realization caused him to wonder why the man was still a patient in a children's psychiatric facility.

"Where did you learn that?" Driscoll asked.

"Colm! He knew everything about insects. Near the end of his stay we had a mosquito problem at this pond. Real bad. Lazarus wanted to spray DDT, but Colm said it would kill the songbirds and other beneficial insects. He ordered a batch of dragonfly eggs, a variety from South America. Those dragonflies, they were like tigers! Each one gobbled up nine hundred mosquitoes a day. In a month, the mosquito problem was licked. That was Colm for you."

"Quite a guy."

"Yeah. Nobody else like him."

Etteridge's face grew somber. He became silent, staring into the darkness of the pond.

"Tell me, Mr. Etteridge, do you like it here?"

"They let me make the coffee." His face beamed. "It was Colm who showed me how to work the dispenser. He knew everything about the stuff. Did you know coffee was discovered in Ethiopia?"

"You learned that from Colm?"

"He talked about coffee all the time. Mr. Pierce, senior, was a coffee importer and a great dad to Colm."

"Did you know him?"

"Not too well, but I know Colm was close to his dad."

"Did his dad visit often?"

"He practically lived here. And Miss Langley was always pleased to see him."

"Who's Miss Langley?"

"Colm's nurse. It was Miss Langley that encouraged Colm to become a doctor. It sure made his dad happy. Boy, I sure miss her and those visits to her house."

"You went to her house?" This man was a wealth of information. Screw Lazarus and his obstinance. Driscoll's prayers had been answered.

"His dad would take us there. Miss Langley would make French pastries. We'd all sit at the kitchen table and eat them with hot chocolate, and then Colm and I would play Scrabble for the rest of the evening."

"And Colm's dad and Miss Langley?"

"They'd go into the bedroom and watch Ed Sullivan."

"I sure would like to have a talk with her. Does she still live in the same house?"

"I think so."

"Could you give me directions?"

Etteridge did.

Chapter 81

The gingerbread cottage seemed more like the residence of an elf from Tolkien than a nurse in retirement. Driscoll found the doorbell. It was carved ivory, etched in the shape of a musical note. He depressed it. Chimes echoed, but his call went unanswered.

"Lookin' for old lady Langley?" a voice sounded.

Driscoll turned to find a small boy, no more than five or six. He was crouched on the slate steps of the house next door, sharing his lollipop with a Brittany spaniel.

"Is this her house?"

"Sure is."

"You think she'll be back soon?"

The youngster pointed to a small cemetery on a double-sized lot at the end of the block. "That's her over there, feedin' the birds."

Driscoll walked briskly toward the cemetery and Miss Langley. Blue jays, sparrows, pigeons, white tailed doves, two mallard ducks, and four Canadian geese fluttered about the woman, screeching for crumbs.

"Saint Therese of the Birds," Driscoll exclaimed.

Silence was his reply and he realized he was intruding on a mysterious and private ceremony. He'd wait until her service was completed.

The crumb distribution ended, yet the birds lingered, insatiable and rude. The woman opened an instrument case and produced a silver flute, which she began to play. Pastoral and rustic was the melody. As if in a trance, the birds listened.

The melody stopped and the birds flew away, perching themselves on the branches of the surrounding elms and oaks.

"Bravo!" Driscoll cheered. "Those are some lucky birds. Not only lunch, but a concert."

The woman stared at him. "Quiet!" Kneeling, she whispered:

> *"Confiteor Deo omnipotenti, beatae Mariae,*
> *semper Virgini, beato Michaeli archangelo,*
> *beato Joanni Baptistae, sanctis apostolis*
> *Petro et Paulo, omnibus sanctis, et tibi,*
> *Pater, quia pecavi nimis cogitatione, verbo*
> *et opere, mea culpa, mea culpa, mea maxima*
> *culpa."*

Then she rose and faced Driscoll. "These grounds are my confessional," she said. "Where do you go to ask for forgiveness?"

"The barroom at Sullivan's."

"Another soiled soul. Well, it wasn't my music, nor my transgressions, you came to hear. I saw you ringing my bell a moment ago."

"If I knew I'd hear a masterful flute solo, I'd have come here first."

"Thank you. I used to teach musicology at Juilliard, but then my son took ill and I had to change careers." The woman smiled. "And you are?"

"My name is Driscoll. Police Lieutenant John Driscoll."

"Wait a minute. You have that big-town aroma about you. Let me guess, Chicago . . . no, Philadelphia."

"New York."

The woman showed surprise. "A little out of your jurisdiction, aren't you?"

"I'm conducting an investigation into the death of a young girl as a result of an automobile accident."

"I'm at a loss," the woman said. "If she died as a result of a car accident, what's there to investigate?"

"Doctor Colm Pierce was at her bedside when she died."

Understanding registered. "Sweet Lord! What are you saying? Are you accusing Colm?"

"Not at all. I just have a few questions."

"It was at my knees he learned the catechism, Lieutenant. Colm was taught to confess his sins before he committed them. What is it you're after?"

"I understand you were Colm's nurse at Wellmore."

"My care for the boy was ages ago. What does that have to do with anything happening now?"

"We're doing a background search of all the physicians on call that afternoon. Routine investigation. Nothing to be alarmed about."

"But how did you find me?"

It was the question Driscoll had hoped she would not ask. "On my visit to Wellmore I met Gunther Etteridge, and he sent me to you."

"I see. How is dear Gunther?"

"He misses Colm."

The response brought a smile to Langley's lips. "Well, let's get on with the questioning."

"I want to know more about Doctor Pierce. How is it such an accomplished radiologist got his start in a psychiatric facility for children?"

"The dear boy's early years were an abomination. A regular horror show. And then there was the fire that burned down his family's home, and all that happened there. Colm O'Dwyer, that was Colm's true name. He became a ward of the state in some squalid institution until Wellmore took him in on a philanthropic scholarship funded by the Pierce estate. That's when Edgar Pierce entered the picture. He took a liking to the boy. In a strange way, the boy resembled Edgar and could have passed for his legitimate son. The jet-black hair, those aquamarine eyes, the cleft in his chin. You could say, as soon as Edgar saw him, he saw himself. And in some ways, emotionally, he had already adopted him."

A regular horror show, thought Driscoll. What was it Sheriff Karp had said? The occupants of the boy's house were into pain. Lots and lots of pain. That meant the boy was brought up in an abusive environment. So abusive that he torched his house and killed his family only to end up in squalor as a ward of the state. Any Behavioral Studies graduate from Quantico would tell an inquirer that he was witnessing the birth of a psychopath.

"Driscoll. That name has its roots in the Old Sod. Do you speak the language, Lieutenant?"

"Some."

"Colm loved the water. *An loch ag crithlonraigh ina ciuineas glaoighean se ar go leor croi uaigneach,*" Langley recited. The lake shimmering in its stillness calls to many a lonely heart.

"That's beautiful. You write poetry?"

"Not I. But Colm the Bard did. At sixteen the boy won a national poetry contest."

"He wrote in Gaelic?"

"He was fluent. Still is."

From psychopath to serial killer, thought Driscoll. "Regarding Wellmore, how is it you fit in?" he asked.

"Edgar wanted it that way."

"Why you?"

"Edgar promoted me to Director of Children's Services, with a special responsibility to act as surrogate mother to Colm. We had something in common, Edgar and me. We both had lost a son. That's what brought us closer together. On a cruise to the Galapagos Islands, Edgar was restless, not his usual jovial self. I found out what was troubling him. He confessed that he had fallen in love with me. From there on, he was part of my life. He never wanted to discuss his home life, and that was fine with me. I was like a second wife to him, and he was a dream husband. It was an idyllic time, filled with wonder. And then Alzheimer's came between us. He would forget appointments. Miss meetings he had called for. And then one day he woke up and didn't know why he was in my bed. He got dressed and left. I never saw him again." She sighed. "But you're not here to do research for a romance novel, are you?"

"No."

"This is more than just idle curiosity, isn't it?"

"Miss Langley, like I said, I'm investigating this patient's death—"

"I realize that," she said with a smile. "But Colm's

temper was never directed at children. He would never harm a child."

"Would he harm an adult?"

"You know Lieutenant, I think Alzheimer's might just be a little contagious." The woman had just slammed another door in Driscoll's face.

"As a nurse, Miss Langley, you may be doing an injured man a great deal of harm."

"The afternoon was lovely, Lieutenant. Thanks for the company." She then turned on Driscoll and walked away.

Driscoll stood alone in the cemetery, collecting his thoughts. From his conversation with Miss Langley he had discovered Pierce's mastery of the Gaelic tongue, and that he had a fascination for bodies of water. Was it not Gaelic that the derelict had heard? And was it coincidence that Monique, Deirdre, and Sarah's bodies were found near water? He had also learned that Pierce had been reared in an abusive home. So abusive that he had probably snapped and killed his family. And the man had a temper. That information came directly from his surrogate mother. Who better to know him? He thought of Margaret. A chill ran through his body. He unpocketed his cellular and called his office. Cedric Thomlinson answered the call.

"Where's Margaret?" Driscoll blurted.

"She's with Pierce. He invited her to his home."

Chapter 82

The mansion stood at the apex of a circular driveway. Margaret had seen photographs of similar structures in the pages of *Architectural Digest,* but had never imagined she'd ever be inside one.

"A place like this usually charges admission," she said. "Does it come with a tour guide?"

Pierce grinned.

"I gave him the day off." He approached the door. "I'm home!"

"You didn't tell me about the kids," Margaret teased.

"Heaven forbid! The door opens on voice command."

A marble-tiled vestibule welcomed the pair. Pierce ushered Margaret into a living room filled with plush sofas, soft leather armchairs and Louis XVI highbacks arranged on Tabris carpets. Armor adorned the walls.

Margaret felt uneasy. Was it simply because she had never visited such luxurious lodgings? Or was something else at play?

"It's not much . . . but it's home," said Pierce.

"Yeah, right!"

"May I offer you something to drink?"

"I'll pass."

"Come, then. I want to show you my collectibles."

Collectibles? Margaret's mind raced.

The level below them contained a large chamber with many glass cages showcasing bird skeletons and illuminated by halogen spotlights. Margaret found the display to be ghastly.

"That hummingbird is a *Calypte anna,* native to Rhodesia." Pierce pointed to the far corner of a glass cubicle.

"You mean, hummingbird bones."

"Stay perfectly still. You'll be able to hear the vibration of its wings."

Margaret couldn't hear the vibration of its wings. She heard only the sound of her own rapid heartbeat. This was way too weird. "I won't budge an inch," she managed.

The pair stood frozen, eyes fixed on the suspended assemblage of bones. "What in heaven's name is that?" she asked, breaking their trance.

"*Lanius ludoviscianus,*" Pierce said, sidling up next to her. "The butcherbird. That guy impales his prey on thorns and barbed-wire fencing."

"Well, he's got the right name." Margaret felt a rush of adrenaline course through her veins as Pierce continued to gush over his collection. This was just too much. The thought struck her: what other collectibles might he have?

"The *Lanius* has to eat, too," he said.

Margaret let the remark go unanswered.

"After a particularly difficult week at the hospital,

I'm drawn here just to gaze at the birds. It's like meditation. Muscles, skin, and feathers once swaddled these skeletons. But now this is all that's left of these beautiful creatures. You might say I've become a caretaker of their bones. A curator, if you will. But it got me into trouble last month. A water main broke a couple of houses down. The town dispatched a bulldozer with an enormous jackhammer to tear up the asphalt. Despite the solidity of my home, one of my Peregrine falcons fell and shattered because of the vibration. I called the Department of Environmental Protection and lodged a formal complaint. They couldn't have cared less. I was forced to take matters into my own hands. I scuttled the damn bulldozer with a sixteen-ounce bottle of maple syrup. Someone must have seen me and reported the incident to the police because shortly after that, I was arrested and charged with destruction of town property. You think the butcherbird is ferocious? You haven't met Griffith, my lawyer."

Was that a preemptive strike? Margaret wondered. Had he anticipated her curiosity about his arrest? The Lieutenant was right. Pierce was a man to keep on a short leash.

"What is it, Margaret? You look as though you've seen a ghost."

"Do I?"

"Your face has lost its color."

"I guess I wasn't prepared to view your collection of bones."

Pierce's gaze fell back on his exhibit. He grew silent. Margaret watched as his eyes closed down to tiny slits. The only sound that could be heard was the thumping noise her heart was making as it continued to pound forcefully inside her chest.

"But you know all about my arrest already. Don't you?" he said eyeing her with what Margaret read as contempt. He turned his attention back to his exhibit. "This is the twenty-first century. A girl would be reckless not to want to know about the guy she's dating. How were you to know I wasn't another Ted Bundy? Tell me, what did your search reveal?"

"The bulldozer incident, and nothing more."

"I lead a very boring life, as you can see."

"Why the fascination with bones?" she asked.

"It's the nature of my profession."

Margaret reasoned that not every radiologist had such a collection. A thought nagged at her. Since he had gone through the tedious task of assembling the skeleton of each tiny bird, she was sure he'd be capable of doing the same with human bones.

"The end!" Pierce announced, flicking a switch and leaving the pair in near darkness.

Margaret rummaged through her purse and re-leased the safety on her Walther PPK firearm.

"The birds prefer the darkness," Pierce whispered. "It feeds their hungry souls."

"But I'm a fluorescent light kinda gal, Colm. Would you mind putting the lights back on?"

Pierce hit the toggle switch again, bathing the room in incandescent light.

"What say you and I go upstairs to the dining room for some lunch?" he suggested.

"Fine. Just as long as you're not serving chicken-salad sandwiches."

"Heavens, no! I'll be serving duck."

Chapter 83

Pierce pushed his plate forward and gazed across the table at Margaret.

"Any new developments in your murder investigation?" he asked.

Was this idle curiosity Margaret wondered, or was the Lieutenant right? Was Pierce the Medicine Man?

"We're making some headway," she said. "The killings have stopped, and we think we know why."

"And why is that?"

"We think the killer is feeling remorseful. And if we're right in our thinking, now would be the time for him to come forward and confess his crimes."

"He could just be vacationing from his sport. No?"

"He may be. But, murders like these usually feed the frenzy in the killer's soul. Without the insertion of guilt his desire to kill becomes insatiable, and usually goes on unabated until the psychopath is caught. We're hoping he's feeling guilty enough to confess."

Margaret was baiting Pierce by design. Referring to the killer as a psychopath would certainly incite the man if the Lieutenant was right about Pierce being their killer. And now would be a good time to get a confession out of him. Perhaps that's why they were brought together in the first place: fate generating restoration.

"Psychopath. That depicts a rabid sort. Someone under the will of an uncontrollable force. I wouldn't think these types ever show remorse. But then, I'm not in the profession of apprehending criminals."

Margaret thought she caught something in Pierce's glance—a glimmer of disdain. It lasted for only a second and was gone. But she was sure it was there, nonetheless.

"The DA, I'm sure, would show leniency to a man, even a crazed killer, who came forward and showed repentance for his crimes."

"Would he, now?"

Pierce got up from the table to clear away the plates. When he returned he was carrying a plate filled with cookies.

"Sweets for the sweet," he said, placing the plate before Margaret.

Margaret selected a seven-layer marzipan and bit into it.

Pierce took his seat across from Margaret and stared intently at his guest. "I don't think your killer is ever going to confess his crimes," he said. "I'd say something unforseen intervened, and it'll be just a matter of time before he strikes again."

It was Margaret's turn to stare intently into Pierce's eyes. Was she now being baited?

"Like what? What could have intervened?"

"An unexpected interloper, perhaps."

Moira. The son of a bitch is talking about Moira. "How's that?"

"Judging from what I read over the Internet, the last victim was the Benjamin woman. Am I right?"

"Yes."

"There's your answer."

Eyes locked. This cat-and-mouse game was taking on huge proportions. How would anyone but the killer know that the Benjamin woman was out of pattern? *An unexpected interloper,* as he put it. Margaret's heart began to race again.

"My guess is the Benjamin woman intervened in some way, and your killer thought it best to remove her from the playing field." He was playing her. The grin on his face said, *I'm your man. Catch me if you can.* "That's purely a guess on my part," said Pierce. "You'd know better than I if I'm even remotely correct in my assertion."

"What makes you think the Benjamin woman was out of pattern?"

"Call it a hunch. Nothing more. Another cookie?"

"You know, I meant what I said about the DA being lenient on a killer who confesses to his crimes."

"Margaret, if I didn't know you better I'd say you're looking for me to confess. I'm simply a radiologist with a passion for bones. I'm certainly not your bone collector."

"That's also a trait of our killer."

"What's that?"

"A passion for bones."

"Human bones, Margaret. As you have witnessed my passion involves the skeletal structure of birds."

"It'd be a short bridge to cross."

Pierce eyed Margaret. There was that look of disdain

again. In full fury, this time. "In a way, I'm flattered that you consider me a suspect. That's what you're alluding to, is it not? It'd be my guess that you think I've got another chamber where I have a second collection of skeletal remains. Human remains. I have to tell you, the thought chills me to the bone."

Chilled to the bone. A subtle play on words. Was he toying with her again? "You seem to know so much about the case it's logical to reason—"

"That I'm your man." Pierce finished her thought. "If I were, would I align myself so closely with the police, the enemy, so to speak?"

"There are any number of reasons why a criminal would align himself with the police. I'd be a convenient way to keep tabs on the investigation."

"The information I've shared with you has been collected from various news articles."

"But the Benjamin woman?"

"Mere speculation, and nothing more."

"A killer like the one we're after is looking to be caught."

"Is that a fact?"

"It is."

"Well, then, get out your handcuffs. You've got me. I'm all yours. I confess. I'm your man. I deserve to be punished for my actions. What'll it be? Lethal injection? Electrocution? Perhaps a firing squad?"

He was mocking her and Margaret didn't like it. "I meant what I said about the authorities being lenient on a criminal who confesses."

"Would that be true for someone who preys on innocent women, stalks them, and bones them? Somehow I don't see that happening. That sort of viciousness would surely be punished. As you put it, to the full extent of the law."

Margaret stared across the table at Pierce. The disdain he had exhibited earlier was gone, replaced now by a look of bewilderment. Were Driscoll's instincts wrong? Was Pierce not the depraved killer he thought him to be? Was she having lunch with an innocent man who was simply a radiologist with a passion for bones? Or was Driscoll right about Pierce? Was he a ruthless murderer? If so, she was now sitting a mere four feet away from a madman.

Chapter 84

"Did anyone call?" Doctor Pierce asked as he scurried past the Department of Radiology's reception area.

Grabbing a stack of messages, Alicia Simmons, his secretary, tagged along behind him. "Dinner date, 6 P.M., at Bruxelles. Doctor Meyers called to confirm. Jimmy down at Crown Motors called, the Mercedes will be ready on Thursday, said he's sorry for the delay, something about waiting for a part. Your tailor called, your suits have been altered and are ready for pickup. And a Miss Langley called, sounded urgent."

"What was that name? The last one?"

"Langley, Priscilla Langley. Here's her number."

Pierce reached his office and fell back in his chair, staring at the rose-colored slip of paper. It had been ages since he had spoken to her. What could be the matter? An ominous and unsettling notion crept into his psyche: this could only mean trouble. Who was stirring things up? he wondered. The parents of the now

BONE THIEF 347

shattered teenaged interloper? The inquisitive Margaret? The dogged police lieutenant at the helm of it all? A whirl of emotions enveloped him. He willed it to go away, but it persisted, and the telephone number on the slip of paper became etched in his mind. He reached for his phone and punched in the number. Priscilla Langley's voice sounded in his ear.

"Is that really you?" he panted.

"Son, there was a man here in South Dorset, a policeman, asking all kinds of questions."

"Questions?"

"About a girl who died in your hospital."

"Patients die here, it's a goddamn hospital! What's this policeman's name?"

"Lieutenant John Driscoll."

Pierce thought his pounding heart was about to rupture. Frenzied thoughts emerged, ran rampant, and collided inside his brain. He could feel his entire body trembling. He brushed back the hair from his furrowed brow, only to find it dampened with perspiration.

"Colm, are you in some kind of trouble?"

The question went unanswered.

"Colm?"

"Yes?"

"You are. You're in some kind of trouble. Talk to me, boy."

Pierce couldn't control his trembling. He pounded his fist against the side of his desk.

"Colm?"

"I have to go now," he said slowly and deliberately. "You're not to worry. I'm not in any kind of trouble. I'll see to it that this policeman is reprimanded for causing you to worry."

"But, Colm—"

Pierce hung up the phone. His eyes fell, once again, upon the scribbled message. He crumpled the sheet of paper in his hand and flung it against the wall. He stood up. A dizziness overcame him. He sat back down. He pounded both fists on the top of his desk. The disturbance brought Alicia Simmons into the room.

"Is everything all right?" she asked.

"It will be," Pierce said, dismissing her. His eyes became fixed on the wall in front of him. His heart was still beating rapidly inside his chest when he heard his father's voice, distant at first, but gathering volume.

"What's keeping those eyes, Colm?"

A shriek came from atop the basement's shelving, shooting splinters of fear up my spine. A skittering sound followed.

"Bugler, what was that?" cried Mother.

"Daddy, we got rats!" Becky whimpered, her brown eyes pooling with tears.

"That ain't no rat," Father grinned.

A second shriek, more bone-piercing than the first discombobulated me. The box leaped out of my hands, launching the agate eyes into their own frenzied trajectories. My father's face went through a transformation. The muscles of his jaw knotted. A furrow cut deep into his forehead.

"Now look what you've done!"

He stood up. My heart burst.

His face became warlike. He let loose a cry, unfathomable and archaic, like the howl of a Celtic warrior.

My sister and I watched in horror. I knew my life hung on his very breath. He could choke me with his brute hands or spare my life.

He ground the strewn eyes under the heel of his hiking boot, leaned his distorted face into mine and said, "I could snuff you out, son. And it wouldn't matter much to the sun, or the moon, or the stars."

Father scraped fragments of glass from the heel of his boot and sprinkled the translucent dust on my head. Then he bolted upright, the tumor clawing at his intestines. "I spawned you, son, and I can snuff you out," he said, staring inquisitively into my eyes, examining my pupils like an ophthalmologist. His attention had been drawn back to his taxidermy. "This gutted pheasant, needs brown eyes," he murmured, inspecting the blue of my irises. "You've got your mother's eyes, Colm, and Rebecca's got mine, brown."

A piercing shriek tore through me. A vulture had leaped from the murk of the cellar's joists, swooped down, and clenched in its claws the entrails of the gutted bird.

"Ain't she a beauty?" Father boasted. "Just a week ago that critter was scanning the Alps for a stray lamb, and now this honey is mine. A real live lammergeier!" The sneer returned to his face. "Becky, come over here and give your Daddy a wet one."

Without warning, Father grabbed hold of my sister and flattened her body on the gurney. He poured some liquid on a rag and brutally smothered her face with it. Becky whimpered. But the noise slowly ceased as my sister fell into unconsciousness. Father then reached for the melon scoop and plucked out both of her eyes.

I grabbed hold of Father's sleeve, restraining further assault on Becky.

"Let go of my arm," he growled through clenched teeth.

Holding the rag he used on Becky, he turned his attention to me. Soon I too fell victim to unconsciousness.

It was the coppery scent of blood that nauseated me, waking me from my deep sleep.

Becky was still on the gurney. Two of Mother's abandoned tailor's mannequins stood, oddly enough, on either side. The *newly mounted pheasant was staring at her through new eyes, and Becky returned the stare through two gaping holes, each one oozing blood.*

I needed something to clog the holes. Mother's ping-pong balls! She had numbered them. They were stored in a vat and picked every week at the church lottery. I ripped open cartons, tore through boxes, and pried open metal cases until I found the keg in which they were stored. Rummaging inside, I pulled out two balls and raced toward my sister, squooshing the balls into her eye sockets, praying they would stop the bleeding.

The effort had sapped me of all energy. The chemicals on the rag I had inhaled were still taking their toll. I drifted into an agitated sleep.

Time passed.

"Colm," Becky screamed, in pain.

I woke up.

"I'm here," I said.

"I can't see!" she shouted.

"I'll be your eyes."

"It hurts," she sobbed. She was shivering. "It's so cold," she said.

Just outside the murky dungeon, the furnace lay dead, starving me and my sister of heat. It squatted, dumb and oblivious to our needs, for it too had abandoned us, despite my prayers for its fire and warmth. Terror filled and numb with cold, we waited for the dawn. But there was no sunrise, only the faint glow of a dingy twenty-five-watt bulb that flickered intermittently, threatening the cellar with total darkness.

Fever ridden, Becky coughed and wheezed. Her breathing had become a rattle.

Her condition worsened as the bleakness of our days led into the darkness of our nights. Eventually her breathing ceased. My sister was dead.

As I held her lifeless form in my arms, the door to the cellar creaked. It was my father. He descended the stairs, brandishing a hunting knife, eyes on Rebecca.

"You leave her alone!" I screamed.

The force of his blow knocked me against one of the tailor's mannequins, dismantling it. My mind was set on one thing: I had to protect my sister from his sinful hands. I grabbed the mannequin's severed arm and charged my father. The limb smashed against his kneecap, sounding as though it had crushed bone.

"You little bastard!"

He lunged for me. But his fractured knee wouldn't support his bulk. He collapsed, holding the injured joint. "I'm gonna kill you if it's the last thing I do," he seethed.

Another blow felled me. I turned my head before passing out from the pain. My eyes caught Mother's grin and the rolling pin coming at me again.

When I came to, a rope was cutting deeply into my wrists. Pain racked my head. I was hanging from a meathook like a leg of lamb.

Father had skinned Becky. The vulture was standing on the gurney, pecking at her bones. Cutting my sister's ligaments with its beak, it freed the humerus and tossed it into the air, watching it crash on the concrete floor. The bone cracked apart. The vulture then leaped on the scattered fragments and gobbled them up. Soon, there would be nothing left of my sister. The creature eyed me, ghoulishly.

I kicked my feet wildly, loosening the hook screwed into the moldy beam, and fell to the floor. I grabbed another of the man-

nequin's limbs and threw it at the bird. It croaked and flew away, perching on top of the shelving.

I embraced the skeletal remains of my sister. It was now up to me to care for her soul and prevent her bones from further assault. I decided to cremate her. It was the only way to protect her from either predator.

In the murk of the cellar I sniffed the stagnant air for signs of fuel and combustible material. There was a pungency emanating from a darkened corner of our confines. I followed the odor to its source: an abandoned canister of turpentine. Corrosion had fastened the cap tightly, resisting my efforts to open it. I found a clothes iron and brought it crashing down on the can. Turpentine soaked my shirt.

I wielded the iron again, striking the skin of the mannequin. Its guts, clumps of dried wood shavings, spilled out. I scattered them over Becky's bones.

I unscrewed the lightbulb and pried open the socket. I was rewarded for my efforts by a flash of pain. My eyes, though, hadn't missed the burst of bluish light that emanated from the tips of my fingers, nor the orange sparks, nor the stench of caramelized insulation wire that seared my nostrils. I'd harness this lightning and direct its bolts at Rebecca.

What witchcraft, what wizardry I was contemplating!

I tore the cable from its mooring and separated the two wires. Solemnly, I approached the heap of bones, sensing their urgency, their longing for rebirth.

As I connected the wires, spears of light cascaded around me, filling the cellar with a haunting luminosity. Fueled by the turpentine, flames blossomed. The lammergeier shrieked as the fire devoured the cellar's accumulated treasures. Becky's bones were being embraced by flames, serenaded by fumes.

In the distance I thought I heard my mother scream.

Chapter 85

Driscoll returned from Vermont, frantic. Margaret was missing. In his mind, he played back the voice mail she had left him. She had said that Pierce knew the Benjamin woman was out of pattern. That news was as enlightening as it was unsettling, considering he didn't know the whereabouts of Margaret. He had left three voice messages on her cellular, and had called her beeper twice, but she hadn't responded. Where the hell could she be? It was very unlike her not to answer his calls. As he watched the narrow red hand on his office wall clock sweep away the seconds, he worried more and more.

The door opened, and Thomlinson walked into Driscoll's office holding a magazine. "Old Brookville. You know what an average house goes for in that community?" he asked.

"Why the sudden interest in real estate?"

"$3.9 million! That's the going price. Location, location, location."

"You got a career change in mind?"

"That's where Doctor Pierce hangs his hat. He's got his home there."

"That much I know. It's the only rock I haven't looked under. But there'll come a time."

"Some house. Made the cover of *Architectural Digest* . . . June '98. Here, check it out."

Thomlinson placed the magazine on Driscoll's desk, open to a photograph of a palatial facade.

Driscoll read the caption below it: "On the corner of Lilac Grove and Primrose Lane lies the eighteenth-century residence of Doctor Colm F. Pierce."

The Lieutenant pushed aside the article and stared at Thomlinson. He was about to speak when he was interrupted by the electronic voice of his computer: "You've got mail" it sounded.

"Let it be Margaret," he prayed.

It wasn't. It was from someone called Paradox. Driscoll looked at Thomlinson, shrugged his shoulders and clicked the Read icon.

Darling Lieutenant,

Bad karma with Godsend, you ask? Well, you can bend me over and tan my hide if I tell you a lie. I went and answered the man's ad hoping to find my first love. All looked promising until I met with the dude. Seems he wasn't too thrilled I was . . . shall we say . . . less than what he was expecting. I'm what those ratty-ass people call a tranvestite. A rootin' tootin' he-she! Well, anyway, your Godsend takes one look at me, rumples up his whitey-ass face and speeds off . . . The bitch. That sucker done me wrong, dude! Dissin' me. Can you believe that shit? Call me, honey, my number is 718-545-2134.

Paradox

Driscoll reached for the desk phone and punched in the number. A husky voice answered on the third ring.

"This is Lieutenant Driscoll. Is this Paradox?"

"It sure be, sugar."

"I just read your e-mail. You're telling me you saw the man?"

"The monkey-faced white dude, you mean? Yessir. I saw him. He took me for a hundred dollars, that mama's boy, and there ain't no way I'm gonna get it back."

"If I scan you a photo of the man could you ID him?"

"I was hopin' for a picture of you, sweetie-pie."

"Me? You don't wanna see me. I'm ugly."

"But your voice sounds so pretty. I bet you're tellin' me a big old fib."

"Paradox, I'm gonna scan you the photo of Godsend right now. Let me know if he's the man who took your money."

It took Driscoll all of two minutes to scan Paradox the bulldozer incident mug shot, and half that time for Paradox to ID Pierce as Godsend.

"That be the dude, you honky-tonk man, you."

"Paradox, you've made my day. I'm gonna cut a petty-cash voucher for a hundred dollars and have it mailed to you. I'll need your address."

Driscoll jotted down the Queens County residence and ended the call. His wristwatch read 7:05 P.M. He called St. Vincent's Hospital and was told that Doctor Pierce was out of his office and wasn't expected back until morning. He punched in Margaret's cellular number one more time. When her voice mail announcement echoed in his ear, his eyes fell upon the *Architectural Digest* photo of Pierce's palatial estate.

"Cedric, you hold the fort. I gotta get into that house. I got a bad feeling about this. What if the son of a bitch is holding her captive?" Driscoll said a silent prayer, grabbed hold of his Burberry, and headed for the door.

Chapter 86

It had become the Lieutenant's habit to keep tabs on all ex-cons he had arrested, especially those who chose residence in his city, and Lazlo Bahnieski was no exception. After his release from the state penitentiary at Attica, Lazlo had exchanged his talents at breaking and entering for the pleasures of fishing for blues in the waters that surrounded Brooklyn, trading in his cat burglar's ski mask for a captain's hat.

Every dawn, he'd sail his trawler, *Born Again,* as it hosted amateur fishermen on a day's outing a few miles east of the Verrazano Narrows Bridge. It was a living and, with the help of Jack Daniel's, Lazlo was a redeemed man.

Driscoll knew that all the fishing boats returned to harbor before dusk and that by 8:00 P.M. Lazlo would be stretched on his boat's hammock, downing his favorite booze. In the now somber Sheepshead Bay marina, the *Born Again* was easy to find. At 8:15 P.M., Driscoll leaped onto the deck of the twenty-six-footer and rang the ship's bell.

"Hold on, pardner!" the voice bellowed from below. "Next charter leaves at six A.M.!"

"All hands on deck!" Driscoll hollered.

The door to the cabin creaked open. "Well, as I live and breathe, if it isn't Lieutenant Driscoll."

"The hat suits you, Lazlo. It hides your ugly mug."

"Lieutenant, that's the nicest thing you've said to me since lockup."

"I'm here on business."

"You're getting married, and the bride wants a wedding at sea?"

"I'm investigating this guy, and I need your help. It's time to sober up. I've got a job for you. I gotta get inside his house."

"What you need is a judge and a warrant."

"Already got it. But the place is likely to be more wired than AT&T. My attempt to get in might lock it down. I can't have that. I'm depending on you to get me in and out without any problems."

"What's in it for me?"

"Word on the street says O'Hara doesn't give you much breathing room."

"That parole officer is worse than a leg clamp."

"I could see he gets a new assignment."

"Let's drink to that."

"No time now. Someone's life may be at stake."

"OK, where's the house?"

"Old Brookville. Let's get a move on."

It took Driscoll fifteen minutes to reach the residence. He parked the Chevy on the street, and he and Lazlo scurried along the property's stone wall to the gated entrance.

"So far, so good. The grounds are alarm free. I didn't pick up any signals," Lazlo muttered, displaying an electronic scanning device.

They had reached the gate. Driscoll pressed the bell. No one answered. He pressed it a second time, producing the same results. Pierce was either not at home or wasn't answering the door. "Here's where you come in, Lazlo. How 'bout this gate?"

"Piece of cake." the ex-con said, eyeing a digital keypad on the metal frame. He produced a miniature screwdriver from his knapsack and removed the unit's cover, then stopped. "This is an import. And if we fuck up, we activate that camera," he said.

"What camera?"

"That one!" Lazlo pointed at an electronic eye imbedded in a brick. He then produced a miniature handheld computer, connected an alligator clip to a black-and-white wire inside the unit, and fingered a tiny toggle switch. "That'll do it," he grinned as Driscoll watched a whir of red and green lights flicker on Lazlo's handheld computer. "We're in!"

The gate opened before them.

"Let's get a move on," Driscoll urged.

The entrance door's lock quickly surrendered to the ex-con's manipulation. Lazlo's scanner detected no alarms inside the house.

"Here's where you take a breather, Lazlo. I'm goin' in alone." Driscoll's stomach churned as he pondered Margaret's fate.

"Just like you to take the fun outa things. What am I supposed to do now?"

"Here's a fifty for your troubles. The Long Island Railroad stops six blocks north of here. Take the train and head back to the marina. I might be a while."

"Aye, aye, sir." In a flash, Lazlo disappeared into the night.

Driscoll was now inside a marble-tiled vestibule, the starting point for his excursion inside Pierce's house. He called out Margaret's name. It prompted no reply.

Driscoll followed the beam of his flashlight and reached a dimly lit circular room with four staircases leading from it, like four spokes radiating from a wheel's axis. The room boasted a frescoed cupola depicting what looked like a feminist resurrection. He wondered if it would be safe to turn on the lights. He groped the walls for a switch, but found none. There was a drawn curtain under one of the staircases, which stimulated his curiosity. He peeked behind the curtain. It concealed a large antique birdcage. The bird within it was three feet tall. There was a brass shingle with carved letters at the base of the cage. It read: LAM-MERGEIER. Driscoll had studied such a bird in an adult-ed class on avian behavior at St. John's University. The bird was a vulture whose diet included a preference for bone marrow. At the bird's feet lay a bone. Driscoll reached for it. That's when the bird attacked. It was swift, but fortunately for the Lieutenant, off-target. Driscoll's fingers must have been an irresistible sight to the bone-hungry predator.

To whom did that bone at the bottom of the cage belong? Although it was a shattered fragment, it looked vaguely human, maybe a tibia or some other elongated limb bone. He wished he could get his hands on it. But the lammergeier was not about to part with it readily, and Driscoll was in no mood to wrestle with the beast.

Thoughts kept gnawing at him. Was that Deirdre's tibia? Or Sarah's femur? Or Clarissa's ulna? Or, God forbid, Margaret's radius? Does Pierce go on hunting expeditions for his pet? Does he stalk malls or parking lots or supermarkets looking for food for this bird? If that were so, then Driscoll had walked in on John Audubon's worst nightmare. And were there any more raptors lurking?

He released the safety on his Glock 9-mm revolver and eyed the giant bird. As he stood, momentarily frozen, he prayed his fears about the bone were incorrect, but the anxiety wouldn't be easily dismissed, and it was not a simple task to focus on the moment.

He shouted for Margaret, and floodlights illuminated the majestic cupola. The room was sound sensitive. Driscoll opened a door that led into a library. Leather-bound books lined varnished shelves. In the middle of the room, a Louis XVI desk gleamed under his flashlight. He caught the shimmer of a tiny dot of light emanating from a rectangular metal box connected to an antique telephone. Driscoll played the messages. A reedy academic voice thanked Pierce for his largess toward the construction of a cardiac wing at Saint Finbar's Hospital Center. A man with a thick Italian accent promised the delivery of a new Lancia that would be offloaded at the port of Elizabeth, New Jersey, on the thirty-first. A secretarial voice from Chelsea Chemicals confirmed the delivery of order #69732-B to his home address. The machine ceased.

Driscoll wondered what order #69732-B contained. Perhaps the Louis XVI desk would hold the answer.

He rummaged through the drawers, finding folders in alphabetical order. The Chelsea Chemicals folder was stuffed with receipts, invoices, product brochures, and letters of credit. Pierce was a frequent customer. Order # 69732-B revealed a large purchase of sulfur trioxide. He made a call on his cell phone. "Cedric, sulfur trioxide. I want to know what it's used for. Call me on the cellular."

Driscoll stomped on the marble floor. The reverberation, like the percussion of a snare drum, indicated a hollowness below. But where was the portal or a trap door, or steps that led downward? No architect would build a multileveled edifice without connecting passageways.

For the next forty-five minutes, he searched every room and every closet inside the house. There were rooms of different sizes, decorated by artful hands. But, in all, no sign of Margaret. He reached a hall more fit for the Palace of Versailles than a Long Island residence. At the end of it, his flashlight exposed a structure of carved wood and gold leaf. It was a confessional booth! Why would anyone have a confessional booth in their home? The sighting made him feel uneasy. He was reminded of his own shortcomings, and that it had been ages since he knelt inside such a booth. As he marveled at the sighting, the ray of his flashlight revealed friezes depicting scenes from the Old and New Testament: the expulsion from Eden, the beheading of Holofernes by Judith, the resurrection of Lazarus, the assumption of Mary, and the day of redemption.

Driscoll opened the door of the booth and stepped inside. It made no sound. It had been well used. His conscience stirred. This was sacred space he was trespassing. An inner voice complained, *You've crossed the line.* He had reconciled with his irreverence before, but this was sacrilege. He knelt begrudgingly and assumed the penitent position. *What are you doing here?* the voice clamored. He heard a clicking sound. Gears were engaging beneath him. The floor gave way, starting a slow descent. *Prayers really are answered,* he thought, as he came to a stop some thirty feet below.

Driscoll stepped out into a spacious wine cellar. His attention was drawn to his right, where a gallery of glass showcases was lit before him. Cranial orbits of birds' skeletons stared at him. He returned the stare, gaping at the ghastly collection. He was filled with a sense of awe as well as a sense of horror. This was a macabre showcase. Its eerie silence was frightening. He read the names of each exhibit: PEREGRINE FALCON, THE BUTCHER BIRD, WHITE HELMET SHRIKE, CALIFORNIA CONDOR. All fierce predators. What purpose did these skeleton's serve? Had Pierce skinned these birds? Like he skinned his prey? The exhibit also made him feel a sense of guilt. It had been months since the first body was found, and he still hadn't caught the murderer. He was not proud of that. Thoughts whirled inside his head. Margaret! Where the hell is Margaret?

His cellular beeped. "Driscoll, here . . . Yeah, Cedric, wha'd ya find out?"

"That chemical you called me on, it's an acid. It's used by taxidermists to dissolve organic matter."

"That fits," said Driscoll.

There was a whooshing sound. It was as though a furnace had kicked in, or a sump pump, perhaps.

A boiler room? he thought. It'd have to be below this.

He returned to the confessional booth. As his knees hit the floor, the booth stirred once more. Sweat collected on Driscoll's brow, searing his eyes, as the booth began its slow but steady descent.

The floor of the cell abruptly struck bottom. The jolt loosened the flashlight from Driscoll's grip. It spiraled, smashing against the wooden floor. Retrieving it, he switched it on. A narrow beam of orange light flickered.

As he shuffled forward, the frail beam from his flashlight was no match for the blinding darkness all around him, yet it exposed a coaxial cable tacked to a stone ceiling. He followed the electrical line as it meandered toward a junction box with a toggle switch. He hit it. A succession of spotlights came to life.

Driscoll was not alone. Two skeletons, standing in individual glass coffins, stared back at him. There were shingles affixed to the coffins. They read MOM AND DAD, RESURRECTED.

Standing before the two skeletons was a mock cave constructed of artificial rock. Assembled around the cave were other skeletons, some erect in their own showcases, some in disarray on shelves. The lammergeier's nest sat in the center lined with synthetic grass, twigs, and a heap of bones. As he stroked the surface of a slim bone, he knew the DNA analysis would corroborate what his sixth sense had already confirmed. He pocketed the delicate bone, wondering which one of the victims it belonged to, and raced to the confessional.

How the hell do I get up? he wondered. But as his knees met the kneeler, the lift began its ascent.

Chapter 87

It was a cloudless, star-studded night. The telltales were flush against the mainsail, gorged by the south-western wind. The ocean buoys clamored, heralding incoming swells, as ridges of salt water crashed against the massive hull of *The Ark*, a thirty-eight-foot Catalina sailboat, its bow dipping deeply into the cascading tide. Liquid notes from Debussy's *La Mer* ricocheted inside the aft cabin. Pierce was at his leisure, and Margaret was still keeping tabs on their number-one suspect. The way Margaret saw it, Pierce may have used the Internet to lure some boating enthusiast first lover out onto the Long Island Sound. As long as she was aboard, she figured she'd thwart that possibility. But she was no fool. The safety was released on her service revolver, and she was ready.

Her telephone purred. "My cellular," she said.

"Go away, world," said Pierce.

"I must," she stated, as she reached for the phone.

"Yes?" Margaret gasped. "I'm not getting you, there's a lot of static . . . what? Did you say a nest? A cellar? What? What about a cellar? Damn it, I've lost him!"

They had found his collection. Pierce was certain of it.

"You're out of cell range, and the water doesn't help," he muttered.

"Can you get me to port? I've gotta make a call!"

"What's the hurry?"

"It's my boss. He's found something. I don't know what it is. It sounded important."

A chill entered the cabin, as if arctic air had seeped into the little room. Debussy's melody faded, replaced by the slapping sound of sea waves crashing against the hull. Pierce's gaze became icy, searching for what was concealed in Margaret's eyes.

"I really have to go!" she pleaded, sensing imminent danger.

"You look like you're about to throw up," Pierce said, his face now starched with contempt.

"The rocking is making me seasick."

Pierce forced a smile and headed topside. "It's time to get you back to shore then. There's some Emetrol in the medicine cabinet. Why don't you help yourself while I turn the boat around?"

Chapter 88

Driscoll was certain the distant bells echoing in his cellular's earphone were the sounds of buoys on a rough sea. There was no doubt about it. Palming the cell phone, he punched in Thomlinson's number, forced the Chevy into gear, and pulled away from the estate.

"Cedric, check your dossier on Pierce. Does the guy own a boat?"

"Hold on a sec . . . Yeah. Here it is . . . A thirty-eight-foot Catalina sailboat . . . *The Ark*. Custom-built in Southwest Harbor, Maine. He keeps it moored at Judson's Marina in Port Washington."

"Hold the fort. I'll call you from the marina."

Driscoll arrived at Judson's Marina just past 11:00 P.M. The place looked deserted except for a blond youth lounging atop the teak deck of a Criss-Craft cabin cruiser.

"Can I help you?" he asked.

"*The Ark* . . . it docked here?" said Driscoll.

"You mean Doctor Pierce's boat?"

"That'd be the one."

"Gone since early evening."

"He go alone?"

"Nope. He had a dark-haired chick with him."

Jesus, he thought. *If you're listening, God, keep her out of danger. That madman is capable of anything, and if something happens to Margaret . . .* He thought immediately of Moira, and with the thought came an adrenaline-fueled rush of guilt.

"Know where they were heading?"

"Probably to his winery."

"Where'd that be?"

"North Fork. It's the only place on the island they grow grapes."

Driscoll tried the cellular again, but Margaret was now well out of range. He called Thomlinson, who answered on the first ring. "Cedric, get me a helicopter. Have it at Judson's Marina in five minutes! Alert the Coast Guard and Suffolk County's Harbor Patrol. Pierce is our man. He's heading for the North Fork, and he's got Margaret with him."

Chapter 89

The Lieutenant was closing in. Pierce was sure of it. He had underestimated the man, and now he felt like a tracked fish being steered toward the net, ripe for the fisherman's grappling hook. This was not the ending he had in mind. One cop below deck, and one in close pursuit. How the hell could he have let this happen? Fate had always been generous. Why not now, goddamn it? Why not now? He felt like screaming, but that would interfere with his plans for Margaret. It would be she that would have to pay for her boss's doggedness. He wished the Lieutenant had learned his lesson with Moira.

Pierce descended to the bilge, crouching in the crawl space that housed the engine. He yanked free the gas line, spilling marine fuel into the cramped compartment. It was time to scuttle the boat and escape. Mindful that he had some unfinished business to attend to, he re-entered the cabin and took from his physician's bag a Bard-Parker scalpel.

Margaret was in the lavatory. The water was running.

"Don ghrian agus don ghealach agus do na realtoga," he chanted, as he opened the door and struck.

Pierce then heard a roar. Giant wings were cutting through the air. He hurried topside. It was a helicopter approaching the sailboat, its floodlight illuminating *The Ark* as though it were day. Despite the din of the whirling blades, he heard a thud. Someone had landed on deck. He turned. It was Driscoll.

The jolt of leaping from the helicopter jarred loose Driscoll's 9-mm Glock, which bounced off the deck and tumbled into the sea. He grabbed the boat's winch handle and lunged at Pierce, slamming the stainless-steel tool against the side of Pierce's head. Pierce dropped the scalpel and brought both hands to the wound, stumbling toward the steps to the cabin. But Driscoll was on him like a slaughterhouse worker finishing off a calf. A roundhouse kick crushed Pierce's rib cage. He gasped for breath but managed a left hook against Driscoll's jaw.

Pierce lumbered toward the sailboat's cockpit, where he yanked the tiller free from its coupling. The Lieutenant tackled him by the ankle and brought him down, his face smashing hard against the fiberglass surface of the deck. The tiller went toppling into the water, and Driscoll renewed his assault with a flurry of punches.

Just then, with blood trickling from a neck wound, an unsteady Margaret appeared, leveling her firearm on the wrestling pair.

"It's over!" she yelled, getting off a round, missing

Pierce's head by an inch. "Give it up," she hollered as she leveled her weapon to fire again.

"Like hell!" Pierce shouted. His left foot caught Margaret in her right shin. The blow upended her, knocking the weapon from her hand, and caused her to tumble over the boat's starboard railing.

"John!" she screamed as her body plunged into the choppy sea.

Driscoll turned his head and was about to follow her when Pierce's teeth sunk into the Lieutenant's right shoulder. The pain was excruciating, but a strategically placed right hook hit Pierce in the temple, opening a wide gash. Pierce then tried to ensnare Driscoll's neck with some rigging, but Driscoll blocked his opponent's thrust with his elbow. Pierce settled for the Lieutenant's arm and quickly knotted a clove hitch around it. With his other hand, Pierce released the line from its clamp, unfurling the sailboat's spinnaker and towing with it Driscoll's body, which was still shackled to its rigging.

A bullet ricocheted off the aluminum mast. Only the rocking motion of the sailboat saved Pierce from the helicopter's sniper. Pierce dove for the cockpit's accessory box, loaded a flare gun, and fired it at the helicopter' s beacon. The recoil knocked Pierce against the dashboard, but the chopper's floodlight exploded in a burst of blue sparks. The pilot gained altitude and skittered away.

Pierce fisted another scalpel and lowered himself into the water in search of Margaret while Driscoll remained intertwined in the sailboat's rigging. The more the Lieutenant tugged at the lines, the more entangled he became. He looked up at the mast. A line had jammed in a pulley a few feet above his head. He stretched out his arm, grimacing in pain from his shoulder wound, and manipulated the rope with his fingers until the line became free. Down he crashed, still caught in the rigging, but no longer its prisoner. He dove into the water in search of Margaret.

Below the surface of the water, Pierce latched onto Driscoll's leg. The cold steel of a finely honed blade sliced into the Lieutenant's calf. But, by jackknifing his body, Driscoll was able to break free from Pierce's hold.

The two men surfaced. Scalpel in hand, Pierce lunged for Driscoll, who deflected the thrust by grabbing hold of the assailant's wrist. The sound of a gunshot rang out.

"Fire again!" hollered Driscoll, spotting Margaret braced against the boat's wraparound railing, her weapon once again in hand.

Another shot followed.

This time the bullet hit its mark. Pierce's arms flailed wildly, then ceased all movement. The scalpel disappeared into the water, and as Driscoll and Margaret watched, a wide-eyed Pierce sank slowly into the murk.

Driscoll climbed back onboard and took Margaret in his arms. "My God! If I lost you too, I don't know what I'd do." Thoughts swirled inside Driscoll's head. It appeared the madman had been slain, and the women in Driscoll's world were safe. He thought of his wife. She would have been proud of him. Moira, who had fallen into harm's way because of him, had now been avenged. She would be smiling, too. And Margaret. He could now start a real relationship with Margaret. For that he was grateful.

The drama of the day ended for Driscoll as police helicopters arrived, accompanied by the blaring sound of a Coast Guard cutter's siren. Spotlights searched the cloudy waters surrounding the boat for any sign of Pierce.

There was none to be found.

Chapter 90

"You and Margaret will meet with the Mayor this afternoon as planned. The medal presentation will be televised," Police Commissioner Brandon directed as he grabbed a cigar from an ivory humidor.

"I'd like you to hold off on that," said Driscoll.

"The Long Island Sound's not about to give up the body. It's in Nova Scotia by now. You know the currents up there."

"That's my point. The Long Island Sound deserves the medal."

"But Margaret shot the bastard. Should she be deprived of hers?"

"Give her mine while you're at it."

"What is this? Professional scruples?"

"Commissioner, it was far from a clean kill. The guy takes a winch to the head, he bleeds like a slaughtered pig, we wrestle in and out of the water, and Margaret shoots him. The next thing I know he slips loose from under me and I lose him to the sea. That's not exactly the proper apprehension of a suspected killer."

"The way I see it, the guy was bleeding from a head wound *you* inflicted, and then Margaret shot him. The current got hold of him, and he was history. Case closed."

"I still would like to hold off on the fanfare."

"Don't be difficult, John. This city is in the mood to celebrate, and I'm not gonna be a stick-in-the-mud. You've earned the medal. Wear it! Say cheese for the cameras and let the women of this city sleep through the night. Now let's get a move on!"

Chapter 91

Driscoll sat in his cruiser alongside a row of rhodo-
dendrons that lined the curb outside of Mary Star of
the Sea Nursing Home. He felt hollow. It was as though
someone had taken a blade and carved out his vital organs. Colette, the love of his life, now lay comatose inside the century-old brownstone. Placing his wife into
the care of the home's hospice personnel was a heart-
wrenching decision, but he knew it was a decision that
needed to be made. He had just left her bedside and
was now offering a silent prayer. A prayer of hope. A
prayer of love. And a prayer of resolution. It was his in-
tention to visit often and remain loyal to her in a way
that she would understand. As he turned the key in the
ignition and slowly pulled away from the facility, tears
blossomed and streaked his cheeks. He gazed in the
Chevy's rearview mirror and watched as the nursing
home's facade slowly faded from view.

* * *

Sullivan's Tavern was bustling. The bar was six deep, and every table in the dining room was occupied. The mood was festive throughout. And why not? The madman that had declared war on the city of New York had been eliminated.

Driscoll and Margaret were seated at Driscoll's favorite table, which offered a panoramic view of Manhattan. They had completed their meal and were both savoring an after-dinner cocktail. A gentleman approached. He was holding a copy of the *Daily News*. Its headline boasted: SERIAL KILLER ANNIHILATED BY NEW YORK'S FINEST.

"You're Lieutenant Driscoll," the patron said, holding forth the tabloid. "Would you mind autographing my newspaper?"

Driscoll grinned. "My lady friend here deserves the credit. It was she who fired the shot that ended it all."

"Wow! A double-header! Would you sign my paper too?" he asked.

Driscoll and Margaret obliged the man, affixing their signatures across the headline.

"You know," said the grateful supporter, "it's because of professionals like you that the citizens of New York can rest easy tonight."

As the man disappeared, Driscoll's cell phone rang. His eyes narrowed. He listened intently to Thomlinson's message.

"Time to go," he said to Margaret as he folded his napkin and shimmied out of his chair. "An hour ago they found two dead bodies in Brooklyn. Looks like we have another crazy on our hands."